Scuba Gold

Ben Thomas

Scuba Gold

ISBN 978-0-945980-90-2

Cover photo by Blanchard Photography
            514 Old Lewiston Road
            Winthrop, ME 04364
            207-377-3829

Edited by Anne Nelson

Printed in the USA

North Country Press
126 Main Street
P.O. Box 501
Unity, ME 04988
207-948-2208

www.northcountrypress.com

"Hey, why you whispering? There's no one here."

"I don't know. Just seemed natural. Here we are in the dark after breaking into a house where jewels have been hidden, then stolen and Jack murdered. Makes you want to whisper."

Matt placed his hand on the banister leading to the second floor. He paused. The tick tock from a grandfather's clock echoed exceedingly loud in the empty house.

"Matt, I feel as though I'm walking through a cemetery." As she spoke she felt goose bumps run along her arms and her heart rate speed up a notch.

With those words Matt felt the hair bristle on his neck. It was easy to imagine someone else in the house watching their every move, some evil shadow, someone who had already killed once and would not hesitate to do so again. He pulled her close and squeezed her hand.

"Stay close, maybe we aren't alone."

With those words McCall felt her heart racing. "My God, Matthew, if you're trying to scare me you are doing a good job." She grabbed his arm and gave a quick look behind her.

"Come on, up we go." Matt pulled lightly on her hand. Each step brought a reluctant groan from the stairs. Each creak thundered in the silence.

Also by Ben Thomas:

Books
> *No Horns Blowing*
> *The Weekender*
> *Hot Blood and Wet Paddles*
> *Your Pocket Guide to the Maine Outdoors*
> *Code Breaker*

Articles
> Canoeing 24 Exciting Maine Rivers-Published in
> Delorme's 1st edition of *The Maine Atlas and Gazetteer*
> Litter Licker Decoys - *Field and Stream*
> The Chamois Mask - *Sno-Goer Magazine*
> Family Canoeing in Maine - *Canoe Magazine*
> Cover Photo - 1st issue *Down River Magazine*
> 12 Hot Rivers - *Maine Audubon Society*
> Canoeing - *Guide to Maine*
> Down East Bow Busters - *Canoe Magazine*
> Hints on Selecting a Canoe Trip in Maine -
> *Post Script Magazine*
> Tap's Tips - *Field and Stream*
> Canoeing Maine Waters - *Maine Life*

Ben Thomas is a graduate of the University of Maine at Orono and holds a master Maine Guide and ham radio license. For ten years he flew small airplanes, landing in remote lakes and ponds.

Over a five-year period, he published three books on whitewater canoe paddling on Maine Rivers. Until *Code Breaker* there have been few current youth and young adult adventure yarns based here in Maine. Come along and enjoy an author whose motto is... *"I'm the kind of guy who would run a hundred miles to look at something.."*---Editor

Remember in life we cannot change the direction of the wind...but we can adjust the sails..._{anonymous}

Dedication

To our grandchildren, Ben and Madelyn Thomas, and to my son, Eben A. Thomas, who is also my best friend.

Acknowledgements

The following people have contributed to *Scuba Gold*:

David and Joanne Tamminen of Yarmouth, Maine

Laura Henry from Winthrop, Maine

Tori Suddeth

Walt and Annie Guerette who established the cover concept

Barclay's Skin Divers Paradise for technical information on scuba diving and equipment for cover photo shoot.
685 Washington Street
Auburn, ME 04210 207-784-7300

Hunter Nolan and Brittany Winslow both of Falmouth, Maine, for their cover images.

Oberlieutenant Hans Deiter's Biber class miniature submarine was rigged to carry two torpedoes but Deiter's boat carried none. He was not rolling and pitching in angry seas to sink ships in Portland harbor ten miles west of his current position. His mission was to rendezvous with two German agents at Parker Point at the mouth of the Royal River deep inside the Gulf of Maine. The risk that the agents would leave before he arrived sent a cold shiver down his back.

Paul Eastman's face registered boredom that can only be accomplished by a private in the army doing a repetitious job, working day after day with no hope of relief. His tour of duty in the Jewell Island 80-foot observation tower this week was from noon to dark. He thought his chances of spotting a German sub this late in the afternoon were slim, especially with visibility through his viewfinder reduced to about 3000 yards.

From this perch atop the tower his view of the Gulf of Maine was obscured only by Half Way Rock lighthouse with its black top and white base, as it rose out of the sea directly in front of his position. Beyond Half Way Rock lay the Atlantic Ocean.

His job was to sweep a powerful range finding telescope across the horizon, moving left and right of the lighthouse and to do this faithfully every five minutes searching for signs of German submarines. Paul Eastman, Pvt. First Class, had been doing this every other week for ten months.

He was there now on August 27, 1944 as bitter rain squalls battered the tower and sloshed stinging rain through the observation slits and plastered his 19-year-old face with wind-driven water. His only inspiration was the fact that two years before an observer had actually spotted a German sub halfway between Jewell Island and Small Point. While this provided an incentive to be alert, his body shook with the cold and his eyes burned from the long hours searching through the telescope.

He checked his watch, noting the rain and mist had caused dusk to fall an hour ahead of time. Even now Half Way Rock was only a blur. He decided one more sweep of the scope would be enough and carefully swung the spotting tube across the sea and let his mind drift to the hot meal and maybe a movie that awaited him back at the barracks.

Oberlieutenant Hans Deiter felt fear cluster in his stomach; the storm had driven his boat under the guns on Jewell Island. For the moment the U-33 was helpless. Rain plastered his blond hair and beard into a mask of running water and his white wool turtleneck sweater, decorated with the Iron Cross, rested wet and heavy on his shoulders. Oberlieutnant Hans Deiter, standing in the open conning tower, was drenched to the skin and shivering with the cold.

Eastman's eyes suddenly bulged and his pulse began to race. He gasped for breath and his fingers on the spotting scope became unmanageable. He pulled his eye away from the eyepiece and stared at the spot just east of the lighthouse where he thought he'd seen an object. He quickly centered his eye over the scope. "Not there," he said to himself almost with a sense of relief.

Then without warning, a submarine rose right out of the sea and appeared full length in the viewfinder. Range 3000 yards bearing 090 degrees. Eastman's arms felt paralyzed as he fired up the radio connecting him to the fire control officer one hundred yards from the tower.

"It's Eastman," he breathed into the mouthpiece. "Submarine... 3000 yards...bearing 090 degrees!"

His range and deflection were immediately converted into a fire mission and the six inch guns located directly below Eastman's tower began to fire.

Deiter never heard the explosion of the shell that chewed a huge divot out of the sea directly astern of his boat. The sound of the first blast was muffled by the second that blew the deck plates off the first four feet of his bow and mangled the conning tower. In the split of time between life and death he thought of his wife and unborn child back in Germany and the fact that Deiter was not his name. Would she ever know what had become of him?

Deiter fell down inside the tower and was dead before he hit the belly of the crippled sub. Water gushed and flooded the forward compartment. When the boat lost buoyancy, the nose struck downward until the conning tower disappeared.

The undamaged electric motor continued to provide power thrusting the tiny boat forward into Broad Sound until rising water shorted out the engine and the bow crunched against a ledge. The Biber class U-33, along with its captain settled to the ocean floor.

1

MESSAGE OF GOLD

The message about the gold came at the same time Matthew Banner's six-foot frame was sprawled on the forward deck of the 20-foot *Dawn Raider*. Matthew's Boston Whaler was at anchor in Casco Bay, a body of water along Maine's shoreline that held hundreds of spruce covered islands. Some bristled with aging summer cottages and elegant new homes; others seemed to float on the green clear water with trees, rocks and shoreline weathering gracefully in the bay.

The boat was anchored just outside Johnson Cove on the southeast corner of Chebeague Island. The sun glared down through a cloudless sky; and while it was unable to smother the sharp chill of the late afternoon, its heat succeeded in covering his tan body, clad in cutoff jeans, with a blanket of warmth.

Matt lay on his back, head propped up on an orange life jacket and slept on the fiberglass deck. It was his day off, a day to rack out and catch some rays, a day away from his job with the Department of Marine Resources (DMR) and the clammy wet suit he wore when working.

Matt had ridden the high trail of high school success, marred by one significant misfortune. That one mischance gnawed daily at his conscience and plagued his dreams. That one episode was also the reason he had accepted the Maine job offer. Actually he had jumped at the chance.

Was he accepting this diving job because of the adventure, or using it as a reason to escape Florida and its problems? Was he running away? He felt only regret and remorse.

Suddenly the ship to shore radio mounted behind the windshield of the Boston Whaler's console squawked to life, uttering a hissing, static bark.

"*Dawn Raider, Dawn Raider*," howled an urgent voice from the gray metal box interrupting Matt's sleep. "*Dawn Raider*, hey, Matt, pick up!"

Matt was surprised at the call, but immediately recognized Lance Williams's excited voice blasting from the speaker. Awake now, Matt scrambled off the forward deck and with two quick strides snatched up the mic. "Lance, you've got the *Dawn Raider*, over."

"Matt, I've been calling you like mad. Where are you...? Never mind...now get this...Jack Kilby found something this morning and if you'll pardon the expression, he hit the *Jack* pot!"

"So, what's happening?" Matt asked.

"Wait till you hear him tell it." He paused for breath. "Jack … get this ... Jack has found a piece of gold!" and his voice rasped with excitement.

"Gold!"

"Yeah, you got it right ...gold!"

"Where'd he find it?" Matt replied, a tiny trickle of excitement tripping through his heart.

"He won't tell." Lance's voice was evasive.

"Well then, how much did he find?"

Lance's voice came down an octave or two, "Actually not all that much."

"So what's the big deal?" Matt answered, a bit deflated.

"It's what Jack is *not* saying that's fascinating. Besides what he did bring in is pretty darn impressive. An 18-inch gold chain with a heavy gold and emerald pendant. You ought to see this thing." His voice became excited again. "We're talking major weight here. That dude is about two inches in diameter and..."

"Did he find it while diving?" Matt quickly interrupted.

"You got that right. Came whizzing up river here to Charlie's yard about a half hour ago. Ran up from the dock with the chain still dripping water." Before Matt could reply Lance burped out of the speaker again. "Get your butt in here, Matt. Got to see this!" Lance made it sound as if Jack had just discovered the Hope Diamond.

Matt looked thoughtful, and then clicked the mic, "*Dawn Raider* out."

Matt had arrived in Maine in early June directly from Florida and instantly fallen in love with Casco Bay, its unusual high tides, dark green water, and rumpled mussel beds that poked through at low water. The tide in the Florida Keys seldom rose above three feet and the flats were golden sand sprinkled with outcrops of living coral. The nine and ten foot rise in the Casco Bay waters fascinated him and he cherished the strange smell of seaweed and mud flats.

He hadn't been on the job a week when late one afternoon Lance Williams had confided in Matt that his main goal in life was to see how much he could get away with and still get to heaven. Matt took his position as team leader seriously and ideas like that worried him.

Lance was also the only member of the team to wear his hat backward. Alex Blanchard kidded him, saying doing that took ten points off his IQ and that Lance didn't have a reserve supply of numbers. While he took the joking well enough, Lance remained an enigma to Matt. Sometimes when he dealt with him he thought Alex's observations on numbers might be true. Lance was sometimes a bit strange–

there were several occasions when Matt believed Lance thought Elvis was still alive.

Lance, however, proved to be an excellent diver and on that score Matt gave him high marks. He had never caught him in a lie but sometimes Lance could enlarge upon what he'd actually experienced. That raised a question about the gold chain and pendant. What had Lance really seen? The word gold had a nice sound but would that pendant turn out to be real or fake?

2

DIVERS AND SEA URCHINS

Matt clipped the mic back in place and gave Lance's words some sober thought. Finding gold no matter what its source was everybody's hidden dream. In fact, finding anything buried or lost was always exciting. Matt and Jack Kilby were divers hired by the Department of Marine Resources in Augusta, as were Big Bob Green, Alex Blanchard, Kiki Malone and Lance Williams...six divers. Shortly one of them would die.

All of them except Matt had graduated in June from Yarmouth High School right in town. Matt had flown in from Marathon, an island in the Florida Keys. All the divers were certified and experienced and there was not one of them who didn't secretly harbor a dream of finding something valuable while poking around the green, shadowy kelp-laden waters of Casco Bay. Now it appeared Jack had located what might be called some *serious* stuff.

Matt's tan body was lean and hard after four years of high school sports, and diving in the blue-green waters of the Florida Keys. It took only a moment for him to scramble to the bow and haul in the anchor, trot to the center console and punch up the power on his 150-hp Yamaha.

He set a course that would lead the Whaler up the channel past Moshier and Lanes Islands to the high bluffs at Parker Point marking the entrance to the Royal River. Charlie's Marina was a mile farther up river. Charlie's ...and ... the *gold*!

The dive teams were based out of Charlie Craft's marina at the head of the river in Yarmouth, a growing yuppy village of 6000, situated between the port city of Portland, ten miles south, and the L.L. Bean-dominated Freeport four miles north.

Charlie, a short fire hydrant of a man with bushy eyebrows and dancing blue eyes filled with humor, had rented office and storage space to the Department of Marine Resources in an unused section of his retail sales building along Route 88 known by the locals as the shore road.

The front of the building, facing Route 88, held a large blue and white sign marked Charlie's Marina. Below and to the right of the door another sign said Harraseeket Yacht Sales. DMR rented the space to the left of the doorway and even though this area was really nothing more than a small rectangular room, the divers had dubbed it the "dive shack".

The ten by fifteen foot wood-floored room housed all their spare tanks, regulators and weight belts. Drying wet suits hung on pegs along one plywood wall. A scarred walnut desk with matching chair that squeaked sat in the center of the room.

The addition of six metal folding chairs and a scratched four drawer metal filing cabinet made up the total inventory with the exception of a computer on the desk, the only new item in the office. One window to the right of the metal door faced the shore road.

Ever since graduating from their respective schools in June the six of them had been diving in Casco Bay, searching for places to domestically farm a three inch dome-shaped shellfish called a sea urchin. Their eggs were a delicacy in great demand by the Asian nations, particularly Japan. On a good day two men picking these urchins could make $1200. With that kind of profit available, divers from all over New England rushed to harvest these little spiny creatures until the urchins were headed the way of the buffalo.

DMR, searching for a solution, hired Matt and his team to look for sections of the ocean floor that could be used to commercially grow the urchin under controlled conditions.

Although Matt wouldn't admit it, the closer he got to the yard the more gold fever trickled through his veins and he asked himself, "What was the source of the gold?" Then the more interesting questions, "Was there more gold where this piece had been found? Would there be gold coins or only jewels? Who else knew where the pendant had been found?"

Matt flipped the fenders over the side of the Whaler, grabbed the dock lines, and hopped over the rail. As he leaned over to tie the knot, visions popped into his mind of broken oak chests with Spanish pieces of eight leaking out of them, maybe chests that had been rotting on the bottom for centuries waiting for some lucky diver to find them.

Matt had a great smile, sort of a Tom Cruise affair. He cracked one now, a broad grin crinkling his darkly handsome face as he sprang up the gangway to shore and hurried up to the center of the boat yard. He knew Jack was an impetuous guy and might already have left taking the jewelry with him.

3

THE GOLD AND EMERALD PENDANT

Charlie's marina contained the usual storage sheds and railways leading from the yard to the water. Discarded wood cradles lay abandoned amid empty paint cans. Twenty-foot Makos, Grady Whites, and Boston Whalers mounted with Yamaha outboards were stacked about in the yard, their blue and green bimini tops ruffling in the breeze.

Matt hurried through the boats toward the sounds of excited, happy voices coming from the back of a long corrugated metal storage building Charlie had painted battleship gray.

Matt walked quickly to a group of yard workers and dive team members clustered in a tight knot around Jack, who was dancing around in the center of the ring, twirling a chain that reflected a soft yellow light, before placing it over Kiki's head. Loud shouts of congratulations were heard in the gathering. Lance saw Matt approach and waved an urgent arm at him to hustle.

Matt strode up, noticing all the DMR crew were still in their wet suits. All except Alex Blanchard, who was decked out in faded creased jeans, army green sweat shirt and unlaced sneakers. Alex was supposed to be diving with Jack today so Matt wondered why he wasn't in dive gear like the rest.

Jack Kilby had a puppy-like demeanor, always full of energy, romping through high school worry free. Jack took each day as it came.

Jack would have made an excellent character in *Grease*. He drove fast cars and was a bit of a player with the girls. Some said his life seemed so perfect he should wear a halo over his head. In his senior year Kiki started calling him *The Saint*.

Kiki Malone, dressed in her distinctive yellow wet suit with orange polka dots on the legs, appeared delighted with the tale Jack was telling. She was clapping her hands and jumping up and down as she did when she was particularly pleased. She turned her head.

"Hey, Matt," she greeted, "get over here." She waited until Matt was beside her and whispered in his ear, "Jack has found something big time!" A huge smile showed a row of perfect teeth. She thought Matt had the deepest brown eyes ever. She liked the turn of his nose and square chin. His mouth, she thought, was especially sexy.

"Hey, Kiki," he returned. The crew was in a festive mood, slapping Jack on the back and snapping high fives.

Kiki was a stunner, her face painted a golden bronze from the sun and glancing rays of Casco Bay. A perky nose, freckles and creases at the corners of her mouth gave her an impish expression. Kiki was a bundle of nice curves, a Taylor Swift in a diver suit.

Matt shifted his eyes to Big Bob Green, the only black diver, who watched the proceeding from the back of the crowd and dwarfed everyone. At six foot six and 240 pounds he'd had his wet suit specially made. His top was off exposing wide, powerful shoulders that would fill a doorway before tapering to his waist.

With his dark skin and black dive suit he looked like a hulking Darth Vader with a scuba tank. Big Bob was just putting in time with DMR before reporting to Loyola's football squad in mid August.

His coal black hair was cropped short and eyes that seemed to bulge from their sockets stared at the necklace as Jack carefully lifted the chain from around Kiki's slim neck and tossed the pendant to Matt.

Matt caught the pendant. His heart gave a short skip when he felt the heavy weight settle back in his hand. That was when he noticed a man and woman standing next to a white van marked Channel 13. The van was parked next to Charlie's office. A good-looking blond in her mid twenties, gold earrings, white blouse and green blazer was packing up gear into a red canvas bag and talking excitedly to her cameraman.

"Who's that?" Matt asked pointing at the two figures climbing into the van.

Jack flashed him a devilish grin, "TV reporter, gal named Mandy Costelle."

"You tell her where you found this piece?"

"Not on your life."

Kiki broke in, "When he wouldn't tell, that reporter asked if she could at least get some close-up pictures."

"You let her do that, Jack?" Matt ran a hand through his unruly brown hair. He had a bad feeling about the answer.

"Sure, why not? Maybe someone will call and tell me what it's worth."

"Yeah, Jack, they might just do that then try to lay out a claim it's theirs."

For a smart guy Jack sometimes made foolish mistakes.

"As soon as the filming was done the reporter packed away the mic, gathered her cameraman and hiked up to that Channel 13 truck," Big Bob said pointing to the street. "She was a bit put out!" They all laughed.

Before Matt tossed the gold neck piece back to Jack he rubbed it in his fingers. The gold felt soft and warm. The pendant was indeed a good two inches in diameter. The chunk of gold was coin shaped with a half-inch bright green emerald fastened to the front. Matt asked himself if he was holding a misplaced necklace or a piece of antiquity.

His pulse jumped and his heart gave a lively skip as images of Spanish doubloons spilling from oak chests flashed again through his mind. *Lance Williams had been correct. The gold was heavy.*

People began melting away from the milling group. Kiki grabbed her gear and headed for the office with the others following behind. Suddenly Matt found himself alone with Jack. Matt had some questions that needed answers.

Jack, at six two, was taller than Matt but not by much and where Matt was dense through the shoulders Jack was reed thin. His wet suit appeared a size too large and hung on him in wrinkles. His blond hair was a shade shy of curly and rampaged around his head.

The blue eyes were full of mischief and dominated a face that was perpetually in motion. Jack wore his usual cocky smile, and while he was considered a clever guy he was Matt's most reckless diver.

"Jack, I don't want to pry and if you want to keep where you found that piece a secret that's okay and it's your business. However, you were obviously diving alone when you found it. That part is my business." Matt had a firm rule for the teams. No one was to dive alone. "Alex was your scheduled partner. Where was he today?"

For just a second Jack had a hard time holding Matt's eyes. He shuffled his feet then said, "Chill out, man, not to worry. Alex had a cold that was giving him problems clearing his ears if he dropped below ten feet. I told him to stay home and I'd just do some scouting. You know how it is, Matt. When I got out there I found this really good-looking spot. I've been diving all my life. I just had to go overboard." He paused. "So I made a mistake." He shrugged his shoulder and threw out his hands.

As team leader Matt had a decision to make and Jack could see him struggling with it. He jumped in before Matt could get started. "Look, I was wrong. It won't happen again. I promise." Jack put his arm around Matt's shoulder. "Hey, lighten up. You can trust me." His voice was deep and sincere.

Matt punched his friend's arm. "All right, Mr. Gold Finder, but never again."

"You got it," Jack replied as he flipped his tank over his shoulder and headed up the grade to the dive shack. Halfway there he stopped and waved to Matt before disappearing around the corner. Considering the events that later unfolded, Matt would wonder then if he should have done something different.

Matt had left his boat only partially tied so he hurried down through the yard to the dock where he ran into Watts Penn. In Arkansas Watts would have been called a redneck or cracker. Here in Maine he was a leathery, tobacco-stained chip of a man who had survived some seventy years fishing lobsters out of Yarmouth's harbor.

His face was weathered parchment, tanned and cured, a face as thin as a knife blade and covered by skin so wrinkled it looked like aluminum foil scrunched up then smoothed out. Watts leaned out over the carriageway rail to the dock below. "Hey, what's all the commotion up in the yard?" he shouted in a voice surprisingly deep for such a small man.

"Jack Kilby dragged up a piece of gold today. Big fuss being made." Matt called up to him. "Had Channel 13 with cameras and the whole works up in the yard a few minutes ago." Matt started to say Watts could see it on TV tonight then remembered Watts didn't have a television.

Watts rubbed his narrow, crooked nose for a second, filing away what he'd heard. Then he hitched up on his black rubber boots and picked up his empty bait pail before he replied, "Yeah, thanks, see ya," and trudged off with the smell of rotting fish following him.

Matt shook his head. Some in town thought Watts was an ornery old cuss, testy and bad tempered, but Matt admired the old man's independence. He chuckled. Watts was so pickled in salt he might never die.

He checked his watch. Six o'clock. Time to quit.

4

KIKI MALONE

When Kiki Malone set her eyes on a guy he was dead meat, zapped and wrapped. She could deliver a hot-eyed stare that fried guys in their tracks. She could turn chameleon, going from demure and innocent to hot and bold in a blink of her eye. That was why she was disappointed and mystified when she failed to get more out of Matthew Banner than a brotherly pat on the head and a peck on the cheek. Kiki promised herself she would try harder.

She wondered if he had brothers or sisters. What had he been like when he was younger? Had he always lived in Florida? She'd have to find out. Guys with broad shoulders and strong muscles intrigued her. Kiki knew she would satisfy her curiosity soon.

Kiki remembered the day Matt came on board. The way he had paced the small space in the dive shack like a caged lion full of pent-up energy, every eye in the room following him as he laid out how they were to accomplish DMR's mission. His words had been delivered as though they had been rehearsed but Kiki didn't think that was the case.

His voice had a vibrant sound, a deep resonance, and he'd let a smile crease the corners of his mouth when he thought he was getting too serious. When Matt was finished, she knew they had a leader they all would follow...a major guy!

Kiki stepped across to Charlie's office where the window faced the docks, in time to see Matt speak with the old geezer, Watts, whom she'd seen fishing lobsters between Green Island and Little Whaleboat.

She had lots of questions concerning Matt. Her information about him was sketchy at best. Last week after Matt had changed into his wet suit Kiki had dodged into the shack and sneaked a peek through his wallet. But all she found were his Florida driver's license, his diver's certificate, and an obviously old photo showing two adults standing behind a Matthew Banner when he was much younger with his arm around a little tow-headed girl. As she slipped the wallet back she wondered why Matt didn't have a more recent photo...weird.

The few weeks Matt had been in Maine was too short a click of time to fully measure someone and she wanted to be fair in her assessment, which so far had disclosed some disturbing observations. He seemed totally cool and had a great sense of humor.

She noticed how quickly the other divers followed Matt's ideas on how to map the ocean floor for Aristotle's lanterns, how he was thoughtful and listened to their ideas. Yet she noticed that he seemed to be struggling with some kind of internal problem he would not share.

She also wondered why this compelling guy had been placed in charge of the dive group. She figured he must have a ton of experience because Alex and Big Bob belonged to the Portland Divers Association where long hours under water were required for membership. In addition, Lance, heck, he could *weld* under water!

She had to admit Matt exerted a firm command on the group. Even Big Bob, who was a real hardnose, said he'd follow him anywhere. There was a kindness in Matt, too, a gentleness she had not seen in the others.

Still there was that dark side, that sudden sadness that slipped like a mask over his face when he thought no one was looking.   Sometimes he seemed to be punishing himself.

Kiki shrugged off her thoughts and hung up her dive gear, showered in the small attached bathroom, then jumped into jeans and T-shirt, smiling with satisfaction at the low whistle she received from Alex. She winked a small drop of encouragement in his direction. "Got to keep your options open, Malone," she said to herself then skipped out the door to her yellow VW.

Kiki poked her pretty face out the window and waved, "See you guys tomorrow." She kicked the little car around on the tar and made a pledge with herself that she would find out what made Matt tick.

5

SCUBA GOLD

The day following the Fourth of July celebrations the sky continued clear. Fair weather clouds drifted over Charlie's yard; a gentle northerly breeze wrinkled the river causing the boats at anchor to point their sterns down toward the bay.

Jack Kilby waited until the rest of the scheduled divers were down at the dock before slipping a note into Matt's mail slot in the dive shack. Then he gathered up the rest of his gear and trotted down to the shore to meet Kiki at the boat.

Matt was off duty that day but around ten o'clock he stopped by the shack to finish up some paperwork. He checked his mail slot and was surprised to find a letter poking out of the box. That had not happened since he had arrived in Maine.

Word from Florida could only be bad news and he frankly could think of no one else who would write. He hesitated, before sweeping up the envelope. There was only a single word in the address space....*Matt*. He tore off the end and quickly pulled out the single sheet from inside.

Matt, I need to see you tonight at my place 8:00. I have something to show you and I might need your advice......Jack

Just before eight that night Matt drove up town past neat white houses with small lawns and short driveways lining the street.   Jack's white colonial seemed large by comparison.

His parents, both teachers, were on a sabbatical some place in Europe, leaving Jack the run of their sprawling four-bedroom house.

During the last few weeks Matt had learned Jack was practical, fiery and aggressive. He was also a hurrier, often walking so fast he had to wait for automatic doors to open. Some fellows Matt knew were slow to make decisions. Not so Jack Kilby and as a result he often got into trouble. Matt turned into the driveway and pressed the doorbell, wondering what had inspired Jack to leave the note.

Jack opened the door and with a hand on Matt's arm hauled him inside. Matt could sense his excitement. Before Matt could say hello, words exploded out of Jack's mouth, "You ready to see something that will tear your eyes out?!" Before Matt could reply Jack grabbed his arm and dragged him through the living room.

Matt hid his surprise, "Yeah, sure...what have you got?" Matt replied, practically running after Jack upstairs to a bedroom at the rear of the house.

Matt wasn't ready for what came next.   Jack had arranged a dark green cloth over the foot of a four-poster bed that was literally weighted down with gold.   The original pendant he'd found was arranged as a centerpiece around which Jack had placed a stunning group of ruby and emerald rings, followed by two platinum broaches studded with more emeralds and diamonds.

Gold bracelets and necklaces, that transcended the original find, were crammed along the outer edges of the cloth and shimmered in the soft glow of the low table lamp. Stacked in a loose pile were a dozen gold coins.

Matt's eyes opened wide with astonishment. Then he tore them away from what had to be a king's ransom and looked to Jack for an answer.

"Impressive, isn't it?" Jack responded in a whisper voice. "Think how I felt twenty feet under water pawing around in green waving rock weed when my dive lamp suddenly illuminated an unusual object in the mud. I reached out and gave it a tug. When the mud cleared I held that necklace," he said, pointing to the center of the bed. "Gold, Matt ...solid, heavy gold!"

As Jack's story unfolded, Matt's ears were doing battle trying to listen and at the same time keep his eyes focused on the gold displayed on the green cloth that seemed alive!

"Then in spite of your promise not to dive alone you went back after work. Probably dove all day on July 4th... back where you found the pendant." Matt could feel his blood pressure ratchet up twenty notches.

"Can you blame me, Matt?" Jack breathed out. "Just look at this stuff. I couldn't leave it. Everything seemed to be going super but after that TV reporter ran the story on the pendant I got a thousand phone calls. Now for two days I've had the feeling someone is following me."

"Cool it, Jack, what is this, *CSI* ? What do you mean, followed?"

"Just that. Nothing I can put my finger on. Just a feeling," and he shrugged his shoulders.

"What do you want from me besides keeping my mouth shut?" Matt asked.

"I need you as a witness that I found this stuff diving over a wreck and didn't acquire it by stealing."

The word *wreck* instantly piqued Matt's interest. "What kind of a wreck?" Then before Jack could answer, "Do you have any idea who owns this treasure? How can you be sure it isn't stealing?"

Jack laughed. "Let's just leave it as a wreck for now and for your second question," he pointed at the bed, "stuff's very old! I doubt anyone is alive that can lay claim to any of it."

"How can you be so sure?" Matt's brow creased with concern.

"You see, I ran into something on the floor of the bay that indicated these pieces were being transported and the boat carrying them sank. I could tell that the ship had been there a long time." He gave a conspirator's wink.

"You sure these jewels were not in some bag that might have been stolen from a bank?"

Jack smiled. "Nothing like that."

"Maybe a chest?" Matt couldn't get the Spanish doubloons out of his mind.

"You could call it that." When Jack replied Matt had the feeling he was getting only part of the story or some truth and some fiction.

Matt pressed him. "You actually found all these pieces in the same spot?"

An even set of teeth flashed as he gave Matt a wide grin, "The same exact spot! You betcha!" Matt didn't know if the heat in the room had been turned up or not but he was sweating.

Pushing once more, he inquired, "All...this...?" He said, spreading his hands toward the bed.

"That's not a bad thing, is it, Matt?"

"Whew, I guess not! But I don't figure you brought me here to tell me where you found it."

"Not yet, Matt," his voice turned serious. "More as a witness like I said... and,"...he paused ... "in case something happens to me you'll have some idea of why."

Matt gave him a worried look. "Do you have reason to believe you're in danger?"

Jack didn't answer right away. Then said, "Not right now, but if word of this leaks out all that could change, that and the sense I'm being followed."

"What are you going to do with all this loot?"

"That's the problem, Matt, I can't tell anyone where I found it. At least not until I figure out how to obtain legal custody."

Matt suddenly realized what Jack was not telling him. "You mean there's more where this came from, don't you?"

Jack bit his lip and raised his eyes. "Yeah," he admitted. "There's a whole lot more." He flashed a broad smile. "My problem right now is figuring out a way to dispose of this stuff."

"So until you decide how to keep this legally, how are you going to hide it?"

"Simple," Jack replied. "In the most obvious place. I've cut out the center of five books here on the shelf. I'm filling the space with the gold coins and jewels."

Matt picked up one of the coins. His eyes shot open when he read the date: 1710! It was only a short leap of faith to his Spanish doubloons but he kept his mouth shut.

With that said, Jack asked Matt to help him make out an inventory. They made two copies. Jack gave Matt one to keep. "Just in case," he said as he handed the paper to Matt.

Back in his pickup the dashboard clock glowed green in the cab. Matt was surprised to find it was ten thirty. He bounced over the tracks to the lower village then down the hill by the old fire station. At the bottom he steered the truck along Route 88 for a short distance before returning to his studio apartment in Harvey Winslow's two-story cape. Harvey and his wife were traveling out west for the summer and had left Matt as sort of caretaker.

He opened the door to the small apartment attached to the side of the house. The kitchen, like the rest of his digs, was sparsely furnished. One porcelain-topped table and two wooden chairs. The combination living room bedroom was equally sparse in furnishings, one couch, side chair and bed. The only new fixtures were his CD player and the 30-inch TV sitting on the floor. The walls were painted a pastel blue and at some Precambrian period the wood floors had been finished. The dishes at the sink, however, were clean and stacked neatly on the sideboard to drain.

He stepped to the refrigerator, opened the freezer, and extracted the Folgers coffee can that he kept in there for freshness. Matt popped off the lid, and stuffed the folded inventory list inside the can before returning it to the freezer. With a hiding place secured he flopped on the bed. Matt propped himself up with a pillow and thought about what Jack had told him.

Was the gold stolen or could he accept Jack's version? Where was this *wreck*? What did he mean when he'd said the treasure came from a period of time *long ago*? And that bit about finding the gold in a *chest*. What had he meant? Matt cursed himself for not asking more questions. One thing was certain, Jack, while diving for Aristotle's lanterns, had instead found... *scuba gold*!

That night the dream came again.

As always, he was back home in Florida. He could see his room, the bed with no headboard; bookshelves painted red provided a startling contrast to the oyster white walls. A football sat on the top shelf signed by all the players and the coach. In his dream his mind read the inscription written in bold black across the center of the ball: *Mr. Touchdown 2009.*

Books on diving filled in the spaces left and right of the ball. Speech and debate awards were pinned above the bookcase. The dream at this point always switched to his boat.

At first the call would come from a great distance, muffled and indistinct, then like an approaching train the voice grew closer and louder until he could make out... *"Matthew...I need you...wake up...wake up...wake up!"* But as usual his mind was drugged with sleep, unwilling to respond.... *"Matthew...I'm dying...please come help me...Matthew it's Lisa...Lisa...Lisa!"* At that point his mind would snap to attention. He'd lean over the rail and peer under water, and like always, she was there... *waving*.

That's when Matt always awoke from the nightmare. He shivered and cursed the dream that plagued him and made the nights a guilt-ridden passage.

6

PIRATES

In the morning with the sun's first feeble rays peeking from its easterly home Matt arose, slam-dunked down his toast and coffee. He hurried from his apartment and drove his DMR truck the short quarter mile to Charlie's yard.

The question of where Jack had found the gold was driving Matt and his dive crew crazy.

Jack had admitted last night there was more to recover but Matt had promised Jack he wouldn't reveal to the dive team what he knew. Jack might tell them but in his own good time. However, like the other divers Matt really had no clue where the pendant had been found.

Alex, Big Bob, and Lance trooped in at six thirty a.m. followed shortly by Kiki Malone. She never failed to cause Matt's heart to bump. Her long blond hair tumbled down her back, the front edges cut just shy of her tanned jaw line along her heart-shaped face.

This morning she wore her V-necked T-shirt cropped short exposing a flattering midriff followed by yellow fringed shorts and gold thong sandals. Matt knew she could shine light into the dark corners of a male's heart and not even know she had thrown the switch.

The musty smell of wet suits drying on their wall pegs swept through the small room and crowded around the divers. Matt could hear sounds of Charlie's yard workers arriving. Laughter spilled through the thin walls. The early morning light had just trickled through the single window

facing the street when Kiki began speaking. Her voice was
almost a hush as she fastened her bright blue eyes on the
group lounging on the fold-up chairs. She was seated facing
the guys who were strung out in a ragged line in front of
her. Kiki took a sip of her coffee. Then with eyes staring
from under her bangs asked, "Do you really think he found
the gold under water as he said?"

"If Jack said he dug it up out in the bay then that's
where he found the stuff, Kiki, even though he's not telling
us where. Jack's always been a straight shooter. He
wouldn't lie." With that Big Bob got up, grabbed his wet
suit from the wall peg and checked to see if it was dry
before turning the spongy rubber right side out.

Of the group Bob was the least difficult to figure out.
He was a straight ahead guy and Matt liked him, but it was
Alex Blanchard that Matt found amusing and brilliant.

For example, Alex was always asking questions that
seemed to have answers but didn't. Last week when they
were diving together, he'd looked Matt in the face and
asked, "What should I do if I see an endangered animal
eating an endangered plant?" Or, "Could vegetarians eat
animal crackers?" Matt had never seen anyone eat carrots
fat end first but Alex did. Alex could be a real enigma. A
guy who ran algebra problems through his head for
relaxation yet never fixed the blinking clock on his DVR.

Lance Williams spun on his chair and faced Alex.
"What's your explanation?" his face a question.

"Well," Alex replied with a tone that said he didn't care
much for Lance, "could be loot lost when rum runners used
Casco Bay to hide from federal revenuers. Dutch Schultz
and Baby Face Nelson were into brewing moonshine and
bank robbery."

"Pretty far out!" Lance practically sneered. "Maybe if Jack had found money that might make sense but not that necklace."

Matt knew from what Kiki had told him that Lance was crude where girls were concerned. He simply didn't understand the word "No". Except when diving he wore the same set of skate boarder baggy pants and dirty long sleeve black sweat shirt with Dallas Cowboys stenciled on the back. Matt thought that if Lance's parents had really observed him they would have said, "Lance is no good, we should sell him!"

Matt, who had been quiet up to now, cleared his throat. They all swung their heads in his direction.

"Maybe Alex is right; at least what he said is logical.

"When I knew for sure I was coming to Maine, I did some research on the islands of Casco Bay. Know what I found?" He paused. "Many of them were settled in the 1700s and farmed for hay or used as fishing outposts."

Matt let a small crinkle form at the corner of his mouth then continued letting the words leak out slowly. "But some of them are reputed to contain *buried treasure*!"

"And just who was supposed to have buried this treasure?" Lance asked, the expression on his face one of amusement.

Matt turned a blank face in Lance's direction and gave him a one word reply. "Pirates."

7

SUNKEN PIRATE SHIPS

"Pirates...awe, come on, Matt, give me a break!" Kiki burst into laughter, rose from her chair and re-deposited herself on the corner of the desk, giving Matt a dazzling look.

"Well, think about it. What other explanation do we have that's less crazy?" Matt answered.

Kiki responded. "I'm not sure, but really, Matt...Pirate treasure?" Her voice turned soft and Matt could see the freckles on her nose.

"You know, guys," Alex smiled. "If Matt is correct, that means there might be more treasure buried out there. I've never read about pirates burying only one necklace!"

Alex seated himself in front of the computer, fired it up and clicked through the dive schedules. "Matt, look," he said tapping the screen, "Jack and I were supposed to dive out by Whaleboat Island the day I called in with the ear problem. I'm sure he went there first."

"Even if we knew Whaleboat is the right spot, that still leaves acres of sea bottom--like looking for the proverbial needle," Lance said. He faced the group. "You know that if Matt's sunken pirate ship theory is correct, Jack is going to find a whole lot more gold!" Matt thought, "*If you only knew!*"

Before they could continue, Jack's truck burst into the yard and disappeared in a cloud of dust toward the docks below. "What in the devil is he doing here today?" Lance wondered. "He's off duty."

Alex and Matt exchanged glances. Matt knew where Jack was going and while he had the power to stop him he somehow didn't have the heart to do it. Then knowing he had to do something to prevent Jack from diving alone, Matt rushed out the door and ran to the dock.

He was too late. Jack's boat, with its new name, *Black Beard* was already tooling past The Cannery Restaurant and headed out to the bay. He glanced up at Route 88 and the early morning commuter traffic. It was time to work the DMR schedule for the day. He would have to deal with Jack another time.

8

HEINRICK VON BROCKNER

At first Brockner didn't budge, just sat rigidly in his high, wing-backed chair, holding the paper with hands that showed a slight tremor as he concentrated on the AP wire report. He was seated close to a fireplace so large that if he had chosen to stand in its center his head, broaching better than six feet, would have failed to reach the apex of the opening.

A full head of snow white hair, cropped military short, topped an aristocratic face. Shoulders were rounded with age. The face that peered at the paper was non-descript. Eyes that were used to probing were a cold, lead gray, steel-rimmed glasses were hooked behind ears built too close to his head.

Light from the flickering fire mingled with the glow of the antique lamp beside the chair. The room in the castle was of church proportions, with tall, vaulted ceilings, and niches along the walls that held burning gas torches. A suit of armor gripping a shield and lance stood stoically in a corner. Rich tapestries hung from the stone walls. The room was medieval.

As Brockner read he could feel excitement build and his facial muscles quiver as he sensed the treasure that had eluded him for so many years might finally have surfaced.

He re-read the article, paying particular attention to the description of the pendant.

Brockner paused in his reading, strode to a large metal safe hidden in the wall and extracted a manila folder, creased and worn from years of use. The metal clasp had long since broken off. He had repaired the packet with scotch tape but this too was dry and brittle.

He withdrew six single-spaced sheets that had been typed on by a manual typewriter in 1944. He flipped through the yellowed pages until he found the one he wanted, then carried it to the light by the chair and seated himself. He tipped his glasses forward on his prominent nose and compared the description from the typed list to the newspaper article.

The nearness of the comparison caused heat to course through his body. He suddenly found it hard to breathe and the hand holding the pages began to shake again.

The AP news article Brockner had been reading reported the discovery of a gold necklace with a two-inch pendant. Jack Kilby's discovery had been picked up by the international wire service. For most readers the article was no more than an interesting filler piece. *Diver Jack Kilby, of 48 West Elm Street, finds gold piece...speculation on its source causes minor furor in small village of Yarmouth, Maine.* The article held far greater significance for the German.

As his electric blue eyes and razor sharp mind followed the words once more, he penciled notes on the exact location in Maine and the name and address of the diver. His face held a scrape of nobility but was a pasty, sallow color hinting at an indoor occupation, a banker or maybe an accountant or lawyer. However, he was none of these. Heinrich von Brockner was a retired German military intelligence officer with rank of Oberst, the equivalent of an American full colonel.

It was no accident that Brockner rose rapidly through the German military system. He made himself indispensable, ran errands, solved political problems, all done with German precision. He sabotaged the careers of those behind him in rank and destroyed those in front. The result was a meteoric rise to power all done with a benign smile.

Brockner lifted the phone from its European cradle and dialed.

Karl Richter answered the phone, his bald head nodding as he took notes from Brockner. "*Ja, ja*, I understand, *Mein Herr*." Richter hung up, and quickly redialed to make air reservations for two from Frankfort to Portland, Maine. Then Richter placed a second longer call to the United States securing a Budget rental car. On the advice of the rental agency he made a long-term reservation at the Down East Motel on Route 1 in Yarmouth, Maine.

9

LEE THOMAS MCCALL

Born in the foothills of the Crazy Mountains of western Montana, Lee Thomas McCall was a strong, self-reliant young lady well used to rough cowboy jobs on a working 100,000 head cattle ranch. There were few if any experiences that fazed L.T. McCall. She zipped through high school, kissed her share of boys, and in general managed her world to her satisfaction.

Until today!

McCall breezed in from the horse barn and wiped sweat from her forehead. Inside, the ranch was a cool welcome relief from the heat of the stable. She walked with a certain sense of herself, secure in who she was, not like her high school freshman year where she'd felt awkward in the shadow of the upper classmen.

As she strode past the fireplace McCall glanced at the photo of her sister on the mantle. While Paige was two years younger, McCall was struck by their similarity. The girl in the photo was tall and athletic, green eyes, a large shock of unruly red hair, slim neck, and nicely molded mouth with sensual lips. The face showed a certain cockiness. She had to admit Paige had a neat figure.

McCall held the gold framed picture in her hand and nodded, "Yeah, that's me except for the red hair." Showing the difference, she swung her head to one side allowing her soft, honey blond hair to swing free at her shoulders. "And my legs are definitely better!"

McCall replaced the photo and snapped on the TV, grabbed a Coke from the refrigerator and flopped onto the couch where she watched the Channel 2 newscaster ramble on about the mid-east crisis before switching to national news.

McCall suddenly snatched up the TV remote from the coffee table and turned up the volume. Her mouth popped wide open in surprise, her heart shot into her mouth. She was at first bewildered at what she'd heard then struck speechless by the image on the screen. Her bright eyes stretched open in shock.

What L.T. McCall had just seen on television was impossible!

The camera zoomed in again as the TV reporter, Mandy Costelle, held up a gold pendant. As she spoke the pendant spun on its heavy gold linked chain exposing a large green emerald fastened to the backside.

Costelle's voice held a touch of mystery and awe. "...*at this point all we know is that a sea urchin diver, Jack Kilby, found this gold piece somewhere in Casco Bay near the town of Yarmouth, Maine.*"

McCall's heart felt suspended between beats. She could not fathom what she was hearing. "*While on one of these underwater mapping explorations,*" the announcer continued, "*Kilby dredged up what could well be a historic find of impressive proportions. Unfortunately, Kilby is keeping the location of his discovery a secret, at least for the present.*"

McCall scooped up a note pad and swiftly scribbled down the names, Kilby and Yarmouth, Maine. Her mind bolted back ten years when as an eight-year-old girl she had flown to Rheims, outside Paris, France, to spend the summer with her grandmother, Countess de Largent.

She would never forget that summer. The Countess had shown her a painting of a pendant done by a well-known artist, who had captured the soft tone of gold against a background of black velvet. Exactly in the center burned a large emerald.

The painting had been lighted with a soft spotlight and the pendant seemed so real she thought of reaching up her small hand to pluck it from the frame. McCall had burned that image of the sparkling necklace and the suspended pendant in her young mind.

The Countess had told her the invading Germans, during World War II, had confiscated the necklace and she had never seen it again. That painting had been all that remained.

Two years later her grandmother died. Now ten years after her visit, McCall had all but forgotten the necklace, until now, when it suddenly reappeared in all its brilliance on the TV screen. McCall had seen it with her own eyes!

Branding was over and the cattle were out on the range for the summer. Her parents were in Alberta traveling. There was only her brother, James, and a foreman at the ranch. Her sister, Paige, was visiting a friend in Arkansas. McCall's hand shook as she texted James and Paige explaining she was... *headed to Maine to check out our grandmother's lost pendant...will call when I get there and explain it all...Love, L. T.*

10

SHOTS FIRED

Two weeks after Matt met with the divers to discuss Jack's source of the gold, the blond Channel 13 reporter found herself regretting her coverage of Jack Kilby's find. The local station continued to broadcast images of the pendant, resulting in a blizzard of phone calls. The heavy gold piece took on a life of its own, one of those cute little news clips that shot out of Channel 13 and suddenly went worldwide.

The fact that the coin-shaped metal looked old and Jack's refusal to disclose where he'd found it made the story even more provocative. Questions flooded into the station faster than Mandy could research them and reply. *How old was the pendant? Where had it been found?* Moreover, the most often asked, *What was it worth?*

Overwhelmed, she finally diverted some of the public outcry back to Jack by announcing his home address. Secretly she hoped enough pressure would be brought to bear that Jack would relent and tell the world where he had discovered the gold.

On the same day Mandy was cursing her luck, and long before she had even thought about the upcoming day, Watts Penn carried a meager lunch and a liter bottle of Pepsi to his dinghy tied to Charlie's floating dock and rowed to the *Sally Anne*. Watts' boat had once been carefully painted but that was a long time ago when his hand was steady, the hull was smooth, and milk was sold in glass bottles.

Clouds of thick rolling fog cruised over the river and mixed with the morning darkness. Watts released the *Sally Anne* from her mooring and turned the bow down river. With the skill of sixty years he poked his weathered face around the windshield and sniffed into the wet air.

When The Cannery Restaurant slid past his starboard rail he leaned the leaky boat through the bends in the river, steering the peeling hull past lobster pot buoys and channel markers until the bow swung even with Parker Point and the opening into Casco Bay.

Not long after Watts went down river, when dawn was only a promise in the sky, Matt Banner used his company-assigned Global Positioning Satellite unit, known as a GPS, to guide him through the closing fog to the town beach on Cousins Island. He drifted his Whaler along the edge of the channel by the bridge leading to the mainland. The morning was turning out to be wet and cold, covering the *Dawn Raider*'s white hull with woolly fog and plastering the deck with dew.

He drew a deep breath, smelled the sea and watched a pale hue wash across the horizon where the sun struggled to break through the low hanging clouds. His quick eyes scanned the water on the shore side of the boat observing the oily smooth surface and the beach slathered with foam, a residue from last night's wind.

This was Matt's honey hole, the place where huge striped bass cruised the shoreline ready to attack schools of blue backed herring. Ever since Charlie had introduced him to fly fishing he had become overwhelmingly absorbed by the sport. He wondered if wanting to fish every waking moment was a sign of obsession, and if so, was it curable...and if it was ...did he want to be cured?

Suddenly the surface ripped open. Water erupted in a wall of white. Matt snatched up his fly rod and sent the fly in a curving line on top of the rising fish.

The bass struck the instant the fly landed. Matt laughed in excitement and carefully played the fish to the boat then cursed when he saw the hook was fouled in the fish's gills. When he lifted the bass on board blood dripped onto the floorboards. The striper was too short to keep so Matt was forced to release the doomed fish overboard.

That was when he saw her!

At first he mostly sensed a movement along the beach. Visibility was poor with the shoreline awash in dull grays, a combination of dense mist and dawn struggling to haul daylight over Casco Bay. There were no colors, just moving silhouettes in black and white. There were two of them.

One was a dog that bolted ahead of the girl's gliding feet. He would dash down the beach then fling himself into reverse, haul around in the sand and lunge back to the girl, where he would spring on his hind legs and bark for her attention. The girl paused in her run, snatched up a stick and threw it for the dog.

On her present track the runner would pass fifty feet from his boat. There was no wind, no sound, as her heels pounded into the beach throwing sprits of sand away from her flying feet. She ran with a smooth, graceful motion, no hitches to her stride. She wore a dark halter top and cut off shorts. Hair bounced just shy of her shoulders and flew wildly around her head. Matt sensed a nice body with rounded, shapely legs.

Matt could feel the adrenaline flowing as he stripped in his line and stowed the rod. "Hey, good morning."

"Good morning yourself," she replied effortlessly between breaths. Her voice carried easily in the still air

"You run here every morning?"

She turned her head looking back at the drifting boat, then flipping him a hint of a smile said, "Sometimes."

Then before Matt could start the boat and catch up she gave a quick wave, whistled the dog and sprinted through the trees to the tar road that led to the interior of the island.

Farther out in the bay, off the tip of Whaleboat Island, Watts Penn motored along his trap line in a fog that continued to blanket his boat.   Worm ridden, barnacled lobster traps were stacked on the transom waiting for Watts to bait each parlor with foul smelling herring.

This foggy July the fog continued so thick the gulls that normally followed his boat begging scraps of bait remained perched on ledges and pot buoys holding close to the water.

Watts speared a piece of bait, lifted the lid on the wooden trap, and secured the herring in the parlor before closing the door. Then with one smooth motion he shoved the lath box over the side, stepped smartly to the wheel, pushed up the power on the four-cycle Jeep engine, and nudged the boat ahead.

The sun was now two fingers over the horizon cranking out enough energy to split open the dense mist when he heard the other boat. A hint of breeze registered on his cheek. Not only was the fog impossible to see through but it had an uncanny way of masking the direction of sound.

The first sign of the other boat was a gentle ripple from its wake. A tiny surge of water crossed the distance between the *Sally Anne* and a dark spot in the fog bank. Watts shut off his engine and turned huge, leathery ears toward the sound of an idling motor confirming the presence of the other boat.

Just as a breeze rippled the surface the sound of three shots, dull thuds in the fog, reached Watts. The sky suddenly brightened as a brisk wind blew a small hole in the mist. Watts could make out a figure struggling with a line attached to another boat. Watts' rheumy eyes, whites yellowed with age, could still spot a shag on a lobster pot at a mile so he had no difficulty in identifying the second boat.

Before Watts could seek shelter in a fog bank a pair of binoculars from the other boat focused on his face then swung to the name *Sally Anne* painted on the stern. He quickly kicked the Jeep engine to life and motored into a covering fog bank, but the damage had already been done.

If he had been worried because he recognized the second boat he was truly frightened by the shots and the fact he'd been seen. His mouth felt dry and fear grabbed him in the pit of his stomach as realization dawned that he would have to hide, sleep on board, and drop out of sight.

Back at the beach Matt felt his heart give a short lurch. With the momentary glimpse and the poor light he doubted he would be able to recognize the runner again in the daylight so he was left fantasizing and half in love with the mystery girl on the beach.

He scuttled the thoughts of fishing and as he readied the Whaler his mind was on the girl. *How will I find her again? Where does she live? How old is she? Heck, I don't even know the color of her eyes!*

As it does so many times the half-light of dawn suddenly slipped away; the sky filled with the rising sun and daylight chased the last of the fog clear of the bay. Matt spun the boat away from the beach, thumbed up the throttle and pushed the Whaler until the screaming motor left long curving streaks of white trailing in the wake.

He shivered as scraps of wind cheated past the windshield. He pulled his sweatshirt tighter before skippering the *Dawn Raider* in and around lobster pots and channel markers to Charlie's yard.

Ten minutes later Matt arrived at the marina, secured his boat to one of the floating docks and spent an hour repairing a broken depth finder cable. He was surprised to see the day had slid past mid-morning and had just finished putting away his tools when suddenly Kiki's frantic voice pealed down onto the dock.

"Matt...Matt!" Kiki screamed from the top of the ramp. She was out of breath and her voice shook.

"What's the matter?"

"Matt, we've hunted everywhere...we can't find him...Jack's missing!"

11

JACK'S MISSING

A tiny drop of dread trickled through Matt and a tightness formed in his throat as his mind suddenly flashed back to Jack's bedroom. He could hear his voice asking...*Do you have reason to believe you are in danger?* Jack had paused...*Not right now.* Then Matt switched troubled eyes back to Kiki. "What do you mean...missing?"

"He was scheduled to dive with Alex and me at eight o'clock and never showed up. I called his house and got his answering service but no Jack! Then we checked and his boat wasn't at the dock. Matt, something terrible has happened, I can feel it!" Her voice was shrill, high pitched with anxiety.

Matt hopped out of the boat and raced up the gangway, grabbed her arm and asked hurriedly, "Why do you say that?"

Kiki turned a stricken face up to Matt, "Alex and I drove over to his house...the front door was open..." She buried her head in her hands. "Matt...his place has been ransacked! A tornado couldn't have done more damage." She threw her hands out to the side, "Drawers were pulled from bureaus and the contents dumped in the middle of the room. Books were torn open, his closet stripped bare. God, Matt, stuff was everywhere!" As she spoke tears flooded down her cheeks.

Matt's mind sped over the events of last night. The piles of gold stacked on Jack's bed, the hints he had been followed but how he felt safe for now. Jack had been wrong. He had been in danger. "Did you call the police?"

"Alex did. He's with them now at Jack's place."

Mandy Costelle hadn't done Jack any favors when she'd photographed the pendant and given out his name and address. Costelle had put all slime bags in the world on notice a cool piece of change could be found on West Elm Street. All they needed to do was call upon Jack some dark night and help themselves. Then Matt thought Jack might be lucky. His boat was missing so he could have been out in the bay when the break-in occurred.

Matt hurried back down the gangway to the Whaler's console, turned on the radio, and called Lance and Big Bob on their dive boat. *"Ram Charger...Ram Charger..."*

"Yo, Matt, we gottcha, come back."

"Either of you guys seen Jack this morning?"

"Nary a hair, chief," Lance replied.

"He never showed up for his dive schedule this morning. Kiki and Alex got worried and checked his house. He wasn't there but the house had been ransacked." Matt tried to mask his concern then added, "Now we find his boat is missing from the yard. We were hoping you'd seen him."

"Not so far but if you'll recall you sent us up into Maquoit Bay. I've never seen Jack over this way. We'll keep an eye out though. You think anything serious has happened to him?"

Matt wanted to say, *"Damn right I do,"* but instead replied, "Nothing we can put our fingers on but ever since that TV gal ran his name and address I've worried someone might try to steal that pendant."

"You got that right. We'll keep looking...keep us posted...*Ram Charger* out."

"What do we do now?" Kiki asked, wiping away the tears with the end of her T-shirt and looking at Matt for direction.

"We'll do some looking ourselves. Come on, help me get the *Dawn Raider* ready."

She climbed down the ramp, boarded the boat, untied the dock lines, and then flipped the fenders on board while Matt started the engine. He backed clear of the other boats and in a matter of minutes they were speeding through the channel at the mouth of the river.

Kiki's shirt ballooned and snapped in the wind, "Where are we going?" she asked, pulling strands of wind-driven hair away from her eyes.

Matt's face was serious. "I wish we had some starting point. I do know that, Jack accepted every chance he could get to dive over by Ministerial, Stockman or Whaleboat Islands. We'll begin there." The wind tore his words apart, forcing Kiki to lean in close to catch what he said.

The sun climbed high overhead and wind ratcheted up to twenty knots as they crossed Broad Sound. Spray bounced away from the bow of the plunging Whaler and short, choppy waves gave way to long, rolling swells. Kiki's blond hair whipped in the air that skidded around the windshield and she had to cling forcefully to the chrome grab bar to keep her balance.

Matt was forced to slow down and even so they could not hold binoculars steady in the pitch and roll of the boat. Kiki snapped down her sunglasses from the top of her head and stretched her eyes into each cove searching for signs of the boat assigned to Jack for the summer, a 20-foot Grady White.

The sun glanced off the waves and Kiki was having difficulty seeing into the short reach between Stockman and the cove on Bangs Island lying in the distance. In ten minutes they had searched both shorelines. Kiki could sense Matt was about to turn east. On impulse she swung her face, dripping with salt spray, in his direction.

"Hey, how about one more island before we quit this section?"

Matt hesitated, then nodded and swung the bow in the direction of her pointing finger. A minute later they approached the cove on Stave Island. Kiki pushed her dark glasses up on her nose, shaded her eyes and squinted into the glare.

"Matt, is that a boat on the rocks?" She pointed to a row of exposed ledges along the tide line. "There...see...yes, it is!" she shouted. Kiki fastened her eyes on the boat just as a huge swell surged against the hull and pushed the boat sideways farther onto the rocks where it hung for a moment then slid stern first back into the seething water.

Matt steered the Whaler in close to shore. He was close enough now to hear the fiberglass tear on the rocks. Recognition splintered into his mind. There was no question. It was Jack's boat. After finding the gold piece, Jack had changed the name to *Black Beard* and, like its namesake, it hung on rocky gallows with the sea slowly pounding the hull to pieces.

"Oh, my gosh, Matt, it's Jack's boat!" She covered her mouth with both hands. Kiki found her breathing cramped in her chest and she was unable to swallow the lump in her throat.

Matt shifted the engine into neutral, letting the following sea thrust him into the cove toward the struggling craft. Then he held reverse power as the Whaler slipped in closer to the boat. Kiki leaned over the rail and tossed a quick look inside. "It's empty," she said in a strained voice. "I don't see any signs of Jack," she added staring into the kelp and barnacle ledges that reared ugly heads each time a swell receded. Then she grabbed Matt's arm and searched his eyes with a frightened unasked question on her face. *What has happened to Jack?*

"Quick!" Matt ordered, "Get a line out of the forward compartment. Make a big loop. See if you can throw it around that stern cleat on the Grady." The boat was awash to the floor boards. Grady Whites were supposed to be unsinkable but unless they hauled it off the rocks in the next few minutes there wouldn't be enough left to sink.

Matt wasn't sure why he felt the pressing urge to save Jack's boat--he just knew a voice inside screamed at him to hook up and get it to a lee shore.

Kiki surprised herself. The second cast landed over the cleat and Matt backed both boats out of the wind toward the back side of the Island. He was at mid-channel when Kiki threw both arms around Matt and buried her head in his shoulder. He felt her wretched sob explode against his chest.

"Oh, Matt look!"

At first Matt thought the dark green blob floating in the water on the starboard side was a garbage bag or lost jacket. But it wasn't. Kiki had found Jack and he wasn't ever going to dive again. As the body rolled in the waves Matt could see three bullet holes stitched across his back.

12

LT. CRAIG MILLER

The Coast Guard had responded immediately to Matt's radio call on the emergency channel 16, retrieved the body from the water and turned Jack's boat over to the Portland police. The waterlogged but floating boat remained impounded for a week before they released it back to Charlie's yard where the *Black Beard* was repaired and moored once again in the harbor as if nothing had happened.

Monday, the day following Jack's funeral, Lieutenant Craig Miller, of the Portland Homicide Division, decided to question Matt and his divers. Kiki, Alex, and Lance waited along with Matt in the dive shack while Big Bob was being interviewed in one of Charlie's inner offices.

Lance glanced at his watch for the tenth time in as many minutes. "Bob's been in there almost an hour. What's that cop asking him that could take that long?" His voice was tinged with uncertainty about his own upcoming meeting.

"I'm not sure," Kiki replied with concern. "This waiting makes me nervous." She wiped her hands across her sweatshirt, an anxious, fearful expression on her face.

Always the rational one, Alex offered, "If I were running this investigation, I'd want to know the last time any of us saw Jack and what he was doing, did he act strangely, did he mention meeting someone. You know, stuff like that, looking for some clue."

"Do you think he suspects any of us?" Kiki asked.

"My guess is he will keep that avenue open for awhile," Lance replied.

Big Bob suddenly banged open the door.

"Hey, Bob, how'd it go?" Kiki burst out.

"You don't want to know. Be on your guard. This guy is after something and may not care who gets hurt while he's looking." Bob's face looked strained. His usual jovial voice came out flat and angry as he slammed the door behind him and drove off.

The bang of the door knocked a wet suit from the hanger. It lay crumpled in a black pile, a dead rubber body. Kiki hung the suit back up then cast a worried eye at the group while the rest of the divers looked at each wondering what fate awaited them in Charlie's office.

Matt had his own demons to confront. He agreed with Alex on the questions Miller would ask. He would have no honest answers to any of those, especially where he was the last night Jack was alive. He'd been with Jack, that's where, and there was no way he was going to admit to that.

Charlie Craft's weathered face appeared at the window. He tapped the glass and motioned to Matt, beckoning him to follow. Matt stood up. As he walked toward the door he felt a weakness in his legs, and a strange tightness gripped his throat that made breathing difficult.

He wondered if the others had the same sensations and decided, no, they had not been through the grueling interrogations he had endured in Florida where the police had tried to pin the accident on him. Matt was about to relive those moments. Tension flooded through his body, tightening every muscle at the thought.

Charlie's office was full of cluttered papers. *Sail and Power* and other boating magazines lay about in huddled masses on every flat surface. Out-of-date calendars were pinned to the wall wherever a space could be found, old days gathering new dust. The man behind the desk was different. He had brushed Charlie's papers to one side leaving a clear space.

Lieutenant Miller wore tan, dress khaki pants with a cuff. His carefully combed, long silver hair framed a charismatic face and curled behind his ears. Matt thought he needed a haircut but had to admit the hair provided a good contrast to the ruddy complexion. His tailored blue blazer with gold buttons was accented by a bright, red and blue power tie that was too long and hung down below his belt.

The Rotary pin in the lapel said he was *connected*, that he was *important*. In point of fact, Craig Miller *was* connected. The fact he was a dapper dresser didn't make him any less shrewd, forceful or clever. When Miller spoke it was vintage cop with an Ivy League twang and with his first question Matt knew he was in trouble.

13

INTERROGATION

The lower part of Miller's face opened and closed, lips barely moving, an empty, unreadable face pointing at the words as he asked, "Now, Matthew Banner, where were you the night Jack was killed?"

Just like that. No introductory questions, no warm ups, just flat out, "Where were you?" Matt had been ready for this question, popped the answer right back and hoped the fact it was a bold-faced lie didn't show.

"Working on my boat." Then he pointed out the window, "At the dock, fixing a broken depth finder cable." The broken cable part was true and he knew the best lies contained some shred of truth.

Miller pursed his lips, gave Matt a benevolent smile, before asking, "Anyone verify that?"

Matt gave an impatient shrug as though thinking but since he hadn't actually been at the dock the Lieutenant's question provided Matt with a real problem. There was no one who could verify seeing someone who had not been there. Then he had an idea and trolled it out, not much more than a weak red herring, but it might buy him some time.

Matt felt his heart doing the rumba in his chest, "Don't think so... maybe Watts Penn," he replied, giving Miller a bland face. The answer was a safe bet since everyone knew that when Watts was fishing lobsters he might not come back into the river for days at a time. Miller had a chore in store for himself before he'd be able to deliver Watts for questioning.

Miller's eyes said he didn't believe him which scored one for the eyes. He scribbled some notes, then asked, "Did you see Jack the day or night he was killed?"

Another zinger but easier. "No." *Just a simple lie.* His experience with Florida police readied him for Miller's next move as Miller hitched forward across the desk resting his sizable frame on his elbows. That maneuver put Miller's nose right in front of Matt's face. If that move was suppose to strike terror in Matt it failed miserably.

Matt suddenly thrust the chair away and jumped to his feet. "You through with me?" Then with one hand on the door he turned and pointed a finger at the officer behind the desk. "Lieutenant Miller, I want Jack's killer more than you do. We all do, but hassling the divers is not the way to solve this crime. I'm the team leader, they respect me, look to me for guidance and leadership. If you want information, I'll talk to the crew. But stop threatening us!"

Miller looked stone-faced, tapped a pencil on the desk, realizing he'd gone off half cocked. "Okay, suppose we start again." He motioned Matt to sit down. "What do you know that could be helpful?" A small ghost of a smile creased his lips.

Matt sat down. "Sometime around the first of July Jack went diving by himself, strictly against regulations, and found a gold necklace with an attached two-inch pendant. He brought it directly from his boat at the dock up into the yard where he gave each diver a chance to hold the chunk of gold."

Miller interrupted, "Was Charlie there?"

Matt had to think. "I believe he was sort of standing in the background but yes, he was there. Anyway, about then I saw a good-looking blond packing gear into a van. Turned out she was a television reporter from Channel 13. Jack obviously didn't tell her where he found the gold but he did let her film the pendant. I remember thinking that was a poor idea."

"Why was that?"

"For two reasons. It put his ownership in jeopardy. With that close-up anyone could step forward and claim it."

Miller nodded. "Good point. What was the other reason?"

"She ran that film clip every night begging the public to come up with ideas about who might have owned the necklace and what it might be worth. No one responded so to put pressure on Jack she broadcast his name and address. Nice person, that girl. Indirectly I think she is responsible for his death." Then he added, "Even without an established price that piece of gold was obviously valuable."

"You think some junkie broke in. Maybe Jack caught him and got shot for his efforts?"

"Something like that."

"How do you explain why Jack was found way out by Stave Island?"

Matt had worried about that and he had no solution so he offered no reply other than a hunch of his shoulders.

Miller ran both hands over his silver gray hair smoothing it into place. He took a deep breath. His eyes burned into Matt's as he asked, "Do you think he found more than this one necklace?"

"I can't confirm that so I'd rather not say." Another lie. Matt wondered if his nose was growing.

"Okay, that will be all for now. Here's my card. If you find out anything, give me a call."

Matt got to his feet, then with one hand on the doorknob, turned to face Miller.

"Lieutenant, no more hard ass stuff, okay? I've got a gal out in the shack scared to death and there is no need of that. I'm not sure what you said to Bob Green. Whatever it was I hope he forgives you."

Before he could reply Matt was out the door thinking Miller was so narrow minded that if he fell on a pin it would blind him in both eyes.

Miller was surprised at the heat in Matt's voice. He remained at the desk, bouncing the eraser end of the pencil on his notes and wondered what experience Matthew Banner had had that gave him a rod up his back when facing an officer of the law. He made a mental note to find out. He made another to locate Watts Penn.

14

DIMILLO'S AND McCALL

Matt's watch showed ten o'clock when he charged out of Charlie's office, leaving the dapper dressed Miller with some work to do. He was so absorbed with the meeting he barely nodded as Lance loped by for his turn in the hot seat.

Matt yanked open the shack door, then slammed it closed and leaned back against the rough wall. Kiki could see the anger turn his face bright red, and the muscles along his jaw stretch rope tight.

Alex could see Matt was in a pool of anger, deep enough to lap around his ears, and maybe about to do something he'd regret. "Hey, guy," he said with a glance at Kiki. "Remember, character is the wisdom not to do foolish things," and raised his eyebrows in question.

Matt remained at the door then blew air out through his nose and smiled. It was hard to stay mad at anything when Alex was poking wisdom in his ears. He grinned, "Don't worry I'm not about to shoot myself in the foot."

Kiki laughed, relieving the tension then asked, "What happened, Matt? You look terrible."

"Our Lieutenant Miller fancies himself as a hard-ass, that's what. He's looking to pin the murder on the first person he can find who remotely has a motive and can be put at the scene of the crime. The motive he says is a no brainer, the necklace. The problem is, I don't have a good alibi for the time he figures Jack was killed.

"I get the feeling he sees me as *numero uno* for the crime. So what I need right now is a place to forget all this. I'm headed to Portland. Where can I get a real Maine lobster dinner?"

Kiki and Alex laughed and answered together, "DiMillo's Floating Restaurant on the waterfront. It's on Commercial Street."

He scratched down directions, waved good-bye, then climbed into his truck and drove off south on Route 88. Matt had another reason for going to Portland. With luck he would have time to relax for an hour or two, eat his lobster and think about questions he wanted to ask Professor Russell at the University of Southern Maine.

A contact at DMR had fixed an appointment with the head of the history department who Matt hoped would help solve the mystery surrounding Jack's gold.

DiMillo's was actually a huge, converted ferryboat retrofitted into a floating restaurant. The boat appeared enormous, over a hundred feet long, painted white with a stripe of blue curling along the water line and upper deck.

Inside Matt found himself in an oval dining room full of brass rails, ships' lanterns and maroon carpeted floor. The walls had port holes rigged as windows. Old ship wheels and compasses finished off the nautically decorated dining room.

Soft and mellow music floated across the decks and drifted over tables covered by expensive white tablecloths and real napkins. This, Matt realized, was definitely not McDonald's!

A waiter, dressed in black pants with dark silk stripe, white shirt and black bow tie, seated Matt with a view of the water. He waved away the menu. "Lobster, clams and iced tea."

Matt sat facing a striking girl at the next table who was about to engage in a one on one combat with a two-pound, steaming red lobster. She wore a white, sleeveless blouse with a simple gold necklace. Sunlight caught her gold bracelet and bounced a streak of light erratically past the port hole.

He could see sneakers and a bare leg beyond the tablecloth and noticed she had protected her blouse from flying juices by tying the standard plastic bib around her neck. Beyond that she seemed completely bewildered.

McCall had noticed Matt the instant he had entered the restaurant. He seemed devilishly handsome, tall with wide shoulders and rangy body. She could see an appealing face light up as he gave the waiter his order.

McCall stared at the red-shelled creature draped across her plate. She had never eaten a lobster and was overwhelmed by the process required to break open the shell.

At that moment she glanced up to find the guy watching her. McCall thought she detected laughter in his eyes. His face was bronzed by the wind and sun and his dark eyes seemed to hold a secret expression. He was definitely what her best friend would describe as *cool*.

For a long moment she gave him a frank and admiring look and found herself strangely flattered by his interest. McCall dropped her eyes again to the lobster that reclined on her plate, red and inert, and concentrated on how to get what was on the inside to the outside. No experiences in Montana had prepared her for battle against the red armored shell.

He nodded. She nodded back. *Old friends*. He gave her a smile. She allowed her face to break into an open friendly smile to match the one on his face. A grin overtook his features.

Matt inched forward on his chair watching her struggle with the lobster. Finally, when he could stand it no longer, he rose to his feet, strode over to her table, swung out a chair and sat down facing her. "Hi, I'm Matt, and you are in big trouble," he said, motioning toward the lobster. A deep chuckle greeted him as he seated himself.

McCall felt an odd ripple of excitement. Her voice was mellow as she replied, "You've got that right, Matt. Is that short for Matthew? No last name?"

It was Matt's turn to smile. "Matthew Banner," he held out his hand. She carefully wiped her hand on the cloth napkin before placing it in his.

He tipped his head in her direction.

"Oh, sorry. It's McCall. Well, actually L.T. McCall...Lee Thomas," she added as an afterthought. "But everyone calls me McCall." As she said the words he saw humor flicker in her eyes.

"Well, *actually* McCall, right now I'd say the score was ten for the lobster and zero for L.T." His voice held a trace of laughter, deep and warm. Up close McCall could see his dark tousled hair was cut short and there was strength in his face.

McCall frowned, looked quizzically at the lobster on the plate then tore off the large claw, "Ouch!" she cried. "Damn!" She sucked her finger where the spines from the claw had drawn blood. Her reaction seemed to amuse him.

Matt took her hand to inspect the cuts. "Shall I call for help?" He raised his eyes in mock seriousness before noticing her hand was warm.

"No, Matthew, I'll survive but I will take some help with this red critter!" She smiled and tilted her head.

As he instructed her on the approved methods of eating a Maine lobster he'd learned from Alex, he gave some serious thought as to why this girl was leaving hot tracks on his heart. He didn't think it was her honey blond hair, although that was important, or the soft crinkle at the corners of her mouth when she smiled, or even the pink lips over even teeth or cheeks with their healthy tan. No, Matt decided reflectively, it was all of those things.

The waiter suddenly arrived with a question on his face wondering where to put Matt's meal. "Join me by all means, Matt," she said, waving a hand at the empty place across from her.

As he broke into his lobster and demonstrated for McCall the secrets of attack, he knew he was looking at a perfect canvas, each brush stroke carefully applied, almond shaped eyes the color of jade under arched brows, slightly tipped nose, a smear of freckles more pronounced with the tan and a nicely rounded chin.

She had swept her soft hair behind one exquisite ear that supported a twinkle of gold. He doubted soft candlelight could improve her complexion.

Matt ate and listened but mostly watched her tanned hands and slim fingers slip bits of lobster into her mouth.

"What are you doing in Maine?" he asked.

"How do you know I'm not from Maine?" She raised her eyes from the lobster. "Oh, the accent."

"Western?"

She slipped a straw between her lips before she replied. Matt watched the liquid glide up the tube and listened to the ice cubes tinkle as she stirred them with the straw.

"Montana. A little place called Two Dot, about a hundred miles west of Billings. Grassland, cow country. We own a ranch. Now what brings *you* to Maine?"

"The accent thing again, right? Maine boy has a Florida twang? Hail from an island in the Florida Keys called Marathon which is about fifty miles south of Miami." His gaze lingered on her face as he replied.

"What brings a Montana girl to the northeast?"

"The story is so weird you'd never believe it."

"I've got time and I'm a good listener. Try me."

"Well, there I was racked out at the ranch watching television when the guy on the six o'clock news starts talking about a gold necklace a diver named Jack Kilby brought up from the ocean floor. They gave a close-up of the gold piece and when they did I leaped off the couch, grabbed a pencil and wrote down everything I could about that diver."

With the words *gold piece* Matt felt a cold chill. "What was so special about the pendant?"

"Belonged to my grandmother," she said between mouthfuls. "Delicious," she said smacking her lips.

"Don't leave me hanging, McCall. What happened next?"

"I booked a flight to Portland, rented a car at the airport and drove to the Yarmouth Town Hall on Main Street. I asked a nice gal there, Patricia Morrill, to direct me to 48 West Elm Street where this Kilby fellow lived. When she asked why I wanted to see him I told her about the necklace."

McCall stopped talking, picked up a piece of lobster and dipped it absently in butter. "That's when she said he was dead!

"I must have had a pretty stupid look on my face when I said, 'Oh, I didn't know that.' McCall paused. "Then she was nice enough to direct me to a bed and breakfast on Cousins Island. I figured as long as I was here I might as well try to figure out the mystery of my grandmother's necklace."

Matt couldn't tell if it was sadness for Jack or frustration at finding him dead that caused her to blink her green eyes, clearing them of mist. Then she added, "Sorry, didn't mean to burden you with my problem."

Before he could stop himself he reached across the table and squeezed her hand.

When he touched her McCall felt the roughness of his hands and was surprised how she welcomed the intimacy that was developing between them. She noticed his high cheekbones and slightly crooked nose. She reached up and traced it with her finger. He smiled, "Football."

Then working on his own neglected lobster, Matt asked, "What was so important about that necklace?"

McCall told him about visiting her grandmother in Europe where she learned the gold piece with the emerald center had disappeared during WWII and the fact she was able to recognize it because she had studied an oil painting of the pendant done just before the Germans looted her grandmother's home.

Secretly Matt doubted McCall would be able to remember something she had seen as a young girl on her first trip to Europe, where she certainly would have been dazzled by a story most likely embellished by her grandmother's imagination, but he kept his thoughts to himself.

"So what do you do?" she asked, a slight tilt to her head.

He went on to explain the Jack Kilby she had just mentioned and the others who worked for the Department of Marine Resources, their mission in Casco Bay and his role as the team leader. Then, leaving out the more gruesome details, he spelled out how he and Kiki Malone had found

Jack. "That necklace disappeared, McCall, and no one has seen it."

"Wow! I certainly stepped into a mess, didn't I?" Matt could see by her expression McCall was possessed by more than vague curiosity as his story unfolded. It was genuine interest that showed in her eyes.

Then with a gesture McCall pointed to the restroom, "I think I'd better fix my face," she said, and walked lightly toward the restroom sign.

Matt dropped his napkin on the table and rose as she left. He noticed she moved with a runner's smoothness. With the word runner came sudden recognition. Not sure what to do with the revelation, Matt squirmed in his chair.

When McCall returned she smiled which erased his uneasiness.

"You look...." he searched for words and then settled for "super." Her tan looked great in white and he told her that, too.

McCall accepted the compliment, "Thanks," and seated herself while noticing how Matt's boyish face could turn old and wise. She knew instinctively that he was safe to be with and liked the humor hidden in the dark recesses of his brown eyes. With all that he somehow looked familiar.

Matt suddenly asked, "Where's your dog?"

"Dog...?" Then, "Oh my God!" she expelled, placing a hand over her mouth as recognition flashed before her eyes. "You're the fisherman from the beach at Cousins Island!"

"Yeah, I'm the one, guilty as charged. I didn't recognize you until I saw you walk to the restroom. You have sort of a ...," he stammered a bit... "cute way with your butt when you move."

She blushed. "Matthew!" However, she saw he meant no offense.

"Then we aren't strangers after all, are we?" He said, a killer grin spreading across his face.

She wrinkled her nose at him and replied. "No." Then with more feeling. "No, not strangers." She reached across and laid her hand on his arm. Matt could feel his world begin to tilt as she teased him and kept him off balance.

They joked away the hour avoiding the waiter's impatient glances. He found she was an avid football fan, then had to confess he knew more about Joseph Conrad and Jack London than about Tom Brady or Payton Manning. He hated diet drinks. She drank only diet Pepsi. He was a jazz man, she followed country western.

McCall laughed at the differences. It was an infectious laugh that sent goose bumps down his arms. The one bright note was when he said in spite of his jazz interest he thought Shania Twain a goddess. McCall laughed, "You only say that because of her bare midriff!"

"Hey, it's my lie. I'll tell it any way I want!" and gave her a devastating grin.

Matt found himself comparing her to Kiki Malone. Where Kiki was small and fragile, with exciting eyes always on the chase, McCall was a head taller, stronger with only mystery in her green eyes.

The waiter suddenly arrived at the table with the bill. Matt dropped money on the waiter's soft leather bill pad and watched him leave. McCall thanked him then busied herself opening her pocketbook to search for her keys. There was an awkward silence as each realized it was time to go. When she stood up Matt felt his heart slip inside his chest.

He walked her to her car. She had the door open and the key in the switch before he could unlock his tongue. "Maybe we could get together and talk about that necklace and what Jack was doing," he said hopefully.

She looked up at the face peering at her through the open window.

Why not, she thought? "Hey, diver, I'd like that." She gave him her Cousins Island address and phone number. "It's the green cottage beyond the trees where you saw me at the beach. The dog belongs to the landlady."

After watching her disappear down the street he boarded his car and headed south toward the University of Southern Maine. A breeze filled his heart and for the first time since leaving Florida he smelled the salt air and freshness of life.

A quick glance at his watch showed if he hurried he still had time to make his two o'clock appointment with Professor Russell. Maybe he'd been wrong and the necklace was just what McCall said it was but Matt didn't think so. He was relying on Russell to confirm Jack's pendant was actually *pirate treasure*.

15

PROFESSOR OF ANTIQUITIES

Ten minutes later Matt swung his car into the student parking lot behind an imposing four-story brick building at the University of Southern Maine. He turned off the key and stared out the window. The more he thought about buccaneers and buried gold the more preposterous the whole idea sounded. How was he going to convince a noted historian when he had his own doubts? He exited the car, walked briskly from the lot and bounded up the stairs to the professor's office.

Matt knew from his reading that no physical evidence of pirate treasure had been found in Maine except for some gold coins discovered on Richmond Island just off Crescent Beach State Park in Cape Elizabeth. That find *was* real. The coins *were* gold. The coins had never actually been listed as pirate bullion but their dates coincided with the historical period when pirates were active.

Armed with those thoughts, he approached a door with an opaque window, the kind with tiny wires running through the glass. The name tag under the window said Dr. Paul Russell, Professor of Antiquities. He knocked and was ushered in, receiving a firm handshake and warm welcome from a friendly looking man that Matt judged to be somewhere in his late fifties.

"Matthew, nice to meet you," Russell said with an authoritative voice.

"Good of you to take the time," Matt replied, his heart kicking up a beat as he wondered how he was going to broach the subject of lost pirate gold without feeling like a complete idiot. His only introduction to the Professor had been by phone when his boss at DMR recommended he give Russell a call. After the one quick look he decided the professor was a far cry from scholarly looking, no thinning hair or reading glasses perched low on a nose, or messy desk and book-strewn room.

Russell stood an erect six feet with an athlete's wide shoulders. Pure white hair topped a ruddy, weathered face that directed a pair of piercing eyes at Matt then motioned him to the couch. As Russell walked to his desk Matt noticed his tan pants and light green V-necked sweater.

Matt dropped onto the couch, surprised to find the cushions were covered in genuine leather. The office was efficient and orderly; books lined the wall from ceiling to floor, each volume carefully labeled.

Matt knew he was in the presence of a keen mind used to research and facts. He wondered how the professor would respond to conjecture and vague unsupported ideas. Matt suddenly felt like a poodle in a car with a Great Dane.

The sun shone brightly into the room from the only window to the left of Russell's desk. The combined light from the desk lamp and the sun gave the room a warm glow. As he relaxed on the couch Matt began to search for a good opening.

Russell leaned back in a worn chair, propped his glasses on top of his head and observed the young man who obviously had something to say, yet seemed uncomfortable with his thoughts. He stared at the alert, intelligent face made more interesting by a crook in the nose, slightly uneven teeth and a grin that was infectious. Matt hadn't said a word, yet Russell was already intrigued by his bearing and composure.

"Matt, what brings you to see me? And why did you choose me in the first place?" As he asked the questions, Russell pulled a note pad toward him and picked up a pencil.

Matt had his opening and he hitched forward on the couch, "Sir, frankly I didn't know who to contact. I asked Tom Hippler, my boss at DMR, if he knew someone knowledgeable about old gold coins and jewelry that might date back to the 1600s. Your name popped right out."

Russell smiled. "I know Tom. He's an old fishing buddy. A good man."

Matt continued, "DMR employs six of us to dive in Casco Bay where we are mapping possible places to commercially farm the depleting sea urchins. We work out of Charlie Craft's marina in Yarmouth." As he finished the sentence Matt caught a surprised expression on Russell's face, a narrowing of the eyes.

Professor Paul Russell suddenly realized Matt was one of the team of divers mentioned on Channel 13's nightly news report featuring a gold necklace with a monstrous two-inch emerald pendant. The diver who had discovered it had recently been found dead. If Matt had been wondering how to pique the Professor's interest he had found the way. Russell wondered what Matt would say next.

Then getting back to Russell's opening question Matt said simply, "I want to ask you about pirates, buccaneers and buried treasure." In spite of his uncertainty Matt felt his words were firm with conviction.

The reply was completely unexpected.

16

LOST TREASURE

"Arrgh...what might yer name be, matey?" Russell suddenly blurted out, voice miming the old salt, Long John Silver.

Matt snapped his head back in surprise. Then smiled, "Why, I be Jim Hawkins, sir," Matt replied quickly, playing along with the *Treasure Island* characters.

"You're way ahead of me, aren't you?" Matt said sheepishly, looking at the floor. "I must be transparent."

Russell pointed a finger at him and said, "Just as soon as you mentioned diving out of Charlie's yard I remembered that gold necklace Channel 13 has been harping on in the news."

"You need to know, Professor Russell, I'm feeling pretty ridiculous sitting here offering that necklace as evidence of pirate gold. I might as well have come here and asked you to help find the Ark of the Covenant or the Holy Grail. You know when I tried this pirate idea out on the other divers I got laughed out of the dive shack. But all the other explanations seem just as far fetched--gangster loot, the tourist or sailor dropping it overboard theory."

"So you want me to prop up your pirate notion, right?"

"Well..."

Russell interrupted. "I might be able to do that." He reached behind him to pluck a book from a lower shelf.

"That sunken gold stuff can fire your imagination, Matt, and I'm no more immune from the lust for treasure than anyone else."

Russell continued, "Gold appears in pure form rather than as a compound so it's easy to find. Darn stuff is incredibly attractive all by itself.

"Now you take this substance that is actually a cold buttery looking metal but so rare that a single ingot builds hot fires in the imagination, stitch that together with legends of buccaneers, wild women, bottles of rum, and these bootleggers of the sea can tear at your soul.

"They can even bring a hot-blooded young man like yourself into my office breathing down the trail of a possible pirate find." He paused. "Am I right?"

"You got me, Professor!" Then curious about the book, Matt flipped through the index and asked, "What's in here?"

"It's called *Lost Treasure* by Bill Yenne. Read it. You'll find Captain William Kidd is your most likely suspect although there are others. Let me know if I can be of further help."

"So you don't think I'm on some wild goose chase?"

"Well, that remains to be seen, doesn't it, Matt?" Then he added, "If you can't prove something doesn't exist then it exists. That could include your pirates."

Sensing the interview was over, Matt stood up, reached across the desk and shook the Professor's outstretched hand. "Thanks for the book. I'll take good care of it and return it ASAP." With that Matt left the building. On the drive back to Yarmouth his mind raced over the possibilities the book might offer.

Perhaps the greatest boost to his theory, however, was the fact that the Professor hadn't outright kicked him out of the office. In fact, as he thought about it, Russell had showed significant interest. The treasure voice that before had been only a whisper in Matt's ear now began to sound like a loud call to arms!

There were two other thoughts that occupied Matt's mind. One had to do with L.T. McCall and the other with Jack Kilby's death, for in spite of their short friendship Matt had no intention of letting the matter rest entirely with the police, especially in the hands of Lieutenant Craig Miller.

He also needed to find out where Jack had located the gold. Matt had an idea about that.

At the same time Matt was leaving the university, Karl Richter unscrewed the storm shutter at the back of Matt's apartment. He secured a piece of tape to the window directly over the lock then cut around the tape with a glass cutter. With the glass removed he unlocked the latch, raised the sash and stepped inside.

Since the Germans had failed to extract the location of the gold from Jack Kilby, Brockner had instructed Richter to place listening devices in Matt's apartment and a tap on the phone. Just maybe Matt might reveal information that would lead them to the treasure. Even if that failed they would be able to keep track of Banner's movements.

An hour later as he was packing tools in his bag the sound of crunching gravel announced Matt's return. Richter hurried out the way he had come in--except he did not have time to refasten the storm shutter.

17

BLACKBEARD, BILLY BOW LEGS AND CAPTAIN WILLIAM KIDD

Back at his apartment Matt had a quick supper, cleared the dishes, and dropped down on the bed to read *Lost Treasure*. As the welcome relief of the bed enveloped him Matt was suddenly overcome with doubts about pirates that were mixed with similar feelings about his life.

Matt thought of how orderly Alex Blanchard had arranged his life. Never a stumble as he finished high school. He knew Alex was way beyond graduate school with his goals and plans.

Matt shook his head. It was a cinch he had no plan for his future. He was having enough trouble handling the day to day stuff. He was drifting, sailing through life like a rudderless dory, allowing the winds to blow him about at will.

At some point he would have to get his life together and head somewhere, but right now he felt he was a boat tacking toward a shore on which he would never make a landfall. Alex kidded him, saying he had a *steerage* problem and that one day he would fix it.

Night crawled into his bedroom. He snapped on the light and began to read. He found several famous pirates mentioned right away.

He hurried through information about *Blackbeard, Billy Bow Legs* and some suave guy called *Jean Lafitte*, finally settling on *Captain William Kidd.*

Kidd actually had buried treasure in at least two places, one at Gardener's Island off Montauk Point near Long Island where gold valued at £14,000 was subsequently found.

Two chests of treasure were also discovered a short way up the mouth of the Connecticut River, at Clarke's Point. Legend has it that between April and September of 1699 he sailed as far north as Maine, burying treasure as he went.

By now Matt's eyes were gritty and sleep was walking over him. He dropped the book into an L.L. Bean canvas bag beside the bed and stuffed in some data he'd gotten from the Internet at the dive office.

He clicked off the light. Matt knew what he would do tomorrow. He punched the pillow into a comfortable position and listened to the wind as it howled around the house followed by the bang of a shutter along the kitchen wall. After that sleep evaded him. Why would that shutter suddenly start to swing loose in the wind? It never had before.

Had someone tinkered with the screws? Who would do that and why? Matt slid out of bed and fumbled in the darkness for a flashlight. The floor felt cool to his feet as he checked each of the windows along the front of the apartment. They were locked. He checked the bolt on the front door although he was certain he'd locked it. The house made light creaking sounds as the wind continued to blast through the yard.

Matt felt a slight breeze by the window at the rear of the kitchen. He let the light drift up to the lock. It was open. The breeze slipped in through the four-inch hole directly over the window latch. The hair stood up on the back of his neck. Someone had been in the apartment! The room suddenly felt small and full of threatening shadows as he spun the lock closed.

His throat went dry and he found his palms wet with sweat. Had the intruder left or was he still in the apartment hiding? He moved toward the bathroom. Maybe he had surprised the prowler and whoever it was stepped into the bathtub and was there right now concealing himself behind the shower curtain. Visions of Hitchcock's movie *Psycho* screamed through his mind.

Matt felt his heart beat faster and his breath stall as his gaze stopped at the partially closed door to the bathroom. He listened but failed to hear anything, then reached inside along the wall and snapped on the bathroom light. Nothing!

With the flashlight he probed the dark curtain. The color and print blocked the light. He felt a hot temper rise in him, drowning his fear, and with a surge of adrenaline, flung himself forward tearing the curtain to one side. The light flooded the back wall of the shower stall. Empty!

Matt waited until his blood cooled and pulse returned to normal before hiking to the front door where he placed a chair under the knob. Goose bumps crawled down his arms as he climbed back into bed and it was an hour before he could settle down.

When he finally drifted off to sleep, his mind was crowded with visions of greasy, bearded villains with pistols bristling beneath bright colored sashes, dirks in their teeth, swords raised high as they swung from the mast stays before swarming over the side of a helpless ship.

His last thought was more comforting …McCall.

18

GILLIGAN'S ISLAND

In the morning Matt rolled out of bed, pulled on a pair of tan shorts, then slipped on a blue Boston Red Sox T-shirt. He grabbed his sneakers and had coffee brewing before eight o'clock. While he waited for the coffee Matt made a hasty repair on the window and refastened the shutter. A quick survey of the apartment had failed to show anything missing so what had been the point of the break-in?

Back inside he poured his coffee and sat at the table, impatiently drumming his fingers and wondering if it was too early to call McCall. At eight thirty he dialed the phone.

After six rings a sleepy voice answered, "Hello?"

"That you, McCall?" Matt asked, afraid he might have the landlady on the phone.

"Yeah, it's McCall, who is used to getting up with the crows in Montana but had planned on sleeping late in Maine, which, I might add, worked until I met a brash guy from Florida who called me," she looked at a clock, "ugh, before nine o'clock!" She put the pillow over her head.

"Hey, McCall wake up." Then before she could respond, he said, "I'll bring the boat and pick you up at the town beach on Cousins. I'd like to show you Casco Bay...you know, like on a date...see you in an hour," and hung up before she could protest.

McCall met him sharply at ten. She had pulled her blond hair back and caught it in a gold clasp. A white sweatshirt hung over her blue Docker shorts that hugged her hips. Toes were jammed into pink flip-flops. With sunglasses perched on top of her head McCall was stunning!

He couldn't tell if her eyes were made up. Matt didn't think so, maybe a hint of blush on the cheeks. Then he decided she didn't need any makeup, not with her complexion.

He helped her aboard and said, "You look very nice."

"Thanks," she replied simply.

"Here, stand next to me behind the wind screen." With that settled he shouted above the roar of the engine, "I'll give you the guided tour." He spun the Boston Whaler into Broad Sound and rode out into the swells by Eagle Island which, he pointed out, was owned by the family of Admiral Richard Byrd.

The weather continued warm, the sun a soft rosy explosion, splintered against the sharp surface chop. A blue-hulled ketch slid past their starboard rail, sails canting the deck until Matt could read the words *Knot too Many* on the stern. Black-bodied cormorants adorned the channel buoys; gulls twirled overhead, mistaking the *Dawn Raider* for a fishing boat.

To avoid the heaving swells from the ocean, Matt steered the Whaler to a grass tufted spit of land and pulled the boat onto the beach.

"Wow...looks like Gilligan's Island," McCall called, and with the sun striking her face she laughed. Over the years picnickers had constructed a rambling campsite. They had used old fishing nets and lobster pot buoys strung over poles, so it did look like a castaway hideout.

Matt tossed her a smile. The whole island was sand. Tall grass grew green on a low bluff.

With a slight nod Matt said, "It's called Sand Island." Matt squatted on the shelving pebble-strewn beach and stared at the lobster boats tending traps. He was quiet so long McCall waved a hand in front of his face. "Hello...earth to Matt Banner."

"Sorry...thinking about stuff."

"Pirates again?"

"Maybe so."

"What you have, Matt, is gold fever!" she said, laughing.

"McCall, how could you remember exactly what that pendant looked like after, what was it, ten years?" Before she could interrupt he continued, "Jewelry tends to look alike."

"Well, maybe, but what I saw on the television was exactly as I recalled the painting, color, size, length of chain and especially the emerald."

"You're positive? I mean if you were testifying in court, for example, could you say beyond the shadow of doubt that was the same necklace?"

McCall didn't reply just shrugged her shoulders.

He took her hand lacing his fingers with hers and walked along the beach. With one hand McCall pulled off her flip-flops and splashed happily along the edge of tide stopping only to pick up a clam shell. She skipped it across the green, clear water watching the shell dimple the surface.

They found a pretty spot and dropped to the sand, faces turned up toward the sun. She sat close enough so he could smell her soap mixed with salt spray. Matt wondered why this slim wild beauty was attracted to him.

She had an impish smile that hooked his heart every time she grinned at him, which he was beginning to think was quite often. Strands of her hair had come undone and curved just under her jaw giving her a rakish, tousled look.

Matt gazed into her flashing green eyes and realized McCall was exceptionally beautiful.

McCall brushed away the loose strands of hair from her forehead, sat up and hugged her knees. Then she leaned lightly into him, tilting her face toward his so she could see Matt better.

She was fascinated by his tanned face that could look dangerously still, unreadable as the Sphinx, and then in an instant explode into a wide smile letting the little boy inside spill out all unabashed and uncomplicated. She wondered though what produced the dark images.

Matt caught her glancing at him. "What are you looking at?"

"Just you, Florida boy. Wondering why a cloud sometimes passes over your face."

Matt suddenly felt an updraft of feeling he had denied, just a whisper of emotion. The feeling was about to wash away when McCall put her hand over his and said, "Matt, I'd like to hear. Besides you got my life story yesterday at the restaurant." She tilted her head, gave him a secretive smile and squeezed his hand.

He leaned back and made small divots in the sand with his elbows, then stared out to sea so long she thought he would never answer. Then a tight voice began a story.

"Before coming to Maine I had always lived in Florida. My dad was a diver. He specialized in underwater welding. I came home one night to a dark house which was unusual because it was usually lit up like a Christmas tree.

"I knew things were not really good between my folks but I didn't know how bad. However, you can't live under a cannon and not smell the smoke. I just didn't realize how much their marriage had deteriorated." Matt felt a small catch in his throat.

He cleared his throat and continued, "This night was different. The darkness of the house scared me at first." Matt swung his eyes around so he could look McCall in the face. "You know what I mean? I remember walking slowly into the living room bumping into furniture, scared of the dark, and hearing my father crying like it was tearing out his heart. That terrified me.

"I was still disoriented when he suddenly grabbed my arm, pulled me to him and darn near hugged me to death. He told me my mother was gone...just gone! Just a note that said *good-bye* and no phone number where we could reach her. I never found out what happened between them and I never heard from her again." Matt's voice was husky as he spoke.

"Oh, Matt, that must have torn you apart!"

"It did, but the disappearance created a real problem for my sister, Lisa. She'd have been about eight at the time. Lisa could never accept that her mother was totally out of her life. She blamed herself for our parents' problems. Dad got her into counseling and she began to understand the problems were between the adults and had nothing to do with her."

McCall waited patiently. She knew by the expression on his face there was more to the story.

"Unfortunately that was not the end. Dad was welding on an oil rig off the coast of Galveston, Texas. He was cutting away a piece of torn staging. He died when the section broke away and crushed him."

Matt paused, cleared his throat again, then asked, "You sure you want the rest of this? The story doesn't get any better."

McCall replied with a squeeze of her hand.

"The next few years were pretty hazy. We were both placed in the same foster home. But before that I'd found a note Dad had written as if he knew something might happen to him." When he finished speaking Matt dug in his wallet and extracted a worn, creased piece of paper.

McCall took the note, unfolded it and read...*Matt, I love you son, and while I don't want to place a heavy burden on you, I want you to watch after Lisa. You have a much better head on your shoulders...Matt, guide her and keep her safe...Dad.*

Matt wiped at his eyes. A stillness hung in the air and a blanket of quiet draped over the beach. A gull landed on the rocks five feet from McCall's toe, settled its feathers then suddenly realizing it was not alone flew off in a scurry of loud noises.

"Something happened after that, didn't it, Matt?"

Matt took a deep breath, "Yes, it did. Lisa and I became inseparable. I watched after her day and night. I took her for music lessons and went to the movies with her. I was the only family member left to go to her softball games."

Suddenly Matt chuckled, breaking the tension. "I always read her a story before bed. My sister could be funny without knowing it. One night I heard her saying her prayers. She'd folded her hands and was on her knees beside the bed praying to her pastor. *Please, Pastor, say a prayer for our little league team. We need God's help or a new pitcher. Thank you.* She could be really funny.

"My father taught us to dive as soon as we were old enough to walk so that's what we did. Every weekend we'd hunt up some wreck and drop together, suspended in a world where the only sound was our bubbles as they trundled up to the surface. Mel Fisher had discovered the wrecks of two Spanish galleons laden with millions of dollars in gold, silver and jewels.

"Each time we dove I had visions of finding the same kind of treasure. Of course that never happened. What did happen was I lost Lisa."

McCall gave a quick inhale of breath and put her hand over her mouth. "What happened?"

He gave a huge sigh and his lips quivered. Then getting hold of himself said, "We'd been diving over this shallow wreck. It couldn't have been more than ten feet to the deck. We'd been going at it pretty heavy. Lisa had found a china tea cup and I remember how thrilled she was. We swam up to the dive boat, shucked off the tanks and had lunch. We were both tired and decided to take a nap. We agreed neither of us would go overboard without the other."

Matt didn't speak for a minute. He was feeling hollow and bleak inside, his heart seemed to shrink. He turned so he could look McCall in the face.

"When I woke up, she wasn't in the boat. I remember being angry at her for diving alone. I looked over the side and could see her swimming near the hatchway. I jumped into my dive gear and shot down to her. Only she wasn't swimming. She'd gotten caught in a piece of wire rope. I cut her loose but it was no use. I started CPR and called the Coast Guard. I kept at the breathing until they arrived about an hour later. They tried oxygen but it was too late. My little sister was dead."

Matt could feel the pressure on his arm and realized McCall still had her hand there. Her face was posed in sympathy. Then she drew him to her and put her arms around his neck. "And you've blamed yourself ever since?" she whispered.

Matt suddenly felt silly. He reached up and unwound her arms. "Yep, I still do. I should have known she might try to get another cup and maybe the saucer that went with it."

"Matt, she bears some responsibility--you'd agreed not to dive alone."

"I'll give you that and it's that fact that keeps me from going nuts sometimes."   He paused trying to shape his words.

"There's more, McCall. All that happened last April. I had just turned 18 and Lisa was just 14. After the funeral I received a call from a lawyer stating he represented my father. He had something he wanted to read so I said go ahead, not knowing what my father could have left but it seems that Dad had inherited a large chunk of money from his mother. He'd put it in a trust fund.

"The wording in the document was strange. Even the lawyer thought so when I questioned him. It said that I would not be eligible for the money until age twenty-one unless something happened to Lisa. If that happened I could have access to the trust as soon as I turned eighteen."

"So why was that a problem?" McCall asked.

"Detective Steven Negely, who investigated the accident, thought maybe it wasn't an accident. He thought I might have killed her for the money.   He's still investigating.

"When I read about the job with DMR I jumped at the chance to get out of Florida.   That really didn't solve a whole lot because Detective Negely is still smelling along my trail....end of story," and he gave her a wry face. With that he reached down for McCall's hand and helped her to her feet.

McCall brushed the sand from her shorts before she replied. "I never heard of anything so preposterous."

Matt gave her a quick look.   "Thanks for the vote of confidence, but what do you know about me...other than I'm the handsomest guy you ever went out with!"   His good humor had returned along with his quick smile. "Race you to the boat!"

If it had been Matt's plan to beat her in the run along the seaweed laden ledges he was disappointed. McCall was sitting on the bow with a nah, nah expression on her face when he arrived out of breath.

"So you're fast," he said before she could razz him.

Matt fetched the anchor from the rockweed and coiled the line. McCall started to climb into the boat. "Wait, McCall."

He took a breath, "What I'm about to tell you no one knows except me. Lieutenant Craig Miller, the guy investigating Jack's murder, doesn't know so I'm trusting you.

"Jack found more than the one necklace you saw on television." He told her about the night Jack had showed him the other jewels and given him the copy of the inventory. "So with that much loot coming from one location it's doubtful it belonged to some casual tourist," Matt said.

When McCall didn't reply he said, "I know, pirates sounds pretty far out, doesn't it?" He shook his head and shrugged his shoulders.

"Matt, you could sell snake oil but there is no hard evidence and no, Matt, I'm not convinced. Even if I were, that wouldn't solve the problem of where Jack found whatever it was he found. Call it pirate gold or stolen bank loot, or my grandmother's necklace, whatever. You'll never solve the riddle of the gold until you find where Jack located it. That make sense?"

"Yeah, I guess it does and I have an idea on how to solve that riddle. You game to join me? In fairness, someone else may be looking in the same places we are. It could get dangerous. You still want in?"

She placed both hands on the side of his face and kissed him full on the mouth. She let her lips linger for a fraction of a second. Then raising her face replied, "You betcha, Florida boy."

Matt hid his surprise then clamored on board. He fired the boat into wind blowing five knots toward Jewell lsland. Matt arrived on the seaward side and slowed the boat to give McCall a chance for a good look. She stared at the lonely cement tower rising out of the forest. Thin observation windows, like empty eyes cut in concrete, rose for eight stories. "Matt, it looks so...lost," she exclaimed. "So forgotten. What was it for?"

"I asked Watts the same question. He said it was built in 1942. During WWII the National Guard had a coast artillery unit stationed on the island. They placed observers up there with powerful telescopes looking for German submarines."

By the time they returned to the Yarmouth town beach it was late afternoon. Matt explained how to get to Charlie's Marina and instructed her to meet him there at ten that night.

"You are most definitely a rogue, Matthew Banner. But I'll be there ten sharp. Just what are we looking for anyway?"

"Jack's GPS."

19

KIKI AND "BLOOD ON THE BOAT"

Tuesday morning at ten o'clock Lieutenant Miller returned to Charlie's yard. He believed Kiki Malone might have something else to tell him and intended to question her again. He parked his green Ford Thunderbird and hurried into the main entrance to find Charlie seated at his desk. Before he spoke Miller slicked back his silver gray hair with his hand and checked his blue blazer for lint.

Then said pleasantly, "Good morning, Charlie."

Charlie glanced up from his papers and gave Miller his best thousand yard stare. "Just what are you back here for?"

Instead of answering he asked, "Where can I find Kiki Malone?"

"You're in luck, Miller; she's next door in the dive shack."

Miller gave Charlie a drafty look before closing the door. He turned and stepped across the hallway and entered the shack without knocking. Kiki was hanging up her weight belt when Miller burst in. She sucked in air then spat out the words, "What do you want?"

"Take a seat," Miller directed. Kiki made a face then sat on one of the metal chairs facing the lieutenant. Kiki was normally unflappable but today she found herself nervous as she waited for his questions. She felt a flush creep across her chest and up her neck.

"You were the one who told Banner that Jack was missing, correct?" Miller asked, reciting from the notes in his hand.

Kiki nodded her head, "That's right. I was frantic. Alex and I couldn't find Jack and when we discovered the house all torn up, well ...I panicked. Matt is our lead diver so I felt he should know."

"Did Banner appear nervous? You know, worried, out of sorts?"

Kiki thought for a moment and replied, "No, but I did notice something odd in his boat."

"Which was?" Miller encouraged. "What did you notice, Kiki?"

"There was what looked like blood on the floor boards." Once the words were out Kiki felt a surge of disloyalty to Matt.

"Blood?"

"Yes, I stepped on it. I pointed to the blood and asked what that was all about, and Matt laughed saying he'd foul hooked a striper that morning and before he could release the fish, blood dripped into the boat."

"And you believed him?"

"Why not? Matt fishes every chance he gets, so why not fish blood?"

"Where was Banner when you reported Jack missing?"

"At Charlie's dock. Looked like he'd just come in from the bay and was working on his boat...Oh!" she said, suddenly understanding. "You think I interrupted him cleaning up Jack's blood!" Kiki shivered as it suddenly occurred to her she might have later taken a boat ride with Jack's killer.

She quickly ran through her mind what she knew about Matt that might indicate he was capable of murder. She came up with zero, except for the sudden moods and that bit about some brush with the law in Florida.

"What I think is you were a lucky girl. You might have been feeding the fish along with Jack," and he pointed a finger at her. "You wouldn't by any chance have those bloody sneakers?" and he gave her a penetrating look.

"No chance," she replied feeling a sense of relief. I scrubbed them clean with ammonia and water as soon as I got home." She hesitated then continued.

"There is some kind of problem in the Keys, Marathon I think, that's been bothering Matt but I don't know what it is. It has something to do with his sister." As soon as the words were out she felt guilty as if she had again betrayed Matt. She picked up a discarded dive jacket and absently began to pull the suit right side out.

Miller finished taking notes before deciding if a DNA test on the cleaned sneakers was worth the effort. He snapped the book closed and tucked it into his suit pocket, then stopped with his hand on the door. "Want to add anything to that Florida bit?"

Kiki was all done being helpful. She wanted Jack's killer caught but thought Matt was a poor target. "All I know is what I told you. Do your own checking!"

"That I will, little lady, that I will," Miller said as he closed the door.

Outside, he flipped on his cell phone and called the Portland based Coast Guard unit. Miller spoke firmly to the petty officer second class who answered, explaining he had not heard from them on the whereabouts of Watts Penn who was needed for questioning in a murder case.

He was told there had been no sign of the lobsterman. As he hung up the phone, he was suddenly struck by an idea that might make locating Watts unnecessary--someone else who might have seen Matt the night Jack was killed.

Walter Golden, better known in Yarmouth as Zig Zag, or Ziggy, was about twenty-five but Lieutenant Miller had never been able to tell. Every small town has at least one odd person whom it shelters and accepts even though he presents some bizarre behavior.

Ziggy was Yarmouth's *idiot savant* whose claim to oddity and genius was his incredible ability to instantly recall the day of the week for any given date in history.

To test him Miller asked questions he knew the answers to, such as "Zig, I was born on October 4, 1965..." Before he could finish the question Ziggy would say, "That was a Monday, Lieutenant Miller."

Zig Zag was never wrong. Ziggy also collected soda bottles for spending money. He rode his three-speed Schwinn bike over all the streets and behind the stores in both the upper and lower villages at least once a day.

The red canvas bag tied to his handlebar usually bulged with bottles. Ziggy was also useful to Lt. Miller because he not only saw everything that happened in town but applied the same ability to time that he did to dates. And Ziggy knew every face.

Miller cruised uptown where he found Zig Zag digging in a trash can behind Donatello's Pizza.

"Hey, Lieutenant, where you at?" Ziggy spoke through his nose, a nasal twang, not unpleasant just different, then rolled his bike over to the cruiser. Zig wore his hat backwards with the band close down over his large protruding forehead. Bushy brows hung like cliffs over narrow black eyes. A dirty, faded red sweat shirt draped over dungarees and his feet were covered by a pair of Nikes two sizes too large.

"Been looking for you, Ziggy. Wondering if you could help me out?"

"I'm your man, my man," and he chuckled at his wit.

"Yeah, well do you know a guy named Matthew Banner? He's one of the divers working out of Charlie's Marina."

"Sure do. Big, good looking dude. Friendly too, gave me a whole bag of soda cans. Let's see, that would have been two weeks ago, July 13th...that be a....Monday," he concluded proudly.

"Good. Now think back, Ziggy, this is important. He claims to have been down at the boat yard the night of July 5th but I think he's lying. You see him any time that day, say somewhere between six o'clock and midnight?"

Zig Zag's reply came instantly, "West Elm Street. Saw him leaving Jack Kilby's house. I know because I was out back of Jamieson's next door smoking my 186th cigar of the year. Saw him clear as a bell under the street light. Ten thirty that'd be."

Miller felt a spurt of adrenaline. *Gotcha' Banner*!

"Ziggy, like always you're a wonder," he patted Zig on the shoulder, smiled good-bye and called the office. He instructed the dispatcher to have Detective Mike Baker place a call to the police in Marathon, Florida, to inquire about any charges pending against a Matthew Banner.

Twenty minutes later Miller returned to his office and found Baker missing but a sticky note on his phone. "I'm at the court house, be back in an hour. Call Detective Lucas, Marathon police."

Miller shucked off his coat and hung it neatly around the back of his chair. He removed his notebook, extracted a pen and seated himself on the comfortable swivel chair before dialing.

While the phone rang, he removed his name tag from his blazer and placed it next to the photo of his wife and two kids, the only decoration on the desk. He perched the portable phone under his chin, walked to the coffee pot. By the time he returned to his desk and pulled his tie loose Detective Lucas was answering.

Questions flew both ways. Miller's book was filled with hastily scribbled notes, some underlined, some starred and circled. Before hanging up, he promised to call if he found more information connecting Matthew Banner to the murder.

He pulled out a yellow pad and wrote out the evidence gathered to date: Banner had lied about where he was the night of the murder, possible incriminating blood had been discovered in his boat (he penned himself a note to verify that with the lab), he was a suspect in the death of his sister.

He wondered if that would be enough to get Judge Lester Wood to issue a search warrant for Banner's apartment.

20

THE BAD GUYS

At the agreed upon time Lee Thomas McCall crossed over the Cousins Island bridge and headed for Charlie's Marina. Ten minutes later her bouncing headlights picked up Matt's pickup parked in front of the dive shack.

The idea of entering a vacant house of a recently dead person sent shivers along her spine but, while it was scary, the hunt for Jack's GPS sounded exciting. When she thought about the dark shadowy rooms that awaited her she shivered again.

She parked next to Matt's truck, climbed out and popped his door open. Once inside she pulled it shut behind her. McCall squirmed sideways facing him. She had changed into a pullover sweatshirt and dark slacks and wore her hair down, allowing the ends to brush along her shoulders.

The first thing McCall noticed was Matt's powerful shoulders and thought how his change into jeans and dark sweatshirt made him appear tough, lean and dangerous.

Matt's heart gave a flip when she entered the truck. A soft feminine smell wafted past the steering wheel. "You sure you're ready for this, McCall? I don't really believe we'll be in danger but I can't promise."

McCall gave him an infectious grin and stuck out her tongue. "I'm no 'fraidy cat, Mr. Diver. You just drive."

"OK, you're on, McCall."

"Matt, just what is this GPS thing we're looking for and how will it help us locate the source of the gold?"

As he drove he explained. "GPS stands for global positioning satellite system. Signals are broadcast from twenty-four satellites that circle the earth, at least four are in range at all times." He drew circles in the air as he spoke.

As the truck bumped over the railroad tracks to the upper village Matt dug into his jacket pocket and handed her his GPS, which was the size of a television remote. "Jack's will look like this one," he said, "A Garmin. DMR assigned one to each diver so we could accurately pinpoint sea urchin beds. At the end of each working day I would download their days work into the computer in the dive shack."

"How does it work?"

"That little red button turns the unit on. When the *mark* button is pressed the exact *latitude* and *longitude* of that precise spot on the earth is logged into the memory on the GPS. You can save the location by pressing the *enter* key." He pointed out the buttons as he talked.

"What is this *GoTo* button?" She asked. Before he answered Matt parked under some low hanging trees one street up from Jack's house.

With the engine off he replied, "If you press *GoTo*, a list of saved *waypoints* comes up. Waypoints are previously stored places saved by the GPS user. Each waypoint has its own longitude and latitude. You can move the cursor to any one of these points, then press *enter*. When you do that, a straight line will appear on the screen *from* your present location directly *to* that waypoint."

"So if Jack marked the location of the gold it would be one of the waypoints in his GPS. All we would have to do is press *GoTo* then put the cursor on the waypoint and push *enter*. *Voila*, a line would go to the pot of gold!"

"Right, but remember he could have named that waypoint with some code word. We could be forever out there in the bay. Trial and error could take the rest of the summer!"

"So how is this GPS going to help?" McCall asked again.

"I'm not exactly sure but I know that unit is the key to the treasure."

"Matt, we could be forever tracking all these positions." Her excited smile was replaced by a thoughtful expression.

"Not to lose hope," Matt responded. "Jack was a devious guy but I got to know him pretty well. He took a chance when he confided in me that night he showed me all the jewels. He as much as said he thought his life might be in danger. I think he would have left me some clue.

"Come on," Matt said climbing out of the truck. "No use trying to figure it out until we have the unit."

The interior light winked on as they slid from the truck. Matt shoved on the door until the lock snapped closed. He grabbed McCall's hand and led her through a row of low pine trees that formed a hedge at the rear of Jack's house. Together they approached the back door.

"Matt, how are we going to get in?" she whispered.

"In the movies the detective uses a credit card." As he spoke he inserted a card against the doorframe and leaned on the knob. A sudden click was followed by the squeak of hinges.

"Matt, my hero, we're in!" Then she turned and spoke more seriously. "Matt, are you sure no one is home?"

"After the funeral, Jack's parents took their oldest daughter back to Montreal. I can assure you, no one is home."

Cautiously he led McCall into the living room. Matt was surprised to see how carefully all traces of the mess

Kiki had described had been erased. McCall shined her light along the walls, her eyes taking in the large oil paintings and velvet curtains, expensive furniture and modern lamps. The high ceiling gave the house a ballroom look.

McCall whispered, "Matt, this house is enormous. Where do we start to look?"

"Jack's room is upstairs. I think he would have kept the GPS close to him. It would be stashed somewhere Jack considered safe. Remember I told you he liked to hide things in obvious places. We need to locate an obvious place."

"About as likely to happen, Matt, as finding a snow ball in an avalanche!" McCall whispered.

"Hey, why you whispering? There's no one here."

"I don't know. Just seemed natural. Here we are in the dark after breaking into a house where jewels have been hidden, then stolen and Jack murdered. Makes you want to whisper."

Matt placed his hand on the banister leading to the second floor. He paused. The tick tock from a grandfather's clock echoed exceedingly loud in the empty house.

"Matt, I feel as though I'm walking through a cemetery." As she spoke she felt goose bumps run along her arms and her heart rate speed up a notch.

With those words Matt felt the hair bristle on his neck. It was easy to imagine someone else in the house watching their every move, some evil shadow, someone who had already killed once and would not hesitate to do so again. He pulled her close and squeezed her hand.

"Stay close, maybe we aren't alone."

With those words McCall felt her heart racing. "My God, Matthew, if you're trying to scare me you are doing a good job." She grabbed his arm and gave a quick look behind her.

"Come on, up we go." Matt pulled lightly on her hand. Each step brought a reluctant groan from the stairs. Each creak thundered in the silence. McCall suddenly giggled.

"What's so funny?"

"Just that it would be impossible to sneak up on anyone with all this noise we're making."

Matt swallowed, tightened his lips and took another step. He hugged the wall as they maneuvered to the top of the stairs where he lingered and expelled a deep breath. They were in a long narrow hallway leading to an open door ten feet away.

His shoulders felt tense as he took a tentative step toward the door on the left, the room where Jack had showed him the jewels. Traffic from the street hummed by setting up a flare of light through the foyer windows.

A loud creak suddenly erupted from the room now just three feet away. "Matt, what was that?" McCall's whisper was tense with fear, her heart now threatening to tear out of her chest.

Matt turned his face and spoke directly into her ear. "Don't know. Maybe just the house settling." But he knew there was someone in the room. He could hear controlled breathing and the shuffle of nervous feet. Matt's hand felt damp and clammy as he realized they were not alone in the darkness. He suddenly realized that if someone were waiting in the room another could be waiting for them to come down over the stairs.

His breath became shallow. He could feel McCall trembling with tension against his arm. She felt so alive, warm and vital. Would either of them survive the next few minutes? Strangely he felt no fear, only a detached need to survive. Matt turned an ear sideways, listening.

"Matt, he knows we're out here."

He nodded his head in the dark.

"But he doesn't know how many of us there are." McCall could feel her ear tickle as Matt's lips moved slowly with the words.

"Who are these people, Matt?"

Matt felt a tightness in his throat. His heart seemed to shrink and his pulse rate soared. He dropped McCall's hand. "Stay here," he whispered ignoring her question.

"Not on your life, Matt Banner!" she breathed, grabbing his arm. "I'm sticking to you like your shadow." With that she swept a quick look down the stairs. The light from a passing car lit up the foyer again. In that instant a man's face glowed in the reflected light.

"Matt, there's another one at the foot of the stairs!" She pressed against him, fear making her voice high and tight. The stairs creaked with the weight of the man's step.

"Matt, we have to do something! We're caught here! What'll we do?"

"Okay, it will be the last thing they'll expect," his voice was almost without sound. "There's a door on the far side of Jack's room that leads to what used to be servant stairs, goes down to a butler's kitchen then through a screen door to the back porch.

"We're going to blast into that room where we heard the creak. Don't hesitate. No matter what happens, keep going. Get to the car and get away. He handed her the keys. If we get split up, I'll meet you at Charlie's in an hour. If I don't show up, go to the police. You got that?" As he said the words, his mouth felt dry and for the first time real fear hit him in the pit of his stomach.

"Got it." She gave Matt's hand a squeeze.

Matt guided McCall the last few feet to the open doorway. A slight bit of light filtered through one of the windows into the hall.

Suddenly there was a sound of a board bending from the top of the stairs. Matt saw the movement. "No time to wait, McCall. It's now!" He lowered his head and plunged into the room dragging McCall behind him.

The man erupted from behind the bed where he had been hiding. Matt crouched to face him at the same time shoving McCall at the exit door. "Run!" he shouted.

Matt staggered as a fist hit him with the force of a hammer. His head snapped back with the shock of the blow, his legs buckled and he found himself on the floor. As he struggled to his feet the man grabbed McCall. Her hands flew to his face. She raked her nails downward feeling skin tear away and the man screamed. She wrenched away toward the servant doorway.

As the man reeled away from McCall, Matt attacked, jabbing an elbow into the stumbling figure feeling bone against a nose. The man's knees sagged, but he regained his balance and swarmed over Matt. A huge hand grabbed for his throat. Matt pivoted and struck him a two-handed blow that thundered off a shoulder. He felt the man shudder and hitch sidewise to avoid Matt's second blow.

A passing car's lights beamed into the room momentarily illuminating the man's contorted face. Suddenly he snatched something from inside his jacket and slammed it against Matt's head. Stunned Matt felt himself stumbling to the floor.

McCall had not run out of the room. She swept up a table lamp and slammed it against the man's head. He dropped to the floor in pain and clawed at the glass stuck in his face. The second man broke into the room shouting to the man on the floor. Only the darkness saved Matt from an instant death. His attacker pointed a pistol at Matt, looking for a killing shot that would not hit his partner. Matt, crumpled on the floor, could only watch the arm rise into a firing position.

With one last ounce of strength Matt yanked on the rug, spilling the shooter backwards. The arm shot into the air. The pistol fired, a bright flame spurted into the darkened room, a deafening sound thudded against Matt's ears, while the smell of burning gunpowder swirled in the air. Before Matt could scramble away the arm lowered again and fire spouted from the barrel. Matt felt a hot tugging sensation along his left shoulder.

McCall's voice exploded in the room. "Matt, lights!" The room flooded with brilliant light as McCall flipped the light switch. Her warning allowed Matt to lunge to his feet and follow McCall's voice to the stairway.

The man with the gun, blinded by the light, stalled in his attack. The first man recovered from McCall's blow to the head and lunged after them. Matt spun around and jabbed the stiff end of his extended fingers into the throat of the advancing man. He followed the jab with a sharp blow to the stomach. As the man doubled over Matt struck upward with his knee sending a smashing blow to the face. The man shuddered and flopped to the floor.

"Quick, Matthew, get me out of here!"

21

JACK'S GPS

As Matt dove down the stairs he heard the shot, and felt the bullet zip by, thudding into the wall. He hit the stairs on his shoulder, tumbled into McCall and drove them both down the dark stairwell. A hail of bullets ripped into the wall, plaster ricocheted in the narrow passageway cutting McCall's face. Concussion from the shots blasted her ears and the smell of burning gunpowder crammed into her nose.

McCall reached the bottom first. She grabbed Matt's hand and they raced into the protecting darkness. Matt for the moment did not feel the sweat, his flying pulse or frantic heart beat. What he felt was an intense anger. They reached the pickup. His hands were shaking when he slammed the truck into gear and spun away in the direction of Main Street.

McCall remained silent and glanced frequently out the rear window to make sure no one followed. It wasn't until they bumped over the railroad tracks to the lower village that she relaxed.

"That, Matthew Banner, was too close. No, not close. That was super near!" Her voice held a slight quiver and she found her hands were cold and had trouble keeping her chin steady.

Matt looked across the seat. "You all right?" He held her chin and turned her face so he could see. "You're all bloody. Were you hit?"

McCall flipped down the mirror and checked her face. After a moment she said. "I think I was nicked by flying plaster when the bullets hit the wall. Nothing except my dignity destroyed." She ran her fingers over Matt's eye. "What did he hit you with anyway? You're bleeding."

"I don't know but the second guy through the door nicked me on the shoulder with his pistol."

"Let me look." McCall rolled up his sleeve. "You were lucky the bullet burned a hole through the shirt but missed the arm." She leaned back on the seat. "Well, what now, Sherlock?" She asked feeling her heart settling down. "Call the police?"

Matt was quiet for a minute. Then concentrating on the road said, "I can't do that, McCall. Those guys won't stick around for the police to question and frankly I can't get involved." He looked to see if she understood and then added.

"How would we explain why we broke into a house, especially one where the guy living there had been killed? We going to tell them we were looking for a dead man's GPS so we could locate a fortune in lost gold?" Matt paused. "I don't think so. Besides I have that little Florida problem where I'm a suspect in my sister's death."

McCall didn't have a reply for that so Matt continued, "I think you're safe. Neither of those guys got a good look at you and won't know where you are staying."

Back at Charlie's Marina he brought the pickup to a skidding stop next to her car. "Go home, McCall. In fact you should really go home. Go to Montana. Get away from this mess."

"Matt, when I snapped on the lights I got a good look at the man hiding in the bedroom. He was almost bald, bullet headed, somewhere in his forties I'd guess. I think the man from the stairs was speaking German."

Matt laughed. "Yeah, I got an up close look too, just as I stiffed him in the throat. Had a powerful set of shoulders and some kind of metal tooth shining in his mouth. Funny with all that was happening that I should remember that, but I do. I'd know him in a heartbeat."

"What about the man who shot at us?" McCall asked.

"Not so sure. I had an impression he was older, maybe in his sixties or older, glasses, moved more slowly."

"Well, I messed up the bullet-headed guy's face." She showed him her nails. "A woman's lethal weapon!" McCall could still feel her hands shake yet sitting here next to Matt she felt an emotion stronger than fear. She tilted her head and considered him.

Matt was amazed how the dashboard lights accentuated her cheek bones and cast a haunting shadow into her almond eyes. He wanted to kiss her but wasn't sure it would be the right thing considering the evening.

McCall could see him start to lean toward her then check himself as he pulled in next to her rental car. "Hey, good night, Matt." Then she laughed and piled out of the truck. "When you want to get shot at again, give me a call!"

"I'll call anyway if it's okay?"

"Please, I'd like that."

As she climbed into her car, Matt rolled down his window. "Be careful, McCall. You're growing on me. Don't want to lose you." With that he said lightly, "I'll be in touch."

McCall spun her tires out of the boatyard and sped away up over the hill to Cousins Island. She let her mind drift over Matt and felt her heart laugh. Why had she let herself be drawn to this wild diver with danger stamped all over him?

Matt locked the door to his apartment, checked all the windows and propped a chair under the doorknob. He crawled into bed wondering who the two men were and why they had been at the house. Why had they been speaking German? Had they killed Jack and stolen the jewels? If they were, why were they still hanging around? As he drifted off to sleep a nasty thought crept into his mind. Had the men also been looking for the GPS?

The next morning Matt poured coffee while his mind focused on the problem of the missing satellite unit. The more he thought about where Jack could have stashed it the more he became convinced the unit was not in his house.

Then it clicked. The boat. Right under his eyes, that was Jack's way. Sure, why not? The police didn't know about the other jewels, only the one on TV. They would never look for a GPS because they had no reason. Jack's *Black Beard* was right at the foot of the street, moored at Charlie's Marina. The question was how to search the boat without being seen.

He looked at his watch and found he'd have to hurry to make his morning dive schedule with Alex. He hurried out the door to his car so fast he failed to see that someone had worked at the door. Small pry marks marred the doorframe.

22

MATT BANNER ON TRIAL

Matt could have walked the half mile to Charlie's Marina and his dive schedule with Alex but his truck made it more convenient. He parked and entered the dive shack. Kiki, Alex, Big Bob and Lance were sorting out the morning dive gear and engaged in a heated debate.

Matt was surprised to find Lance there since it was his turn out of the rotation but he found out later he had showed up at Kiki's request.

It was obvious to Matt from the attention directed at Kiki that she had been the one leading the discussion. An absolute, embarrassing silence greeted him as he entered.

Matt stood with his back to the door, his eyes shifting from one diver to the other. Definitely a solemn group. From the looks on their faces it didn't take a genius to guess he had been the topic of conversation.

"Okay, who died?" He asked, before realizing that remark had been in poor taste. Still no one spoke until Alex nodded to Kiki. "Well, tell him," he instructed.

Still the silence. Lance lifted a tank to his shoulder. Big Bob cleared his throat and awkwardly shifted his feet.

"Okay, gang, what's up here? I got two heads or what?"

Kiki finally started, "Matt, Lieutenant Miller was here yesterday. He wanted to know more about the morning you and I went out to look for Jack."

"So what did you tell him?"

Matt could see Kiki was uncomfortable. There was a slight flush along her neck and he knew that never happened unless she was really embarrassed or under stress. "He really pressed me, Matt. Oh, my God, I feel so disloyal to you." She cried placing her hand over her mouth. "I had to tell him about the blood in the boat."

With that said she bit her lower lip and turned wide imploring eyes at him asking for understanding.

"Blood?" Matt looked confused. Then understanding. "That striper I foul hooked?"

"I told him that's what you said but he seemed pleased and wrote it all down in that little book he carries."

Matt studied the group to see what effect her remark had. The blank unfeeling stares told him what he needed. He was hurt to see that people he called friends could even entertain the thought he might have killed Jack. He felt a cold isolation.

"You just told him what you saw, that's all," he finished thinly.

"Then he asked if I knew about any problems you might have had in Florida. I don't know how he found out about that, but he knew." Matt shook his head and blew out a deep breath. "I told him I didn't know about anything except it had something to do with your sister." She looked at him. "You told me that."

Matt felt betrayed. He'd told Kiki a little about his Florida problem but felt it had been in confidence. A dispirited feeling crept over him. One quick pull at the knot and the anchor of friendship had slipped overboard.

Alex spoke for the first time. "Miller just called here, Matt. Kiki took the call. She was just telling us what he said when you walked in."

"What interesting yarn did he have to spin?" Matt asked with a voice that sounded distant and hollow.

"Matt, he said your sister had died under mysterious circumstances." Alex paused, looked at the group then continued in a quiet voice. "He said you were the prime suspect in what actually might be murder." The shack went quiet again, not a sound, all eyes directed at Matt.

Matt hesitated, and let out a huge breath. A calmness settled over him as he flipped a chair around and leaned his arms on the back of the chair. "So, you are wondering if I'm the guy who not only killed Jack but murdered my 14-year-old sister?...Right?"

There was an uncomfortable pause, feet shuffled and eyes that would not make contact with Matt's drifted around the shack. Then he continued, "Since you really don't know much about me all this seems possible or at least feasible. You figure it might be someone who was closely connected to Jack. Someone who might have found out he had more gold pieces and murdered him for them."

"That," Lance said slowly, "and the fact Miller says you lied to him about where you were the night Jack was killed."

Matt looked puzzled. He didn't think Miller had located Watts. Then in answer to his confused look Lance said, "Zig Zag saw you coming out of Jack's that night." Lance's shrill voice made his announcement sound even more damning than it was.

Big Bob spoke up. "Matt, he implied he was close to placing you under arrest."

That was news to Matt and he let it sink in before he shifted his eyes to Kiki. "You are wondering if you have been on a search for Jack with the guy who had just returned from killing him, aren't you?" He could see by the way she lowered her eyes that his remarks had hit the mark.

"Scary thought, I agree but don't let it worry you. I might feel the same way if I were in your shoes." He gave her a reassuring smile.

Matt sat motionless on the chair. His eyes swept over the dive gear stacked and ready for the day. Everything seemed normal, only it wasn't. At least not for him. He had a difficult decision to make and a very short time in which to make it.

The group looked at him, hoping for some kind of denial but he knew that would not be enough. They needed more, especially from some Florida transplant.

Rubbing his hands across his face, he took a deep breath. "Okay, I guess you deserve an explanation. I want you to know I have no way to prove what I'm going to say. Maybe when you hear it all... well, I don't know..."

Their faces encouraged him so he told them about his sister first. The same story he'd laid out for McCall. Then at the last moment he pointed to his mailbox at the back of the shack. "The afternoon of the night Jack was killed I found a note stuck in that box. Since I never get mail I was surprised to find it there. I was even more surprised at what it said."

He told them about his visit to Jack's house and the enormous pile of wealth he'd seen spread out on the bed. "That's all of it." He lifted his hands and shrugged his shoulders. "Miller and Zig Zag are correct. I did lie to Miller about where I was that night. I just didn't see how I could tell him the truth."

Alex nodded his head as though his story had filled in some gaps and made sense. Kiki immediately flew into his arms and buried her face in his neck. Tears appeared in her eyes. He could feel her blond hair tickle his ears. Big Bob and Lance looked at each other. "Makes sense to me," Lance said.

Matt felt relieved at the response. "You still on to dive with me today, Alex?" Matt asked with a question on his face.

"Never doubted you, Matt, but there were holes in my thoughts you were able to fill."

Matt fixed a happy note on his face, "Let's dive!"

23

KIKI'S PHONE CALL

McCall was returning from Yarmouth village to the island after running some errands. As she drove down Pleasant Street she recalled the number of times today she had tried to reach Matt by phone and failed. On the spur of the moment she pulled into Charlie's yard and looked for him.

No one was in the front office and when she stuck her head into the dive shack it was empty. She followed the gravel roadway down into the yard and caught Kiki half way up from the dock.

McCall noticed the sun bronzed, radiant face, blond hair bleached and windblown. The yellow and orange wet suit set off her color. McCall was instantly alert; her female intuition telling her this golden diver would have more than a casual interest in Matthew Banner.

Kiki stopped, shaded her eyes against the afternoon western sun. A striking honey blond gal with a nice bounce to her walk was headed right at her. When McCall stopped a few feet away, Kiki slid the air tank off her shoulder and dropped her weight belt over the top. An attractive girl in tan shorts, white cotton sleeveless shirt with LTM on the pocket and open-toed sandals stood inquiringly in front of her.

A smooth confident voice asked, "I'm looking for Matt Banner. Do you know where he is?"

Part of Kiki wanted to help but after her botched talk with Lieutenant Miller she had become guarded where Matt was concerned.

"Who wants to know?" she replied carefully.

"Oh, I'm sorry, I'm L.T. McCall, a friend of Matt's."

Kiki sized up McCall, deciding she was obvious competition but likable all the same. With her usual bright smile she replied, "Hi, I'm Kiki Malone. I just got in from the bay. Matt's diving with Alex today."

She looked down river past the restaurant. "They should be along shortly." Then giving McCall a sweet smile hoisted her gear back on her shoulder and hiked up to the shack.

McCall wasn't sure what to do. She walked briskly to the docks behind the storage shed and waited. After fifteen minutes she gave up and drove home.

Twenty minutes later Matt and Alex entered the shack, stripped off their dive gear. Matt waited until Alex was ready to leave before he asked, "How about we grab a pizza for supper? I've got a problem and need your thoughts."

"You mean you've got more problems than what we discussed earlier today? Can't believe it, Matt."

"Yeah, well this is a future problem and I need to address it big time quick." Alex nodded, understanding Matt would reveal what was on his mind when he was ready which looked like it would be after they ate.

"I'll grab the chow and meet you at your place. Give me a half hour. You want a loaded pizza?"

Matt nodded yes. Then added, "Make it two. I'll have a friend there I want you to meet." Alex flipped him a salute and tooled his classic 1956 Chevy toward Main Street and

Donatello's Pizza. As he drove up the hill, dull mellow sounds from the doctored muffler echoed along the street.

At the same time Matt and Alex were ordering pizza, Kiki Malone was sitting in her green VW in front of Andy's Handy Store in the upper village. Her head was pressed down on the steering wheel and she was both angry and miserable. Angry at herself and miserable because of what she had exposed to Lieutenant Miller. The dashboard clock showed six pm and the heat from the day still lingered in the tiny automobile. Perspiration beaded her upper lip, but Kiki appeared unaware of the heat. She was lost in thought.

Guilt was not a familiar emotion but she was learning the havoc it could wreak on her soul. Ever since she had faced Matt that morning, guilt had been saddled to her shoulders.

Every time she played back her interview with Miller a hot uncomfortable flush spread across her face and stampeded over her chest. All that day she'd found it difficult to concentrate on sea urchin plotting and her stomach felt sour.

Part of her realized she was obligated to cooperate with the police investigation; however, her conscience kept asking if she had just cooperated or gone beyond into some dark hole where she had volunteered information she knew would be detrimental to Matt. If that were true, what had been her reason?

The stuff about Matt's sister, Lisa, had been offered to her in confidence. Matt hadn't said not to tell anyone, but she had understood it was confidential and could have kept that out of the interview.

Kiki Malone asked herself if she had leaked out that information because she was angry at Matt for not paying more attention to her obvious interest in him or because she had been so afraid of Miller it had just slipped out. In either event Kiki now kicked herself for being a fool.

With that thought she drove down East Elm Street, parked at the last house before the bridge over the Royal River, rolled up the windows, locked the car and with resolve entered her house to place a call. Kiki had Matt's number memorized. She dialed. When his answering machine kicked in, she spoke to the machine.

"Matt." She paused gathering her thoughts, breathing softly into the phone. She hitched nervously and ran fingers through her shaggy blond hair. "I don't know what to say. You mean a lot to me, Matt. I mean a whole lot and I think you know that. I hope my stupid talk with Lieutenant Miller won't change how you feel about me.

"Oh, Matt, I feel so terrible! I didn't need to tell Miller about Lisa,   I feel so ashamed." She placed the phone against her heart and sniffed back a cry.

"You told me all that in trust and I just blurted it all out at the first chance." As she spoke Kiki felt the warm flush of embarrassment. She felt a lump swell in her throat and her voice became husky with emotion.

"You need to know Miller came by again right after work looking for you. He had a search warrant. Said he'd found what he needed to arrest you. Something about a note Jack had written to you and some sort of inventory list he dug out of your apartment.

"I don't know what all that means, maybe you do. I hope I've helped. Can I see you...?" Matt's answer machine timed out. Kiki looked at the phone not sure if it was her friend or enemy. She debated whether to call back but decided against it. Matt knew how to get in touch with her. Maybe he would. She hung up with a sigh.

After giving Alex his order, Matt hurried up the hill to his apartment. He could hear the phone jangling as he parked. He unlocked the door but the machine clicked off as he entered the room. He considered the tiny red flashing light urging him to press the message play back button then decided there was a better chance of bad news than good and for the moment chose to ignore the light.

He opened his cell phone and called McCall. She sounded excited about the pizza. "Be there in a flash." She hesitated, before saying, "Oh, by the way, I met Kiki Malone today."

Matt didn't know what he was supposed to do with that information so he said simply, "Oh?"

"Pretty girl," McCall replied without inflection. Then rang off with "See you in a little bit."

McCall arrived first, followed in a few minutes by Alex, who after pointing to the doorframe said, "Hey, guy, what happened to your door? Looks like the boogeyman tried to get in."

A cold chill swept over Matt. He cast a quick eye at McCall. She looked pale and sat staring at the door as though the boogeyman might momentarily crash into the room, one with a bullet head and massive shoulders.

Matt went to investigate the pry marks before taking a chair at the kitchen table. His face looked serious when he said to Alex, "We'll tell you about it." Then he introduced Alex to McCall. They smiled at each other and said the appropriate words.

Matt had told her Alex could be sort of nerdy on occasion but she saw no signs of it. He wore a gray sweatshirt pulled down over carefully pressed chinos and sneakers with no socks. In fact he had a rakish handsome look, bushy black hair and long sideburns.

His eyes surprised her. Deep pools that seemed to absorb the whole room. Matt had told her that Alex would be his choice as one of his life lines, the friend to call, if he ever appeared on *Who Wants to Be a Millionaire*. Looking at him now, McCall could see why.

Alex switched his eyes from McCall to Matt giving him both thumbs up and mouthed silently, "Very nice! Where'd you meet her?"

"Hey, Alex, I'm here too and we met at DiMillo's," McCall answered smiling.

Matt knew he would have to tell Alex the whole story about their escapade at Jack's if he wanted his help. He looked first at McCall and explained how earlier that day the divers had laid out the evidence Lieutenant Miller had against him, the fact he'd lied about where he was when Jack was killed, the blood Kiki had seen in the boat and how Miller had found out he was the prime suspect in the death of his sister. Then he looked at Alex.

"Okay, here's the scoop on those pry marks." He looked at McCall to see if she agreed they could bring Alex in on the puzzle concerning Jack's death and the lost jewels. She understood and nodded her approval.

As they finished the last of the pizza, Matt completed telling him about the attempt to locate Jack's GPS and their subsequent battle at the house and their narrow escape. As an afterthought he mentioned the loose shutter and broken window.

"So you think one or both of those guys tried to break in last night?"

"They might have except I had propped a chair against the doorknob," Matt replied. "It's strange I didn't hear them though," he finished.

"Scary stuff, Matt," Alex said, shaking his head in wonder. "What about the police?"

Matt explained why he couldn't choose that option.

"Okay, we keep the police out of it, but aren't we getting in over our heads?"

"Probably, but maybe the prize is worth the danger. Remember the loot Jack showed me that night. The jewels alone were worth a fortune. A fortune that's missing right now and my guess is the bad guys located them the night they killed Jack." Alex started to say something and Matt interrupted.

"Think about it, Alex." Matt could feel his pulse quicken as he spoke. "Those guys have that pile of gold and are still sticking around. Now I ask you, why would they do that instead of running?"

McCall suddenly understood where Matt was going. She opened her mouth and pointed at Alex. They spoke together. "There's a whole lot more gold around somewhere!"

"You got it. What they have now may only be chicken feed."

Matt wiggled his eyebrows and made a clicking sound in his throat. "You betcha, there is a ton of it somewhere," Matt said, excitement brimming in his voice.

"Hang on, Alex," McCall interjected. "I think he's about ready to spring his *pirates as the source of the gold* theory on you,"

Alex laughed. "He's tried that out on us before. You still hung up on that crazy idea?"

"I've been telling Matt the necklace belonged to my grandmother," and McCall told Alex why she was sure that's what she'd seen. Before Matt could get in a word she rushed on, "To support his pirate theory Matt says I could never have remembered what that necklace looked like after ten years!"

Matt finally got his turn, "How do you explain the gold Jack showed me? I'll tell you what. If and when we find the gold we are going to find it on the wreck of some ship. Jack as much as told me so. Now who but pirates would be carrying that much bullion of that particular variety?

"Why, you'd have to break into the Titanic's vault to find jewels, necklaces and diamond pendants like the ones I saw." Then added, "Why do you suppose Jack changed the name of his boat to *Black Beard*? Answer me that!"

"OK, Sherlock, how do we find Black Beard's treasure?" Alex asked.

24

HEART BREAK

Matt had no immediate answer for Alex's question. Whatever they did probably would be dangerous and he told them so. When he thought about the possibility of blood being spilled, Alex's question might have been better phrased, Okay, *Shy*lock, instead of *Sher*lock.

Matt shook his head. Suddenly there was no sound in the room. The three of them looked at each other. No one had a ready answer to Alex's question. When she thought an appropriate amount of time had elapsed, McCall spoke.

"As I understand it, Jack's boat is anchored in the middle of a bunch of other boats right off Charlie's dock. Am I correct?" Matt nodded. "And since you doubt the GPS is at Jack's house that leaves the boat. Right?"

"Well then," McCall continued, "if you use your scuba tanks and swim out there underwater you should be able to board Jack's boat undetected." She tilted her head looking for agreement.

Matt cast an inquiring eye at Alex, who shrugged his shoulders and said, "Yeah, maybe." He ran a hand through his wiry hair. "Who goes?"

"I go." Matt replied immediately.

"Hey, it's your funeral." Alex smiled grimly.

"Getting there is one thing," Alex said. "But you have to get back, Matt. From what you said these two guys are nasty. What makes you think they haven't been watching you, waiting for you to find that GPS? If I'm right, there could be quite a reception party waiting on shore!"

"I don't know. Maybe you are right. For all we know they might have found it at Jack's house and have already recovered the treasure but it's a chance I have to take. I owe that much to Jack."

With that statement McCall looked solemn. She reached over and squeezed Matt's hand. She glanced at Alex. "You think it's safe?"

Alex laughed nervously and replied with one of his inane statements, "All things being equal a fat person uses more soap than a thin person."

"Now what is that supposed to mean?" McCall asked.

He grinned and replied, "Well, some things are obvious. Damn right it will be dangerous."

Matt looked at his watch and was surprised to see it was almost eleven o'clock. "We go at one a.m." He looked to the others for approval. No objections came. The next two hours were spent in planning.

At twelve forty-five Matt stood up and noticed again the red blinking light on the answering machine. He was tempted to punch the play button but decided he didn't need any distractions at the moment. "Time to go," he said, heading for the door. McCall followed them outside.

She stood close to Matt. Close enough so he could smell a tinge of jasmine. He could see the invitation on her lips and feel his pulse beating in his ears.

"Hey, diver." she said. "Be careful, come back to me." With that, she melded against his chest and gave him a soft kiss.

As Matt clasped her waist to him he felt locked in some kind of emotional upheaval. Whether he liked it or not McCall was turning out to be an essential part of his life.

"I'll be back," he breathed. Matt had decided to ride in Alex's car to the marina. Then over her shoulder he could see Alex waiting impatiently beside his Chevy.

"Gotta go." He released McCall wondering what love really felt like. At the car he turned. "Hey, L.T. McCall."

She stopped half way to the apartment.

"If that phone rings, take the message for me, will you?"

"Got it", she replied. Then not wanting to go back inside she watched them drive down the hill. No matter what, if those two Germans were watching, Matt and Alex had their lives at risk.

McCall was not sure how long she stood there hugging her arms in the early morning chill. Her feelings for Matt were all mixed up. She had dated lots of guys and had several hook-ups but what she felt for Matt was far stronger and somehow deeper. It affected her whole being. For the first time in her life she wanted to spend every minute with this mystery guy.

When she tried to defend her feelings there was little on the table. She'd known him less than a week yet it seemed a lifetime. He had a smile that lit up his face and a slightly crooked nose that gave him a look that said don't mess with me!

Most of all, she trusted him. She thought she liked that best. McCall wondered if this rousing effect Matt had on her soul was called love?

McCall finally walked back to the house where she noticed the answer machine's red light blinking. Realizing someone must have called while she was out in the yard, she immediately punched the playback button.

She instantly recognized Kiki Malone's voice as it crept hesitatingly out of the small speaker... *"Matt, you mean a lot to me. I mean a whole lot and I think you know that. I hope my stupid talk with Lieutenant Miller won't change how you feel about me..."*

McCall sat on the couch stunned. Her heart seemed to stop. She choked out a cry, "Damn you, Matthew Banner!" Tears came to her eyes as she listened to the rest of the message.

She recovered for a moment, hit the replay and listened to the part about Miller arresting Matt. In spite of her hurt and anger she felt a shaft of fear at the implications for Matt.

Then the ending to the tape blasted into her ears... *"Can I see you..."* McCall paced the room, face flushed with anger.

Matt had been leading her on all the time. Here she was thinking he was the one who had won her heart, kissing him wantonly, throwing herself at him. He must have felt smug accepting all that while he had another girl on the string. Maybe more than one, maybe a dozen!

As she fumed and stamped around the apartment she began to wonder if there were other things Matt had told her that weren't true. What about that story concerning his sister, Lisa? What about the blood Kiki had seen on his boat? God, maybe that really had been Jack's blood.

Then reason took hold. No, Matt could not have killed anyone. But he could be unfaithful. With those twinkling brown eyes he could be running a harem for all she knew.

The kitchen clock showed one thirty. In spite of herself she hoped they both would be all right out in the dark swimming after some piece of electronics that would lead to some unknown pot of gold.

It wasn't hard to imagine a swashbuckling buccaneer standing on a chest of gold with a sword in one hand and a pistol in the other. The whole treasure idea reeked of death and destruction.

McCall felt like going home. Not just to Cousins Island but all the way to Montana. She'd get her tickets as soon as she could and blow this place off. "Good riddance, Matthew Banner!" Startled that she had spoken out loud and at the venomous sound of her voice, McCall plunked herself down on the couch to wait and plan how she would approach Matt.

She had never felt so betrayed and the word trust lay like a spear in her heart.

25

MASK AND FLIPPERS

At Charlie's, Matt used his key to enter the shack. They left the light off and after stumbling around in the dark managed to secure Matt in a black wet suit and webbed weight belt. He flipped the tank and regulator over his shoulders then snapped them into place, grabbed his mask and flippers, then whispered, "Let's go."

There were thirty feet of open ground between the last boat sitting in its cradle and the high tide lapping the grass along the shore. That part worried Matt. Anyone on board one of the boats moored in the harbor or hidden in the shadows on shore could see him when he entered the water.

Alex held a three-cell flashlight. The plan was simple. Periodically Matt was to glance toward shore. Alex would rapidly flash the light three times if they were in trouble. If that happened, Matt was to swim to the opposite shore and climb out through the docks at the Yarmouth town landing. He was to hustle up the landing road to Bayview Street where he would wait for Alex to pick him up. Simple works best but it didn't work out that way.

The moon was low in the western sky, reflecting in the ripple of water ebbing in the tide. The night was clear except for scattered clouds, stars, pinpricks of light. A gentle breeze spun up the river from the bay.

The mission wasn't exactly heart stopping but Matt still felt nervous and he found himself shivering inside the rubber suit. The look on Alex's face didn't encourage him either. "There is really no other way to get to the water from here except to run, is there, Matt? What about the other side by town landing?"

"Same problem and we can't sneak down through the parking lot as far as we've come here."

Matt took a deep breath. His thoughts were in a turmoil bouncing between this was going to be a piece of cake to this could be his worst nightmare. He focused his mind on the shoreline and tried to drive away the feeling he was being watched. All at once clouds slipped over the moon blocking the silver light for a second. Matt chose this the time to move.

He burst out of the shadows, sprinted across the open space and slithered into the water. After a quick glance to locate Alex's position he donned the mask, tucked the regulator in his mouth, took a quick compass reading before sinking beneath the murky waters of the Royal River.

The river was shallow, maybe eighteen feet deep at high tide. He doubted his bubble trail would be a problem even if the moon suddenly flooded the harbor. He quickly covered the one hundred yards and surfaced at the buoy end of Jack's boat. He worked his way aft to the swim platform on the port side.

He could hear an occasional car as it crossed the bridge fifty yards up river and waited for the glare of their lights to recede before propping his mask on top of his head. With a cautious glance in Alex's direction, he hoisted himself out of the water onto the deck. With his body below the gunwale, Matt crawled to the console located in the center of the boat. He peeked over the rail toward shore. No lights, at least not yet.

Heinrich von Brockner watched from his position on shore near the large storage shed and saw Matt slip inside Jack's boat. He lowered his night vision binoculars and signaled Richter to enter the water. The listening devices Richter had installed in Matt's apartment were now paying dividends but Brockner was worried. His plan had been to strike quickly and return to Germany carrying the gold. Richter, however, had killed Jack Kilby before they had gotten the location of the treasure from him, a mistake Richter would pay for later.

Matt's searching fingers slid open the compartment door beneath the wheel and probed through the box-like interior. Failure there sent him to the forward section of the Grady White.

On his boat he used this compartment to stow rain gear and spare anchor. Jack or someone, however, had cleaned it out, leaving the fiberglass space empty. He spun a quick look at shore but all remained dark. So far so good!

Matt popped open the anchor locker located at the far end near the bow and found just the anchor. Discouraged, he had only one place left to examine. He turned on his knees to the box directly in front of the windshield. This was where most of the divers stored their life jackets.

As quietly as possible Matt removed all four jackets then ran a hasty hand around inside the box to be sure he hadn't missed anything but the box was empty. He was about to replace the last of the jackets when he felt a stiffness along the right front of the preserver.

Alex had suggested he carry a small mag light but Matt had said, no. Light carried a long distance at night especially over water. Even held below the gunwale the glow would alert an interested party. Now he wished he had one.

Matt raised the jacket into the dim light of the moon and discovered the stitches had been cut and re-sewn. His pulse rate picked up and he had difficulty controlling his fingers until he finally inserted the blade of his dive knife into the seam and cut into the fabric allowing Jack's GPS to slide into his hand.

A slight breeze swirled across the channel swinging the boat up river against the tide and the hull gave a slight shift as it bounced on the mooring line. Ignoring the motion of the boat Matt removed a waterproof bag from his suit, unzipped the top and dropped the GPS inside and sealed the bag.

Just then Matt felt the deck tilt to starboard and heard the sound of a wet sneaker on the deck. A prickling sensation ran along his arms under the rubber jacket, his mouth suddenly went dry. Matt snapped his eyes to shore and saw one wink of light. There had been no plan for a one-wink flash!

The sneakers eased along the starboard side and the boat continued to list in that direction. Matt slammed down the lid to the box, leaped to his feet, stuffed the GPS inside his suit and made a frantic dive for the rail and safety of the black water.

Before his body dropped over the rail a powerful hand fixed itself on his shoulder. The pain and power of the grip paralyzed him. He let out a deep breath, pivoted on his right foot and swung a stinging blow at the huge shadow that held him powerless.

His eyes looked directly into the man's face as the moon tripped out from behind a cloud. A tooth glinted in the waning light, confirming what Matt all ready knew. The hands that had held his shoulder suddenly switched to his throat. The German was trying to kill him!

In a matter of seconds the vise-like fingers were squeezing the life out of his body. Matt's lungs screamed for air, burned and heaved for a breath that would not come. Bright lights flashed behind his eyes and his mind bellowed commands to muscles that could not respond. He dug his fingers into the hands surrounding his neck but failed to pry loose the iron grip.

He could feel his struggles getting weaker. Then the shock he was dying sent electric sparks through his muscles and with one final movement lowered his head, ducked forward, slamming the regulator with the weight of the tank directly into the German's face, knocking him down. Before he could recover Matt leaped over the side and sank beneath the surface allowing the safety of the water to close over him.

Zipping sounds punctuated his ears. He rolled onto his back to see straight line bubbles punching three feet beneath the surface. The German was shooting at him. Matt blew water from his mask and dove for the bottom. There was no time to decide on the best route. In an emergency the plan called for him to exit on the far side of the river at the town landing but the one flash of light might mean Alex was in trouble.

He checked his compass and struck out for the spot where he had entered the river and five minutes later crawled out of the water into sheltering grass. He ran to the shadows of the 40-foot sloop where he had left Alex.

No movement came from the shadows. He waited a few seconds then whispered, "Hey, diver, whistle up." He waited. June bugs scratched the night air and mosquitoes hummed, but no reply. He needed to hurry. If the German from shore joined the one with the gun they would be in deep trouble.

Suddenly he sprang out from under the shadows of the sloop and hurried to the dark form he now could see sprawled on the ground. He squatted beside Alex. Matt quickly felt for a pulse, and was relieved when Alex uttered a painful groan and put a hand to his head. "Sorry, Matt, never saw him coming."

"You feel okay enough to move? We have to hurry before they come over here."

"They?"

"Yeah, there were two of them."

Matt helped Alex to his feet. "Can you walk?"

"I'm okay. Just my head...hurts like the devil."

"We've got to get to your car. Can't go to my place. I'm sure they are the ones who tried to break in. They know where I live."

Matt hauled Alex up through the yard to the street and tumbled him into the front seat of his truck. Flipping open his cell phone Matt called McCall. While it rang, he shed the air tank and tossed it in back along with the remainder of his gear.

With the phone glued to his ear, Matt slipped behind the wheel and in a cloud of spinning tires and gravel raced out of the yard to Rt. 88. He swung the sharply careening pickup over on two wheels in a mad dash for East Main Street.

"Hey, Matt, what's the hurry?"

When McCall answered Matt shouted, "Get out McCall...get out...don't ask questions, just get out of the house right now." Not wanting the Germans to know where he was directing her he finished with, "The pink house...go...go!"

The swaying pickup lurched into Alex's driveway. Matt vaulted up the steps and thumbed open the door.

McCall looked at the phone as though she couldn't believe what she'd heard. Then grabbing her purse she bolted out to her car. McCall only partially remembered the bit about where Alex lived in his pink house. Was it East Main Street or East Elm Street--she wasn't sure but she would find it. Kiki's voice still rang in her ears, "*Matt, you mean a whole lot to me...*" Just maybe there was a reasonable explanation for the words on the tape...but just *maybe*...!

26

THE FIGHT

Kiki pushed open the door to the refrigerator and poured her third Pepsi in an hour. Before stretching out on the couch, she changed the CD player to put on Shania Twain's *Feel like a Woman*, which she knew was one of Matt's favorites. Sleep overtook her before the CD had half finished.

Kiki was miffed at Matt for not returning her call. Several times in the last two hours she had started to call him back only to lose her courage at the last moment.

She awoke with a sudden start, apprehension tight in her chest. Something was wrong. Matt was in trouble. She could feel it.

"God," she thought, looking at the mantle clock. "It's two a.m.!" Kiki made a hasty, frantic call to Matt's house not caring if he was upset by the hour. When his answering machine kicked in, she hung up. She snatched up the phone book, located Alex's number and dialed.

Matt answered. "Hello?" he asked.

"Matt, it's Kiki, are you all right?" Then realizing Matt sounded wide awake, she asked, "What are you doing up? Why are you at Alex's at this time of night? Is he awake?"

"Hold on, Kiki, Alex and I..."

Kiki interrupted. "Matt, why didn't you return my call? I left a message. I thought sure when you heard it you'd at least respond."

Matt had a mental image of the little red light blinking. So it had been Kiki. Well, whatever she'd said he was probably going to hear again.

"I feel terrible about the things I said to Lieutenant Miller," she continued. "Matt, I need to see you right now. I'm coming over."

"Kiki, now is not a good time..." The phone was dead.

Kiki arrived five minutes later and parked next to Alex's Chevy. Matt opened the door and she hurried inside.

McCall finally located East Main Street and could see in her headlights the outline of a pink house. When she saw Matt's pickup in the yard, she cut her lights and slowly turned into the driveway making as little noise as possible. Her dashboard clock showed two twenty a.m.

There was a light on in the front room where she could see two people talking. McCall was still uncertain she had the correct house so exited her car and crept to the window. She knew that from the lighted room the occupants would not be able to see her.

There was a guy, who certainly was Matt, standing with his back to the window. The other figure, a striking blond, was facing him. There was no mistaking Kiki Malone's startling figure holding the other person's hand with a possessive gesture.

The more McCall studied the guy the more she was convinced it was Matt. Worry washed over her as she thought about the implications of this blond and Matt together at two a.m. However, she was confused. Matt had told her to come. Why would he when he was with this girl?

Suddenly the blond flung herself into the guy's arms, twisting him sideways as she kissed him. McCall's eyes bulged. It was Matt. His arms were around the girl. They were kissing! The girl clung to him, thrusting herself against him. Before McCall could help herself she choked out loud. "Matthew! I trusted you!" Tears leaped into her eyes.

McCall pushed away from the lighted window and stumbled to her car. She fumbled for the keys with shaking fingers just as the door burst open. Matt ran down the steps and grabbed her arm and pulled her from the car. "McCall, what's the matter?"

"What's the matter?" she said coldly. "What's the matter? ...You and that... girl! That's what's the matter!" Her chest heaved with emotion.

Matt flinched at the hurt sound in her voice. "McCall, it's not..."

She felt her fists clench at her sides as she folded her arms and revved up her stare, "Don't McCall me, Matthew Banner, I saw what just happened. I trusted you. I thought we had something special...." Her voice broke and did not finish.

"McCall, Kiki..." Matt began, an almost imperceptible note of pleading in his voice.

"I know who she is!" She paused for breath. "I don't understand. You tell me to come over, a matter of life and death, and then thrust that...that Kiki in my face." Then testily, "Really, Matt, you could have handled that *much* better!" Her eyes misted. Her heart was hammering and jealousy stuck in her throat so hard she could hardly get the words out.

Matt could see raw hurt glitter in her eyes and he suddenly realized how the scene must have played out for

McCall, Kiki with her arms around his neck, her mouth planted firmly on his.

He stood stiffly in front of her uncertain what to say. He could feel McCall's stormy eyes accusing him. Matt knew he was about to lose McCall unless he could convince her his arms had automatically folded around Kiki as she grappled with him, that there had been no feeling, no return of her affection.

Matt groaned inwardly at the task. He put his arms around her and moved close, feeling her breath on his face, her warm and musky smell. When he put his arm around her waist, she gave a small cry and pulled away. "Well, explain yourself!" she demanded, hurling the question at him.

She then pivoted away, ducking her head as she entered the car. "Or maybe you can't," she continued, her face cold and hard.

"McCall, I had nothing to do with what you saw. Kiki and I are friends. We dated a few times when I first came to Maine. I'm afraid she read more into the relationship than there was." Denial flew from his mouth.

"She just pounced on me back there," he said with a ghost of a smile. "First time, too. Hey, McCall, cut me some slack here. It's not what you think." While he tried to make light of the situation his chest felt tight and he found himself clearing his throat as he spoke.

Their eyes made contact. McCall's wavered for a moment. After all she had not really let Matt explain. She turned her blazing eyes at Matt's strained face and stung him with a long unwavering stare hoping there was more of an explanation coming.

All she could think about was her one real love affair back in Montana when she had given her heart to a dashing quarterback. They'd been steadies for six months. Then one night she came over unannounced to find the head cheerleader wrapped around him like a wet noodle.

Her heart had been broken. Vowing never to get that close to another guy, she refused to date the rest of her senior year. Now it appeared it had happened again. She felt hurt and was angry at herself for the strong pangs of jealousy coursing through her body, making her face burn. She had not realized how important Matt had become.

Matt felt he'd been ambushed, shot and bleeding, with no one to come to see if he was dead.

"McCall, I'm not going to explain any further. Either you believe me or you don't. The guy from Jack's house attacked Alex. The one with the silver tooth almost killed me out in the boat. I warned you out of the house because I was afraid they'd come there looking for me."

For a fraction of a second McCall hesitated as she recognized the truth in his words. Then replied sharply, "So you think that explains your ..." She searched for a word, "...entanglement with ...Kiki." Her voice became brittle, "Nice try!"

When he realized McCall was about to drive off he could feel his heart pounding faster. Time seemed to stand still. His nerves were taut as he watched her expression change. The charge of electricity, a live spark between them, crackling and unsafe to touch without warning, fizzled and burned itself out.

He watched woodenly as McCall swept her hair behind an ear, and wiped her hand across her eyes. "McCall, I'm not wrong here. You have to learn to trust someone. I have not violated that trust."

With all her heart McCall wanted to believe those words spoken with such sincerity but she no longer felt warm and feminine. Instead she felt cold and remote, hurt and unsure. She rolled up the window as she spoke, "Goodbye,

Matthew!" The words were smothered off as the window slid closed. Before Matt could decide what to do she backed the car into the street. With a lurch and spin of tires McCall roared into the night, her tail lights two red dots disappearing from his life.

The last thought Matt had, as he turned back to the house, was that love was one of those things about which it was impossible to be wise.

27

SOMETIMES YOU ARE THE PIGEON AND SOMETIMES THE STATUE

Matt dragged leaden feet toward the house. Watching him return, Kiki leaned against the door, her face a combination of awe and confusion. Matt stopped and looked directly into her eyes, "Got any more surprises? Maybe you have a zebra named Spot you'd like to show McCall?"

Kiki looked uncertain, "Matt, I don't *have* a zebra." Then understanding dawned on her face, she lowered her head and said, "Oh."

As he brushed past he saw the hurt reflected in her eyes as she realized his feelings for McCall. "Matt, I'm sorry. I didn't know. She saw us, didn't she?" Kiki placed a warm hand on his arm and gave it a slight squeeze.

"Bulls eye!" Matt responded. Then softened his voice, "Hey, you didn't know. Besides you're a good kisser." He placed his finger on the end of her nose and gave her a friendly smile. "Kiki, you'd be the one if I hadn't run into McCall."

Even though she knew that wasn't true, she said, "Thank you for that, Matt."

His voice was heavy with concern. McCall was strong willed and independent. He knew perfectly well she could be in Montana at the drop of a hat. No goodbye, no contact,

no see you later, not even a "maybe we can work this out."
Like a puff of smoke in the wind...gone! Out of his life.

"Kiki, please go home.   We'll talk about this later,
okay?"

"Okay, Matt. Sorry about the mess. I just needed to tell
you I was sorry I leaked information to Miller."

"It'll work out, don't worry about it."   However, Matt
was not certain he would see McCall again and suddenly he
realized how much that would hurt.

As soon as Kiki drove out of the driveway Matt hunted
up Alex who waited in the living room, a bag of ice on his
forehead. Matt started to explain what had happened but
realized that it was unnecessary--Alex had heard it all. Alex
held a hand up and said, "If I had written all that down I'd
have a great scene for *Friends* or the old *90210*." His grin
split his face wide open. Matt gave him a grim smile. "Not
funny, funny man."   Then in spite of himself he burst out
laughing.

"What's so funny, Matt?'

"Well, sometimes in life you are the pigeon and
sometimes the statue and right now I feel more like the
statue with crap all over me. Might as well laugh."

As he spoke he sprawled on the couch and fished Jack's
GPS out of his pocket, looked at Alex and asked, "You sure
your head's alright?"

"No problem," but Alex winced as he said it.

"I didn't say anything, but before McCall arrived at the
house last night, and while you were getting pizza, Ed
Vance, the director at DMR, called. He has put me on
administrative leave until this cloud Lieutenant Miller has
raised over my head clears up and will send over another
diver to take my place tomorrow. Seems Miller is serious
about arresting me for Jack's murder.

"The Florida cops now think I'm a double murderer and my girl just blew out of my life. On the other hand, in here," he hefted the GPS and pointed it at Alex, "is the key to a pot of gold that cost Jack his life and could make our fortune."

"You sure, Matt?"

"I'm sure. Jack was just lucky when he stumbled onto the gold the first time. He knew that and would not leave it to chance again. No, Jack would have marked a waypoint anchoring down the latitude and longitude." He slipped the GPS back into his shirt pocket and looked at his watch. "Alex, it's two thirty. I'm bushed.

In the morning we need to decide what to do with this GPS. In the meantime I think we are safe, at least for the night. I'm out of a job and if I remember correctly you are out of the dive schedule tomorrow. Want to see if we can find Jack's treasure?"

"Ah," Alex replied expansively, "I owe much, I have nothing, and the rest I give to the poor."

"Who said that, Alex?"

"I don't know, some French humorist," and gave Matt a sly look. "Anyhow, I am broke. A small fortune would fit into my budget quite conveniently!" Then he asked, "What about McCall? Will she be safe tonight? Those guys may have gotten a look at her during the fight at Jack's. Think they have figured out who she is and where she is living?"

"I doubt it. She's staying in a bed and breakfast over on Cousins Island." He thought about calling but quickly discarded the idea. He doubted McCall would answer anyway.

Matt threw a blanket over himself, propped a pillow under his head and prepared for sleep when Alex said, "Jack will have hidden that waypoint. How will we find it?"

"Remember the time when you told me how remarkable it was that cats have two holes cut in their skin exactly where their eyes were located? You never explained and I never figured out how hard you were pulling my leg. Well, it's sort of the same thing here." He grinned and said, "Good night."

28

FOLLOWED

McCall hurried the car down East Main Street, passing houses locked and dark as her heart. She tried to think how the argument with Matt might have ended differently, but each time she tried to paste a clever thought onto the pages of the story the image of Kiki wrapped around Matt and his arms holding her flashed in front of her eyes.

She shivered and wiped away the wetness on her face. The matter of betrayal settled on her shoulders like a velvet cloak smothering her doubting heart.

Then a small trickle of misgiving leaked into her thoughts. She remembered there were two parts to Kiki's message on the answering machine. One, Lieutenant Miller had found Jack's note asking Matt to come to his house on what turned out to be the night he was killed.

Two, he also had located the inventory hidden in Matt's house listing the other jewels Jack had recovered. That much she already knew from what Matt had told her out on the sand island. He had told her about his sister, Lisa, too.

The blood in his boat. That was new. Had she really fallen for a killer who had mercilessly murdered two people? The thought was unsettling. She gripped the wheel and hunched forward on the seat.

Then what about the Germans at Jack's house? How did they fit in? Weren't they the more likely suspects? She thought so and realized no matter how angry she was with Matt he could never have hurt anyone.

All at once she inhaled deeply and put her hand to her mouth. The police hadn't known about the *other* jewels. Had they found out? Would they figure Matt knew about them and had killed Jack?

There was no traffic on the road as McCall drove over the Royal River Bridge. Suddenly lights flashed in her rear view mirror, then went out. The road behind remained empty as she pushed the car up Route 88 past Charlie's yard. Yet as she made a left turn, the lights once again shone in her mirror.

Odd, she thought, but her fight with Matt blocked out further thought about who might be behind her. Again McCall turned left onto the road leading to the bridge and Cousins Island.

As she rounded a curve the light appeared once again. McCall felt a sliver of fear ripple up her back and the hair on her neck stiffen when she realized she was being followed.

The road was dark and lonely with no place she could get help and once across the bridge escape would be impossible. Her only chance would be to dart into a side road and hope the pursuer would miss the turn.

McCall speeded up until a mile separated the lights following her car. Probably it was all in her imagination. With that thought the lights disappeared.

She crossed the bridge and a quarter of a mile later turned into the road to the bed and breakfast and parked. McCall jumped from the car and raced to the back porch. Once inside she bent down below the porch window, then nudging her fear to one side, parted the curtains and watched the road.

Twenty minutes later, her breathing back to normal, McCall was satisfied no one had followed. Had she heard a car door shut? She wasn't sure. McCall shrugged off the feeling someone was still out there watching, checked to be sure the door was locked and crept upstairs to bed.

29

HURRICANE *ALBERT*

Friday morning Matt awoke early, his head stuffed from too little sleep. The sun was just peeking in through the living room curtains, casting meager shadows on the wall, when he flipped off the blankets and raced to the bathroom.

He showered, slipped into his jeans and had bacon and eggs cooking long before Alex stumbled sleepy-eyed into the kitchen and flipped on the television.

Kevin Mannix, Channel 6 weatherman, was just starting his morning report when Alex started to ask if...

Matt waved a *be quiet* hand. "Listen," he pointed to the TV.

"*...Tropical storm Albert is currently in the Atlantic sixty miles north of the Azores tracking west northwest, packing winds of a hundred miles per hour.* The screen faded behind Mannix and a new one popped up showing a possible path over the next few days.

"*Where this storm will hit depends on the jet stream...here...*Mannix pointed *and the cold front moving down from Canada. This storm could swing out to sea...or...*he looked straight into the lens of the camera...*our first hurricane of the season could bang into Cape Cod. If it does Albert will sweep up the coast with an excellent chance of hitting Portland, Maine, head on.*" He closed with, "*I'll keep you posted.*"

"That," Matt said, "could prevent us from searching after Jack's gold."

Alex noted Matt's words but was more interested in what he'd started to say and repeated his question. "Do you remember what I said last night just before you blacked out?"

Matt's mind was plugged with thoughts of McCall and the fight. He tried to see it again from her perspective. In the morning light he realized he could have been more understanding. He was so absorbed he had to ask Alex to repeat the question. When he did, Matt replied, "Bugs?"

"Yeah, you know, the possibility that some kind of listening devices were planted in your apartment."

"Bugs!" Matt repeated again.

"Yeah, whatever. How else would those Germans know we'd be at Charlie's Yard last night?"

"Coincidence?"

"Coincidences like that just don't happen," Alex stated.

"I'll check out the apartment the next chance I get," Matt assured him.

Alex only smiled. "You look, you'll find," was all he said about the listening devices and let the matter drop.

Then Matt's face turned hard and cold. "Alex, in one way or another those two men have cost us a good friend, made me some kind of fugitive and stepped deep into my life. The best way we can retaliate is to get that pirate gold before they do."

He slipped the GPS out of his pocket. "This is our edge. As long as we have it we're ahead of them. Come on, let's go find Jack's treasure."

Ten minutes later they returned to Charlie's marina.

Alex performed a cursory look for Miller. He hollered at Charlie who replied Miller had been a no show. Quickly they loaded their dive gear into Matt's Boston Whaler.

Matt fired the motor and headed down river. The sharpness of the early dawn air was crisp in Matt's nose and he zipped up his jacket against the chill. He was continually mystified how the sun could hide for so long beneath the horizon then suddenly jump into the sky as it had this morning, mashing against the sea, scaring away the wind, leaving the bay mirror smooth.

The eastern horizon turned lemon pink and cast a warm glow over the racing Whaler as the boat erupted from the mouth of the river on the way past Lanes and Moshier Islands. At the southeast tip of Whaleboat Island Matt cut the motor and allowed the Whaler to glide forward into the incoming tide.

"Okay, hot shot," Alex said. "We're out here so turn on that rig of Jack's and...*show me the money!*"

Matt turned a hopeful face at Alex before turning on the GPS and began explaining their problem. Alex knew enough about the GPS to locate his sea urchin beds but somehow never had much interest in it beyond that point.

He knew that every time the *mark* button is pushed on a GPS two things happen at once. One, the *latitude* and *longitude* of the exact spot where the operator is located is recorded in the screen at the top of the unit.

Two, that position, called a *waypoint*, is recorded on a way point list stored in the GPS. These waypoints were numbered sequentially starting with 001, or the operator could substitute a name for the waypoint number like *red buoy 6*, or *dock*.

In answer to Alex's question Matt said, "All we have to do is figure out which one of Jack's waypoints is the one marking the gold and... bingo!" With Jack's unit in his hand, he brought up the *main menu*, highlighted *waypoint list* and hit *enter*. All the waypoints scrolled up on the two-inch screen.

"Those are places Jack marked, right?" Alex asked, with a discouraged voice as he noted there were more than fifty waypoints listed.

"Right. And one of them will lead us to a pot of money, but..."

"But which one?" Alex finished.

30

THE DIVE

Matt shifted the *Dawn Raider* into neutral and turned off the key allowing the boat to bob and slew in the following wake. "To answer your question, I don't know exactly how we are going to find that pirate loot but I have an idea."

"If Jack coded the location we could be forever finding it, Matt," Alex replied. Then added, "Maybe he just used visual landmarks and not the GPS."

"I doubt Jack would have left a buccaneer's dream to memory. Our spot is in here somewhere," he said tapping the GPS.

"So we're left to unscramble some code or stumble around fifty waypoints?!" Alex's voice was discouraged.

"Agreed. But there is a chance, a slight one admittedly, but at least a chance Jack either by design or by error left us a clue. Look at Jack's GPS. Notice the dotted lines behind the square icon that represents the boat. Those dots are like footprints in the snow. If Jack followed them backwards they would take him back where he started, which in his case was Charlie's yard. These dots are called the *track back* log. Look at my GPS. See, it's clear. I erase those dots every day or so because they clutter up the screen. I looked at Jack's last night..."

"And he didn't erase them." Alex finished, face beaming for the first time.

"Right on." Matt held Jack's GPS in his left hand and steered with his right so Alex could see the tiny screen chock full of trailing dots. Some ran in long curved lines, some crisscrossed. The dots streamed out of the bottom of the screen then bent into looping circles where Jack had stopped his forward motion and begun a turn backward.

Watching over Matt's shoulder Alex shook his head. "I don't see how this is going to help. The gold could be anywhere along those dotted lines. They are not even exactly together."

"That's because Jack didn't steer the exact path every time he came here. But," Matt's voice reflected his excitement, "notice how close they are, probably not more than a hundred feet apart. Here," he said, handing Alex a piece of paper.

"I made up this list of waypoints. I took them from Jack's unit while waiting for you to get up this morning. We'll use *Jack's* GPS and let the icon representing our boat move along the dotted lines. Then every few seconds punch *mark* on *my* GPS and our latitude/longitude will be displayed on the screen."

He punched *mark*. "See," and he pointed as the GPS displayed their present position. "Somewhere along those dotted lines Jack would have put in the waypoint for the gold. We'll compare the GPS waypoints from that list I gave you with the latitude and longitude on my screen."

"And when we get a match...bingo!" Alex exclaimed. "Smart guy!"

Matt smiled. "Save the kudos for when we bring up the gold." Secretly he was pleased he had been able to figure a plan that would bring them to the wreck.

For two hours, Matt steered his *Dawn Raider* along the dotted lines. Alex vigilantly compared the latitude and longitude positions. His eyes were getting gritty from the glare of the sun and constant reading of Matt's handwritten notes when suddenly his heart gave a flip. "Matt hold it. We got a hit!"

Matt held the boat steady.   The numbers matched. Before the wind could drift them off the mark he slipped the anchor over the side.

Alex struggled into his wet suit pushing his feet into the objecting rubber legs in a frantic drive to be the first over the side. He slipped the top over his shoulders and zipped up the front.

Matt, a half second behind him, spat into his mask and rubbed the lens so it wouldn't fog, squared the tank on his back, inserted the mouthpiece, and splashed backwards into thirty feet of clear, green water three hundred yards off Bates Island. He struggled to control his breathing as the anticipation of what lay below engulfed him. He could smell the gold; his torso tingled.

He forced his body to relax, then glanced up to see the shadow of the Whaler above disappear as the weight belt gave him a negative buoyancy and dragged him into the darkness below. He switched on his portable halogen light, swept it in a wide arc and spotted Alex swimming ten feet to his right.

The two lights carved a bright yellow path along the muddy bottom rippled by years of running tide. Cold crept into his wet suit, trickled down the hollow in his back and chest then slowly warmed.

His fathometer showed thirty feet. At that depth Matt knew there was no danger from nitrogen narcosis, no need to decompress on the way up. However, other dangers lurked underwater. Currents could shift from zero to ten knots as the tide swirled past the tip of the island which could carry an unwary diver out into Broad Sound.

Old lobster pots with broken, trailing lines dotted the bottom of the bay, a ropy octopus waiting to snare the unwary diver. A shudder swept up Matt's spine as only a pale hue of light remained from the surface. If their lights went out the bottom would wrap a frightening darkness around him, a hug from the underwater boogeyman.

Matt signaled Alex as a dark hump appeared at the extreme edge of his light. At first the shape looked like any other ledge he'd seen, waving olive-colored arms of kelp, tight knots of bubble-encrusted seaweed. But there was something different about this ledge.

As he kicked around the base of the mound, small schools of herring darted away, their silver sides glinting momentarily in the glare of his light. Matt let his feet settle to the bottom. He stared straight ahead. Alex appeared next to him, finning clouds of mud and sand.

A vague shape loomed in the semi darkness. The kelp seemed to climb over a rounded object complete with iron railing. He felt his pulse pick up and heart beat faster. A few quick kicks propelled him along the shape of the object that seemed about thirty feet long.

He checked to see if Alex had followed and found him at his side giving him the high sign, thumbs up. Together they swam closer.

Matt tore loose a waving arm of weed. The tide quickly cleared away the rising silt, exposing a surface that looked like metal. Matt slipped his dive knife from the sheath along his leg and with the hilt tapped the rusty spot. A sharp tink, tink clipped against his ears. He looked at Alex and tapped again to be sure.

Matt nodded to Alex, pointed the knife into the gloom beyond the lights and swam off toward the end of the mound. Together they ripped away more weed until Matt knew he was looking at the hull of a submarine.

The sub was strangled in weed, plated with barnacles and mired deep in the mud. Three kicks pushed him away from the bottom to the top of the cylinder and the mangled remains of the conning tower.

Alex tapped Matt on the shoulder and triggered his light to the side of the turret. With his rubber glove Alex quickly rubbed the barnacle-encrusted metal. A name appeared. Matt read *U-33* followed by a German swastika!

31

FOUND – THE TREASURE SHIP

Alex's eyes glowed with excitement as the flair of light illuminated the rusty hull. With his finger he traced the letter U and number 33 as if trying to make certain his mind wasn't playing tricks on him. While Matt knew what he was looking at, he had no idea what it all meant. Did anyone else know about this submarine?

Most all known wrecks were registered by the U.S. Government. Was this one? Was this where Jack had found his treasure and if so why had what was obviously a German sub been carrying gold?

As algae, rubbed from the rotting steel, floated past his mask he tried to think. All known wrecks were plotted on the charts. Was that true or was it only those that were a threat to navigation? How old was the sub?

Matt swam along the upper deck, noticing a pair of tubes extending along each side slightly below the main cigar-shaped hull. He wondered if those held torpedoes. He had visions of the captain, his hat switched around backwards, commanding, "Up periscope"...then with his arms cradled around the handles, acquire a target and order..."fire one...fire two!"

He swam back to the conning tower and shined his light into the opening. The cover was open but when he put pressure on the warped lid it wouldn't budge. He'd have to find another way inside. Alex swam toward him, his mask flashing in the glare of Matt's light.

Matt nodded at the hole and shook his head signaling no way in. If this was Jack's treasure ship, there had to be another entrance.

They finned back over the side, sweeping their lights carefully along the hull. As Matt descended to the mud floor and kicked along the base of the hull line, bubbles trailed off to the surface and billowing muck swirled around his flippers. His light probed for an opening into the submarine.

Just forward of the conning tower he noticed a difference in color in the out-cropping of weeds. Swimming closer he could see signs of fresh work where someone, probably Jack, had pulled away the encroaching sea cover.

A large piece of plate metal stood open like a door inviting him inside. A slight glow from Alex's light slid over the top of the hull as he searched the far side for another way in.

Matt noticed the edges of the opening were jagged where some sort of explosion had torn open the side creating a hole full of ragged, metal teeth waiting to grip a careless diver. The chain of bubbles that shackled him to the surface stopped their bright flow upward as he held his breath. Matt ducked his head and pulled himself inside.

A sudden shiver crawled across his back. Was the crew still inside? Would he see bones drifting and floating in and out as the tide flowed through the hull? He imagined a hand stripped of flesh drifting into his light, a waiting ghost, ready to grasp him in a bony embrace. The thought made him nauseous.

His entrance had caused mud and silt to funnel up from the floor, obscuring his vision. Loose debris flooded before his mask and for an instant panic seized him. His throat closed and he choked on the mouthpiece.

Bright particles of phosphorous floated away in the beam of his light, causing a pale green glow to erupt from inside the sub. He couldn't see and suddenly had the feeling a hand had grabbed his arm and he swore he could hear someone breathing until he realized the noise was coming from his own rasping regulator.

Then the tide sucked away the cloud and his light once more explored the interior. In spite of the cold water, Matt could feel sweat beneath the black rubber suit.

The halogen beam fell on a box canted on the floor. The top had been cut off and lay propped against the side. One corner of the box had eroded away leaving a hole the size of his fist. The mud and slime leading from the entrance in the hull to the box had been swept away, leaving an obvious path, Jack's route to riches that had ultimately gotten him killed.

Was there a link between the German sub and the two Germans that had been attacking them? Were the Germans the killers? He thought there was a good chance. What connection did they have to the sub? How did they know about the gold?

Those questions hammered inside his skull. Without warning he realized air no longer filtered from the regulator to his mouth. Sweet, carefree air had taken a hike. He sucked and nothing flowed. Fighting to quell the panic rising inside his chest Matt turned to escape the tiny interior of the sub. He had only half a breath, would it be enough to make it to the surface?

As he ducked through the hole he was suddenly wrenched backwards. A jagged piece of the hull stabbed into the hose leading from his tank to his regulator, pinning him inside. His chest heaved, lights began to flash before his eyes.

Matt realized even if he could rip free he would not have enough air to reach the safety of the boat. He was going to die inside the sunken hull. There would be more bony hands to greet the next diver searching for his pot of gold!

He wondered if he would lie here, a piece of humanity like the crew of the sub waiting for a rescue that would never come. He felt giddy and was about to spit out the useless mouthpiece when a light exploded in his face. Alex yanked out Matt's mouthpiece and thrust in his own before freeing Matt from the metal edge jammed in his gear. He buddy breathed him to the surface. When they reached the Whaler, Alex clamored aboard, reached over the boarding ladder and hauled Matt into the boat.

"What was that all about, Matt?" Alex asked in a worried voice. "You freaked out down there. You kept grabbing at your mask. I stuck my air in your mouth. Were you really out of air?"

"Not sure," Matt replied as spasms of panic cruised through his chest. He set his tank on the floor and pointed at the pressure gage.

"Hell, Matt, that still shows full!" Alex cried out, tapping the gage but the needle stayed stuck on full. Then he added, "I was poking around the starboard side hunting for another way in. I didn't find one and just happened to come back to see how you were doing. That was a close call!"

"You said that right. Thanks, you just saved my life!" Matt gripped Alex's hand in a firm shake before examining his tank again. Each diver had several cylinders assigned to them and their responsibility was to keep them full and ready to go.

The diver's name was stenciled in bright blue letters. This one was definitely Matt's. His name was clearly marked. He had filled both his tanks the day before and they'd been full then. This tank still showed full but was definitely empty. Matt wondered if this had been equipment failure or had someone tampered with his stuff. That thought caused a dark cloud to race through his system.

"So what was inside?" Alex asked, referring to the sub as he peeled out of his wet suit.

"Really didn't have much time to look around. There was a box of some sort about three feet square attached to the floor. There was a ragged hole at the base of the box and I noticed the top was off. I could see in the silt where Jack or somebody had been back and forth. I was about to poke my light inside when the air clamped off."

"Do we really know this is Jack's shipwreck?" Alex asked, excitement building in his voice.

"I don't see how it could be anything else. The GPS marks line up. There's a ship, albeit a sub. There are recent marks of entry. Yeah, we got Jack's hidey hole all right." Matt banged a high five with Alex's raised hand.

Both faces beamed with anticipation of what they would find when they dove again. Matt's watch showed four-thirty. "We don't have time to set up a new tank today. Want to try again tomorrow?"

"If I can get Big Bob to do my dive schedule, you're on!" Alex's voice was full of anticipation.

On the run back to the cove they stood side by side next to the windshield, each with his thoughts about tomorrow. Suddenly Alex turned to Matt and shouted over the wind.

"Wonder what that sub was doing in Casco Bay? My grandfather told me submarine nets had been strung between the mainland at Homewood Inn and Cousins Island.

"Ships were sunk in back channels to keep these small subs like the U-33 from sliding into the back side of Hussy's Sound in Portland harbor. He said massive transports, anchored in the deep channel, were lined up as far as the eye could see."

Matt assimilated that new information but remained puzzled. "I can see why there was concern. But the U-33 was nowhere near that net by Cousins Island."

"True, but remember someone sunk that sub before it could carry out its mission. No way to tell its final destination," Alex replied.

Matt added, "I didn't see any signs of torpedoes on board, did you? I checked the tube on my side and it was empty."

"Mine too." Alex nodded in agreement. "So, what's your point?"

"I think the U-33 was on some kind of secret mission carrying massive amounts of gold. But where was it going...? Who was going to pick it up ...and who was going to use the gold?"

"Yeah, and is there anyone alive who knows the gold was never delivered? Those German guys have to be involved somehow," Alex added. "Think about the implications of that for a minute! Maybe we could find out how and when it was sunk. That might give us a clue about the actual mission. I might be GPS dumb but the Internet and I are like that," and he crossed his fingers.

Matt anchored the boat to a vacant buoy in the secluded cove inside Sunset Point, and rowed the attached dinghy to shore. Then chucking the ailing scuba tank into the back of his pickup, he started the engine and headed toward Yarmouth.

"Where could we go to check all this out?" he asked, looking at Alex. "I could try Professor Russell again but I'd rather have more information before I tackle him."

"Easy," Alex replied. "The Yarmouth library is open until nine tonight. Meet you there right after supper."

32

GERMAN *BIBER* CLASS

Matt dropped Alex off at his house and rode uptown to the Village Deli. As he drove he thought the submarine had been amazingly small, not more than thirty feet bow to stern and about eight feet in diameter. The conning tower and short periscope must have been destroyed in the same gun blast that put the four-foot rent in the port side, creating Jack's entry to the gold.

Matt parked. The smell of onions and French fries assailed his nose as he ordered a burger and Pepsi. Twenty minutes later he paid his bill and, checking to be sure he wasn't followed, he hurried off to the library.

The Merrill Memorial Library was an imposing two-story colonial brick structure. He ran along a brick walk, down a couple of steps and entered through a pair of glass doors. At the oak circulation desk he asked an attractive mid-twentyish clerk if he could use one of the library computers. "Second floor near the back wall," she replied with a smile.

Matt took the stairs two at a time, a whole parliament of questions whirling through his mind. What was the sub's purpose? Who had planned the whole affair? Words like *sabotage* and *espionage* slid out of his mouth close behind *cloak* and *dagger*.

At the top of the stairs Matt entered a high-ceilinged room with a soft green carpet. A handmade quilt depicting the islands of Casco Bay hung on the wall by the door. He walked briskly to a small console surrounded by a sea of books at the back of the room.

As he fired up the Hewlett Packard and connected to the Internet, he noticed Alex hurrying across the room. "Sorry I'm late," he said.

Matt hopped up giving Alex the chair.

In an instant Alex opened UBoat.net and clicked through several links. "Bingo!" Alex said when all U-boat losses filled the screen. However, the U-33 was not listed. "Wonder what the U-33's mission was that was so important to make the Germans, even after the war, deny the existence of this particular submarine." He paused for a moment and said thoughtfully, "Why was it carrying gold?"

Alex's eyes gleamed in the reflection from the computer screen. "Hey, Matt, does it matter? The gold is there or at least Jack found a small fortune and there is probably more!" He finished snapping a high five against Matt's outstretched hand. "Yeah! The gold is there all right and right now we are the only guys who can find that sub."

Matt thought for a minute before asking Alex a question neither of them had considered. "Do you suppose anyone is left alive from WWII that knows the gold was on board the sub? And have they made any attempts to recover it?" Alex started to reply when Matt signaled him to wait. "Someone in the German high command had secret plans to use gold and other jewels in the United States before the war ended. What for?"

"I don't know but if I had been doing that," Alex offered, "I'd have made a list of every last item just to protect my backside in case something happened to that chest and I was held accountable."

Matt replied, "And that was exactly what happened. The sub sank, the captain was lost and the gold never delivered."

"How do you know the captain was lost? Maybe he escaped and has been hiding all these years waiting for the lost loot to surface."

"Alex, if the captain escaped he'd have carried away the exact coordinates in his head. He'd have come back a whole lot sooner if he'd been alive. From the looks of that sub my guess is whoever piloted that craft went down with the ship!"

"Yeah," Alex smiled, "but you can't be sure, can you?" and he punched his friend in the arm.

"You thinking of those Germans who have been tagging us?"

"I've been giving them some thought. But if one of them had been captain of the sub he'd be in his late eighties, I don't think the older guy is more than sixty. The one with the bullet head and silver tooth can't be much more than forty. That rules them both out."

All at once the lights flickered and the librarian's voice carried through the room, "Five minutes."

Matt gathered up the printouts and hurried down the steps. Pointing to his hip pocket, he said in a voice hushed with concern, "Little scary isn't it, carrying the position for the gold around in this GPS? The Germans would give a lot to know those coordinates." Matt look solemn as he tapped the pocket. "They were willing to kill for them, remember!"

Before they said good night Alex agreed to meet Matt at nine the next morning at the hidden cove on Sunset Point where Matt had moored the whaler.

Matt knew going to his apartment was probably foolish. Lieutenant Miller was sure to have it staked out. Somehow that reinforced his desire to go there. While Miller might be a menace in his life he was not going to let him take it over completely.   Matt made one exception to caution.   He parked the pickup in a neighbor's yard, and hid the GPS under a rock.

The bushes allowed him to approach within thirty feet of the back door. Open lawn stretched before him like a minefield too treacherous to cross. He felt exposed and wondered if crossing to the house was really safe or was one of Miller's men watching him even now as he paused on the edge of the lawn. He was close to the gold, very close, maybe one more dive.

The woods seemed quiet, no birds disturbed, yet he had no way to determine if someone waited inside. Matt could feel the tension in his neck and shoulders. What he needed was a good night's sleep and he was damned if some rude cop from Portland was going to keep him from it.

He shoved caution aside in favor of a shower and soft bed. With the dive tank over his shoulder he sprinted across the open space, kicked open the kitchen door, and suddenly realized there was someone else besides Miller who wanted his hide.   The Germans!   The apartment, however, was empty.

He placed the tank on the white enamel table, pulled the shades and propped a chair under the door handle before returning to examine the pressure valve where he noticed the seal around the threads had been broken away from the wall of the tank.

With tools from the drawer he twisted off the gauge. The answer to the problem became apparent immediately. Someone had exhausted most of the air then shoved a stick against the valve stem so it would constantly read full. When he thought about who might have sabotaged the tank, he saw the faces of the two unknown Germans.

Then on Alex's advice he carefully searched the apartment for listening devices. He had only a vague idea what he was looking for but when he pried the back off the phone a tiny piece of electronics fell out on the table. Matt continued his search more carefully but was unable to find another "bug" as Alex called them. Even finding the one made the room feel unfriendly, alien.

33

ALBERT THREATENS

The dark shades of night retreated to the corners of Matt's room, but it was not until later when the beacons of early morning light painted gold shafts on the walls that Matt dragged himself into the world of wakefulness. His mouth felt dry and his eyes sticky, he itched all over and was feeling worn after a fitful night's sleep.

He hastily tucked a worn T-shirt into a pair of faded jeans, stuffed his feet into moccasins and had coffee brewing before the fight with McCall and danger from the dive into the submarine wormed its way into his consciousness.

He remembered he'd almost lost his life yesterday and most certainly lost his girl. That was how he'd recently thought about McCall... his girl. Fat chance she would even be in Maine this morning.

When the full impact of what occurred between them registered he felt the muscles along his jaw tighten first in anger at himself for how he had handled the fight with McCall and, secondly, for whoever had tampered with his air tank. He patently wished he could live yesterday all over because Matt was certain his response to McCall would have been far different.

The beeping sound from his cell phone announcing an unheard message caught his attention and Matt thought it strange he had not heard the phone ringing. Even stranger still since he swore he'd not had a minute's sleep. Matt dropped into the wooden chair, flipped open the phone. There were two messages. The first from Alex. "Matt, the new team leader assigned by DMR is a stickler for rules. He refused to let me switch with any of the other divers. Wish you luck, Matt, keep me in the loop." It was easy to hear the disappointment in Alex's voice.

The second call was a wall banger. McCall! "Hi..." Her voice sounded hesitant, uncertain, "Two things, Matt. I'm sure someone followed me home last night and I'm scared. And ..." she paused, clearing her throat, "we need to talk. Last night was a disaster. Call me." Her voice sounded wistful as she left a number.

Matt felt a huge weight lift from his shoulders. McCall had not flown off to Montana. She was here! She wanted to see him! He dialed. "It's Matt," he said when she answered.

Then not knowing exactly what to say, he asked if she could meet him, and not sure if there were more listening devices in the apartment, finished with, "Meet you at the place we first met. Will nine o'clock be okay?"

"Nine's fine."

"Be careful, McCall, if what you say about last night is true you could be in danger."

It was nice to hear the concern in his voice. "I'll watch my back trail, partner." she replied with an exaggerated Montana drawl. "But what about that there Portland sheriff that's pounding down your trail?"

While her voice was playful the reference to Lieutenant Miller was sobering. "So far Miller hasn't showed but he's bound to catch up soon.

"Look, Alex had to cancel out on a dive with me today. I wasn't sure you'd still be here. If you don't mind playing second fiddle, grab a warm coat and I'll take you on a real pirate adventure."

"You found something, didn't you? I can tell by the sound in your voice..."

"Not over the phone," he interrupted. "Look for you in an hour," and hung up.

The second listening device recorded it all.

Forty-five minutes later he drove across the Cousins Island Bridge, turned in to the public beach and left the motor running.

McCall was waiting and lifted a canvas bag out of the rear seat of her car and walked briskly to Matt's truck. McCall paused as she opened the door, blond hair swirling just off her shoulders, a wink of gold at her ears. She wore a blue long-sleeve blouse with a tan sweatshirt tied around her waist.

Matt's face brightened at the sight of her. He wondered if she knew how beautiful she really was. He could feel his heart pick up in rhythm as she slid onto the seat and shut the door. Matt painted her face with the light from his eyes. She caught him looking and blushed.

"Hello," she said softly, watching the play of emotions on his face.

"Hello, yourself," he replied, with nerves taut and a dry burning throat. The soft sunlight filtering through the truck window danced on her face and his breath quickened as he reacted to the defiance in her eyes that said she had not totally forgiven him for last night's episode with Kiki Malone.

Then to his surprise the light in her eyes seemed to change and McCall spoke softly, her lips moving slowly. "Matt, last night...let's put it away somewhere and forget about it."

"Done," he replied with his steady brown eyes fixed on her face, wondering what stroke of luck had placed this beauty with wit and charm in his path.

McCall sensed his feelings and placed the flat of her hand on his face and leaned toward him. A weakness stole over him as he responded to the raw chemistry between them. She gave him a long unwavering stare, then uttered a small cry and slipped her arms around his neck. He pulled her roughly into his arms as his lips found hers.

No words were spoken. For the moment none were needed. He kissed her again, this time more tenderly. Matt had never felt as close to someone as he felt at this moment.

Then she slid out of his embrace and rested her head on his shoulder. There was a comfortable silence before she looked up into his face and whispered in a tender voice, "That was nice, Matthew."

Matt suddenly felt heat pulsing through his veins. "There was more to that than just a casual kiss."

"I know, Matt, I could feel it. I've never felt the way I do right now with any other guy." Then sensing the moment was over and with the specter of Kiki Malone swept into oblivion said, "Hey, Mr. Pirate Man, take me to your treasure!"

Matt wheeled the truck around and headed back across the bridge. A half mile further he turned toward Sunset Point. While he drove he said, "You got that pirate man correct. Wait until you see what Alex and I found yesterday." And he gave her hand a squeeze. "Would you believe a WWII German submarine!"

"No way!" McCall sat up straight and faced him in disbelief.

"Believe it! All thirty feet of her."

She put a question on her face and asked, "What kind of a sub is only thirty feet long?"

"We looked it up last night at the library. Looks like it's a one-man Biber class sub," Alex said. "During the war the islands were strung with a series of submarine nets and ships sunk in channels to keep these small critters out of Portland Harbor.

"Lots of transports and stuff moored there prior to shipping overseas to Europe. Small as they were, those subs carried two torpedoes but we don't think the one we found was carrying any."

"Right now," McCall deadpanned, "might be a good time to tell me again that theory of yours. You know, the one about Captain Kidd and all that malarkey about buried treasure?" She tried to keep a straight face but suddenly broke out laughing. "Sorry, Matt, couldn't help that. She placed her hand on his arm. You were so sincere and I'll admit you almost had me convinced."

Matt looked flustered for a moment then in defense replied, "I was right about the gold coming from the sea. I even suggested once it might have come from a ship."

"Matthew Banner, never in your wildest dreams did you ever believe it would be a submarine!"

"Got me there." And he grinned. At the fork in the road he pointed. "We go this way to the right. Sunset Point. There's a cove surrounded by a bunch of cottages. There're two or three boats moored there. I've sort of hidden the Whaler in amongst them, tied up to a huge styrofoam buoy. There's a skiff on shore. We'll borrow it to row out.

"Lieutenant Miller hasn't found this spot yet but he will. McCall, this may be the last shot I have at the gold from this side of the bars." His voice was serious and McCall thought sounded grim.

"How much gold did you and Alex discover yesterday?"

"Well, you see that's why we're here today. We didn't have time to do more than find our way in." Then he told her about the problem with the air tank and its sabotage. Concern swept over McCall's face. She turned on the seat. "Who do you think is responsible?"

"Probably the same Germans who have been dodging us for the last few days."

"That doesn't make me feel any better about last night. I was beginning to think I was imagining being followed but now I'm not so sure. As soon as I got home I parked the car and ran to the back door. Once inside I waited in the dark watching the shadows.

"I could swear someone was watching me back. I got all tingly and the hair on my neck prickled when I heard a car start up and head back to the bridge."

Matt parked the pickup well under some trees so it would not be visible from the air and led McCall down a short clay bank that ended at a rough, gray ledge. Matt retrieved the skiff from the haul off, rowed to the waiting Whaler and tied off the dinghy.

As the boat drew away from Sunset point, dark menacing clouds formed over the southern horizon. Matt could smell rain and he was spooked by the sudden change in the weather.

The wind freshened up into a steady twenty-five knots. Worry crossed Matt's face and he flipped on the VHS radio and tuned in the weather channel. The marine forecast confirmed Kevin Mannix's prediction. *"Albert is now officially a category one hurricane bearing winds over one hundred miles per hour,"* the announcer said in a flat voice.

Matt leaned down close to the speaker and turned up the volume. *"Unless a cold front from Canada pushes Albert off shore it will make a direct hit on Cape Cod and slide up the shore into Portland, Maine, by late afternoon."*

Matt could see McCall hadn't been listening to the report and chose not to explain his concern. Winds would arrive well in advance of the fast-moving hurricane. The sharp pitch they were experiencing in the bay right now was a result of *Albert's* searching hand.

The speeding Whaler produced a sharp chill and McCall slipped on her sweatshirt, hauling her hands back up inside the sleeves.

"Why do girls do that?" Matt asked motioning toward the dangling handless sleeves.

"You mean this?" And she swung her arms inside the shirt. "I don't know." she smiled.

It's a girl thing, Matt reasoned. He'd never seen a guy do that.

Suddenly McCall's smile faltered. "What if someone followed you yesterday and is right now anchored over the sub?"

34

SKELETONS AND IRON CROSSES

The breeze seemed to blow away the threat of arrest from Lieutenant Miller as Matt skippered the Whaler toward the sub. He gripped the wheel and felt himself relax as the boat sped toward the wind-brushed islands anchored under a sky laden with low-hanging clouds.

It wasn't until the *Dawn Raider* sped over the sand bar between Little and Great Chebeague Islands that he let the weight of McCall's words sink in. What *would* he do if someone were anchored over the submarine?

"You're right, McCall, we were so excited about finding Jack's gold we never gave any thought that someone might have been watching." Matt silently cursed his stupidity.

"Those guys found us at the house," she replied. "They were at Charlie's yard when you went after the GPS on Jack's boat. Seems reasonable they would find out where you went yesterday." She turned an inquiring face at Matt. "They obviously know about the gold. It wouldn't take any genius to figure you'd use the GPS to find it."

When he didn't answer she said, "Well, I hope for our sake you weren't observed," and gave his arm a hug.

McCall turned her back to the rising wind that howled around the windscreen. She reached up to tuck in a flying piece of hair behind her ear and marveled at the beauty of Casco Bay.

Her eyes, used to mountains and miles of waving Montana grass, sparkled as they took in the green islands that peppered the bay. McCall had never seen a seal and gave an excited laugh when Matt slowed the boat next to a ledge covered with fifty whiskered noses and dark eyes. She thought she'd never seen anything so smooth as seals sliding into the water. Gulls soared overhead and she thought them a blast.

While they talked, Matt maneuvered the boat along the eastern end of Cliff Island. He handed McCall the GPS, showed her how to turn it on and asked her to tell him when the satellites locked on. He indicated the bar graph at the bottom of the screen.

Twenty seconds later, "They're locked on," she announced, proud of her newly-acquired GPS vocabulary.

Matt continued giving her a basic five-minute course in GPS operation. When he was done McCall asked, "You mean if I pressed this *Mark* button my exact location on the face of the earth would show up in this tiny screen?"

"You got it."

"Wow, that's pretty neat! Now what do I do?" she asked.

"Push the *GoTo* button." He watched to make sure she followed his directions. "You should see a screen with *waypoints*." While he steered, Matt leaned over and pointed out the numbers. "Highlight *046*, that's the one Jack used to mark the sub. Now press the page button until the map screen comes up."

McCall punched the buttons and watch the screens change. "Matt, there's a straight line from a little square to the number 046."

"That square is our boat," he said pointing. "All we do is follow the line to 046, the sub."

Five minutes later Matt had the Whaler anchored over the U-33. The sky was a tie-dyed mixture of darks and grays, heavy with drifting clouds. The wind that had blown steadily from the northwest suddenly changed to the south.

The sudden switch in the weather worried Matt, the storm was approaching faster than the forecast indicated. Rolling clouds thrust black billowing heads into the upper atmosphere. These clouds were only the forerunners; the main front was still some hours away and Matt could smell rain.

McCall caught him looking. "Problem, Matt?"

Measuring the cloud formation he replied, "That storm Kevin Mannix has been predicting. Looks like he's right. Big blow coming but we should be able to get the dive in before the front hits.

"This German *Biber* class sub is small, only about thirty feet long. There's a box fastened to the floor four feet in from the opening in the hull made by some kind of explosive shell. I shouldn't have to explore any deeper inside."

"Isn't diving alone dangerous?"

"I'd fire one of my crew for doing what I'm about to do. However, with those German dudes pressing us I don't have any choice. Alex can't go. You don't dive. I'm reluctant to bring in others at this point. The water is only 30 feet and I've been there before so I've cut down the odds."

"Still dangerous though, isn't it, Matthew Banner?" she replied with a tone she used when upset. She grabbed the wet suit he'd slid into and shook his arm.

"Matt, this is crazy. What am I going to do if you get into trouble down there?" McCall pointed at the dark green water swirling around the stern. "I've got a bad feeling about this!" Then seeing he was determined, stepped in close, then gave him a breath of a kiss. "Come back."

He slipped the U.S. Divers tank over his shoulder, this one with proper air, examined the Poseidon regular and adjusted the weight belt, then checked to see his knife was strapped to his leg. He grinned at her, "Not to be so solemn, McCall, piece of cake."

He grabbed the net bag he'd brought along to retrieve the gold, held the mask against his face and flopped over the side. Cold seeped into the wet suit down the valley between his shoulders. Icy tentacles trickled through the tunnel at his chest before completely flooding the suit allowing his body to warm the water.

The last vision he had was of McCall standing stiffly at the rail, freckles the color of gold shining from her worried face. Her arms were once more pulled up inside her sleeves. He plummeted downward, barreling through the unfriendly water, where visibility even with the light was limited.

Matt wondered if he would really find the captain of the sub, his fleshless arms draped around the periscope, bony eye socket glued to the tube, ivory fingers toggling the handles. He shuddered as a prickling sensation crept along his back.

Bubbles roared past his ears. Breathing slowly and every few seconds equalizing the pressure that leaned on his ears, he dropped through the lightless green cold. When the sub loomed into view from the yellow halogen dive light, he felt a strange sense of relief.

Silt swirled upwards mixing with the rising bubbles as Matt touched bottom five feet from Jack's entrance hole. His lips felt cold and for a moment terror gripped his soul as his probing light was swallowed up by the intruding dark water.

He felt the muck along the bottom infiltrate his flippers, and kicked to the fractured, gaping shell hole in the port side of the sub. He held his position before entering. Schools of blue-backed herring darted away from the opening and disappeared into the gloom, swimming in unison.

He felt danger lurking beyond the hole rent open fifty years before by an exploding shell. He felt light-headed, and his breath quickened, expelling wasted air into the murky darkness beyond the light.

Holding the powerful beam of his dive light in front of him like a Jedi sword, he followed the yellow beam and swam into the uninviting steel cave. An unexpected shift of tide suddenly tumbled him onto the floor of the sub, unleashing a blinding cloud of silt.

Matt was forced into a moment of confusion. He could not tell up from down. Then a bent metal bar struck his mask, knocking it loose from his face. Muddy water flooded inside the glass, bursting tentacles of panic raced across his chest.

His breath shortened into fleeting gasps and his body felt weighted down with the pounds of lead around his waist and tons of anxiety pressing on his heart as he struggled with his fear in the near zero visibility.

Then training and experience returned. He cleared the mask and bit down hard on the regulator mouthpiece, the air tasted tinny and fear left a copper flavor in his mouth. Suddenly the billowing clouds of debris settled to the bottom and the water cleared.

Matt found himself staring at the box he'd seen on his first dive. A sense of *deja vu* rippled through his mind as though no time had transpired since he was last here.

The water was cold against his face. He could see his fingers begin to wrinkle. The images of McCall on deck floated in front of his mask, her hair whipped and tangled by the wind, her tanned, freckled face showing no fear as she followed him into a dangerous adventure. As he thought of the wind, he knew he'd have to hurry. The storm had granted him favors by laying back as long as it had.

He kicked toward the box, a trail of bubbles followed, rising to the roof of the sub, flicking away small particles of rust that floated into the glow of his light. Matt worried about the structural integrity of the rusting hull that encased him like a coffin. Someday at some unannounced period of time this tube would suddenly, without warning, collapse.

Beyond the box his light revealed a twisted, decaying iron ladder leading to the conning tower. He suddenly forgot about the box! Something was stuck in the rungs of the ladder.

A dark object moved and fluttered with the tide. At once a cold spark of fear gripped his chest and he had all he could do to resist the urge to flee away from the object that seemed to stretch out a hand, beckoning him further into the submarine.

Two kicks put him at the ladder. Matt gave a shudder...he had found the captain!

He trod water, calming himself, getting his breathing under control, concentrating on slow even breaths. Caught in the steps of the ladder were the remains of what had been a white wool sweater now covered with light brown silt.

The arms of the sweater waved from the pulse of water and pushed in front of his body as he advanced. The sleeves, where arms should have been, were empty.

Matt was relieved that no head showed through the neck. He reached out to touch the dark cloth below the sweater and as he touched the material realized he was looking at the remains of a naval uniform.

Trapped inside the narrow hull, surrounded by the pale hue of the light and the remains of a dead man sent chills up his spine. But when he shined the light on the floor he almost bolted from the hole. An algae-covered skull grinned at him from a tangle of bones that had once been the captain. Next to it, half under the mud, peeked the hard brimmed naval hat worn by sub commanders.

Matt reached down and plucked the hat from the silt and shook it. When he did the skull rolled over so only one eye leered at him. A rock crab crawled out of the eye socket moving its claws. For a moment Matt thought the skull had winked at him.

He felt something heavy inside the hat and when Matt withdrew the object he held a wallet and piece of metal Matt recognized as the Iron Cross. The captain, it seems, had been a hero.

Realizing he might be holding the clue to this whole mysterious affair he tucked the wallet and metal cross safely inside his suit. His dive watch showed he'd been down much longer than expected but he still had almost thirty minutes of air.

Still, if he didn't want to spend the next fifty years playing cribbage with the commander of the sub he needed to check the box then boogie out of there!

A foreboding cloud of anxiety suddenly froze Matt in suspension. He stopped swimming and finned just enough to maintain neutral buoyancy. An eerie sensation of danger swept into the submarine, an intense feeling McCall was in some kind of peril. Thoughts of the box vanished as he thrust himself toward the surface.

34

CAPTURED

A powerful sense of urgency drove Matt upward. He whaled his flippers against the unyielding water, grabbing handfuls as he thundered upward. He broke the surface, a black, rubber torpedo, spearheaded by mask and tank. He bobbed once at the surface then swarmed up the boarding ladder into the boat to find McCall with her hands tied behind her.

The German had a dead man's face, white skin stretched taut across high cheekbones. Healing scratches from McCall's attack striped his face, a knife slit of a mouth exposed a lipless smile.

His left arm was wrapped tightly around McCall's struggling body. His right hand curled around the butt of an automatic pistol, its black Cyclops of an eye pointed directly at Matt's heart. The bulbous nose of a silencer protruded from the end of the barrel.

"McCall?"

She looked at him quickly, hopefully. Realizing there was little Matt could do, she shouted, "I'm all right but go carefully, Matthew; he means business!"

Thoughts of rushing the gunman bolted into his mind. He stepped forward. "Not such a good idea, *Mein Herr*." Only *good* came out "*goot*" waxed all over with barely passable English. The barrel lifted ominously. Matt knew instantly the hand and eye directing the gun had done this work before. "Let me introduce myself. I am Kurt Richter."

Matt felt helpless. With the heavy air tank and his feet all fettered up with flippers plus the weight belt, there was little he could do.

"The gold and jewels that are on board the submarine. You will dive again and bring them up or..." He paused. The narrow face of the German got even more fox like. He peeled back his thin lips. As he did the sun escaped the clouds, mashed against the silver-capped tooth igniting a silver fire in his mouth. "...or I will simply shoot the girl."

The foul odor from his mouth made McCall gag and she recoiled away from Richter's face taking the opportunity to mouth a question, "*Matt, did you find the gold?*"

Ignoring her question, Matt focused on a set of crazed eyes and twisted mouth, measuring his chance to jump the gun.

Richter looked emaciated but behind the gaunt look lay a lean, powerful body. Holding Matt's eyes, Richter said, "We know your friend, Jack, located the submarine and with it the gold. All we require is that you deliver the rest of it to us. You see we already have the jewels Jack located."

"You mean you killed him. That's how you got them," Matt said, anger packed around his words.

McCall struggled to ease the tension of Richter's arm, but in spite of her strength he easily pinned her tightly to his body. His eyes darkened dangerously. "Be still, girl. We have a use for you that requires we keep you alive for the moment, but we could alter our plans. Do I make myself understood?" His mouth twisted with the threat and his English was speckled with a German accent where the w's became v's and alive became *alife*. But the meaning was clear. He would kill her.

His small black eyes glittered. "Unfortunately neither of us is a diver. There are at least 200 more necklaces, rings, and priceless broaches down there plus gold coins. It would be awkward to hire someone to bring them up, don't you think?

"How would we explain how we knew about the treasure that's been locked inside that unfortunate boat whose sinking dates back to WWII? Lots of questions we'd rather not have to answer." He crooked his mouth into what passed for a smile.

Before Matt could respond the pistol raised once more, pointing directly at his heart. McCall struggled in Richter's grip. She felt fear and anger knot in her heart as she gasped, "Matt, look out!"

"Be still, *Fraulein*, or I will shoot you," and gave her a violent shake.

Richter pointed with the barrel of the pistol and barked an order. "*Mein* friend, overboard you go. When you bring up the treasure and I have it stored aboard," he said, indicating the twenty-two foot Grady White boat tied to the Whaler's stern, "I will tie you both up and leave. What could be more fair than that? Perhaps one of your friends will get to you before the storm."

The laugh he uttered was only a notch above a squeak. When his mouth opened the silver tooth now looked dull and dead in the light from the overcast sky.

Matt knew they were in a tight spot. He glanced up at the sky where the clouds had thickened, changing from a moving soot color to an inky black.

Pointing to the gathering storm, Matt replied, "No time to dive today, Richter, that storm will be right on top of us in about 20 minutes." He ground the words out between his teeth as he spoke.

Richter surveyed Matt's words. Then with one quick look skyward made a decision.

He prodded McCall with his pistol towards his boat releasing her for an instant while he bent down to untie the line securing the Grady White to Matt's Boston Whaler. He kept the pistol aimed at both of them but for a moment his eyes were distracted as he struggled with the line stuck around the cleat.

In that second Matt made his move on the pistol. He unsnapped his weight belt and threw it at Richter's head, at the same time dodging around the center console. Scrambling along the starboard side he grabbed the hand holding the pistol and wrenched the barrel away from McCall.

Richter, without the weight of the dive gear, was faster and whipped his arm free. Matt tripped on his flippers and crashed against the gunwale. The pistol made a small sputtering sound; a stinging pain sliced through Matt's left shoulder. The shock and force of the bullet spun him overboard.

At first Matt began to sink but without the weight belt the rubber suit quickly popped him to the surface. McCall was more shaken than she realized. She'd been too stunned to cry out but her mind was still working.

While Richter concentrated on Matt, she swept up the GPS from the seat were she had put it and slid the black piece of electronics into her pocket.

The German reached over the side and hauled Matt close to the boat. He then placed the silencer against his forehead. His hand shook and his finger tightening around the trigger turned white. McCall's voice screamed in protest, "Kill him, Richter, and you'll never get the gold. He's your only chance!"

Cold sweat dripped down Matt's face as he watched the German decide if he were going to shoot. Slowly the narrow black eyes steadied. "Yes... of course...you are correct. Very foolish of you, *Mein Herr*. I could have killed you. That would have been wrong, *nein*?"

"Okay, diver," he said hauling Matt on board. "The *fraulein* goes with me in *das boot*," and he pushed her onto the Grady White. "You have until five o'clock tonight to produce the gold or the girl dies!"

"Matt, are you all right?" McCall yelled across the boat, her voice mixed with terror and concern. She could see Matt was holding his wounded arm as he crawled into his boat, his face pinched in pain.

Instead of replying he directed a question at Richter, "How do I get in touch with you?"

Richter dipped his hand into his pocket and shook out a cigarette, struck a light to the end and blew out a lung full of smoke before answering. "Your cell phone," he said, pointing at the unit by the center console. "Read me the number."

Matt reeled off the number. Richter punched the reply into his cell phone. After storing the number he retreated to the wheel of the Grady White and prepared to leave. "I'll call later," he shouted across the widening space between the two boats.

Matt knew that once he'd delivered the gold, he and McCall were as good as dead. There was no way the Germans were going to allow them to live. Where could he turn for help? By this time Miller would have a warrant out for his arrest. If he notified the police the call would get forwarded directly to Miller, who would pounce on him like a cat on a mouse.

Miller would never believe the tale he'd have to tell him of sunken submarines, lost treasures and abductions. Miller would lock him up and throw the key away.   McCall would...he didn't finish that thought.

If there were some way he could track Richter's boat there might be a chance to rescue McCall, but that plan seemed equally remote. Even if he figured a way there was the storm. Unless a miracle happened, Casco Bay would whip up into a rage of wind and water making navigation of a 40-foot vessel impossible let alone a 20-foot, low-sided center console.

He watched helplessly as Richter handcuffed McCall's right hand to the stainless steel rail and turn on the ignition key letting the engine warm up. Then Richter thrust the throttle forward sending the Grady White pounding through the cresting waves.

Matt gave McCall a thumbs up, then watched with a numb heart as the boat receded, getting smaller until it disappeared on the back side of Ministerial Island.

Matt shook his head in disbelief. McCall was gone!

The only piece of information left in the wake was that Richter seemed to be headed to Portland, but that could change the instant the boat dropped out of sight. There were hundreds of islands in Casco Bay. Finding McCall was going to be like locating Waldo in a field of daisies.

Blood dripped from under his rubber suit, staining the deck with a thin red dye. The numbness was receding. His eyes darkened with the pain, his teeth chattered, and his body began to tremble. Matt could feel the burning ache lance across his arm and into his chest.

He eased off the wet suit top and examined the wound, a purplish hole with an angry puckish mouth. Satisfied it was only a deep flesh wound he located the emergency medical kit.

He tore open two gauze packets, placed them on the entrance and exit holes and taped them into place pulling it tight to quell the bleeding. He carefully replaced the suit and zipped it up then tossed down four aspirin to dull the sudden throbbing in his arm.

Matt dreaded what he had to do next but there was no other course. He would have to dive now before his arm stiffened up and he needed to figure a way to get the gold up from the submarine before the storm rolled over his boat. He carefully checked the air in his tank and found he had barely enough to retrieve the gold. The thought of McCall cuffed to the rail, her face a mask of controlled fear, gave him a shot of adrenaline as he dropped to the sea floor.

Now that he knew the way he quickly glided through the hole and immediately poked his light at the box. He gave a few short kicks then held the corner of the box, letting his feet settle to the floor. The cut-off lid was propped alongside the box.

Matt's heart raced as he thought about the gold. He had to clamp down on the feeling of greed that surged through his soul.

The light illuminated the entire box, casting a yellow green incandescence into the corners. For the space of two full breaths Matt stared. Time seemed to stand still as his eyes adjusted to the glare of the light. A numbing cold drifted over him and he noticed the dull ache in his arm. Fear for McCall rocketed into his throat. He felt a great weight pressing on his chest, squeezing against his heart.

The box was empty!

36

WATTS PENN

Watts Penn held his peeling, green-hulled lobster boat into the wind along a sheltered cove on the northwest shore of Long Island. In fact he'd more or less been hanging out there, hiding ever since he'd seen the two men in the fog dump what looked like a body into the bay. He was sure they had read the name on his stern. Watts had been taking no chances.

A few scattered lobster boats dotted the bay. Because of the rising wind only half of those were tending traps. He could see the fisherman nearest him bend over the rail and with boat hook in hand snag a colored buoy. He snaked the line into the hauler, then swung the trap, water gushing through the slats, onto the deck. The man had to steady his feet against the throbbing swells before he could open the parlor doors, drop the shorts over the side, and flip the keepers into a bucket.

Watts didn't need Kevin Mannix to tell him heavy weather was coming. He'd been in so many storms he canted to port as he walked.

Without warning, a white pleasure boat crashed through the heavy chop and burst into view by Little Chebeague Island. Watts felt a jolt of alarm. Not many things frightened Watts but the sight of the racing boat, tossing high waves off both sides of the bow, sent tingling drafts of fear down his back. The last time he'd seen that Grady White had been on the foggy morning where he'd watched someone dump a body overboard.

Visibility in the rain made positive identification difficult but Watts was sure it was the same boat. Watts didn't like hiding and dodging, wondering if someone would sneak up during the night and do him in. He clicked the throttle up to full speed and followed the boat. Ten minutes later the powerful outboard out-distanced the *Sally Anne*.

Watts dug out a rusted pair of binoculars, spit on the lens and wiped them with a crusty shirt tail. His salt spit fingers gave an arthritic turn to the focus knob, then his watery blue eyes caught the boat as it reduced speed. The binoculars followed the white boat in between Great Diamond and Peaks Islands. Then a sudden wall of squall-driven rain laid a curtain across the bay obliterating the boat. Marble size raindrops pounded the surface. He waited until the squall passed and was rewarded by seeing the boat make a landing. He marked the spot.

There had been two people in the boat. One looked like a girl. What would a girl be doing in the boat where murder had been committed? Earlier in the month there had been two men. Who was this girl? Satisfied he hadn't been seen, Watts drove his lobster boat through the protective curtain of rain past Peaks Island into Portland Harbor, losing himself in the fleet of boats seeking shelter from the impending storm.

37

TIME PRESSES

After discovering the mysterious box was empty Matt conducted a panicky search through the rusting hull. He scoured the wreck from bow to stern but found no evidence of the missing gold and reluctantly returned to the surface. Back in the Whaler he shrugged free of the wet suit and hastily re-bandaged the shoulder, swallowed more aspirin and climbed awkwardly back into his clothes.

Satisfied he had done all he could for the moment he dashed to the bow and hauled one-handed at the anchor. Then he hurried to the center console where he popped the engine alive and drove the Whaler northeasterly down Broad Sound around the end of Chebeague.

As he forced the Whaler ahead even faster, dark storm-driven water caromed off the windscreen and plastered his face until the stinging salt water numbed his cheeks.

The missing gold was most likely Jack's doing but he couldn't be sure. Even if Jack had recovered the gold Matt had no way to locate it, at least not in the time frame established by Richter. He had only until five o'clock. The task was impossible.

38

"I'M IN A TOMB!"

The powerful surge of the racing twin motors on the Grady White thrust the bow upward into the air spilling McCall backward against the safety rail. She wrenched her wrist in the handcuffs and tore the skin. She felt the bone grate against the manacles and pain shot up along her arm. In spite of the agony, McCall refused to give Richter the satisfaction she'd been hurt, and treated him to a cold dangerous stare.

He tossed a smirk at her as the boat dropped onto the plane. All three hundred horse power of the twin motors bit into the throbbing water. A final touch of the throttle popped the boat up to top speed. When the driving hull crashed over the white-topped swells McCall was bashed against the rail.

Spray pounded McCall's face with cold salt water, drenching her sweatshirt. She closed her eyes against the piercing spray, feeling utterly miserable.

From behind the protection of the tall windscreen Richter enjoyed her suffering, seeing the drenching water pouring over McCall who was anchored to the rail and fully exposed to the ravages of the storm.

McCall stared at his face trying to figure out what was out of place, then suddenly realized he had no eye brows, which gave his eyes a wide open, surprised look. Richter's shoulder muscles rippled beneath the black T-shirt as he worked the wheel against the wind.

Chained to the racing boat, McCall felt a sense of complete helplessness. She shivered with the wetness and icy wind that tore at her body. Water slopped over the side soaking her sneakers before drifting aft and out the self-bailing hull. Hatred burned in her soul. She promised herself she would make him pay!

McCall wasn't certain how much time elapsed before Richter eased back on the throttle allowing the following wake to catch up. He slipped ahead on the gas, nudged the boat close to a huge stone structure that looked like a Civil War fort which overwhelmed the rocky outcrop of the island it was built on.

Panic like she'd never known welled in her throat. She began to shake with the cold and fearful images built in her mind. McCall was certain she was being taken to her death.

He cut the engine and let the boat drift up to an orange buoy. Richter rushed forward, secured the boat to the mooring and returned to unlock the handcuffs. He prodded her into the rubber, Zodiac tender that had been tethered to the buoy and motored fifty yards to a protected beach. He motioned her over the side, then hauled the rubber dinghy up the slanting shore and tied it off.

McCall had no idea why she had slipped the GPS into her pocket except something had driven her to it. She could feel the hard, square corners pressing against her leg and she tried to remember what Matt had said about being able to locate someone anywhere in the world.

With Richter up on the beach she slipped out the GPS and pressed the red *on* button and waited until the unit locked on the satellites. This part she had done before.

Matt's words guided her for the next few minutes. *Press mark, see how the latitude and longitude are displayed on the screen.* While Matt had been diving over the midget sub she had experimented with that feature. She repeated it now. The numbers scrolled up on the screen.

Richter suddenly raced back to the boat. McCall cried out when his talon-like fingers ripped the GPS out of her hand. McCall hoped the unit was off. Then over his shoulder she could see the screen was blank and she heaved a sigh of relief.

His eyes blazed with sudden anger. His powerful hands grasped her arms in a painful grip cutting off the circulation. She shrank away from the vile smell of his breath.

Richter's eyes were cropped close to a nose that was off center. One eye was higher than the other giving him an inquiring look. McCall decided Richter had no redeeming features and spat in his face.

His slap thundered against her head bringing tears to her eyes as she staggered backwards onto the beach. Richter stood over her. His ugly face twisted in fury but before he could strike again McCall leaped to her feet and raced over the rocks to a large open archway leading inside the stone structure. The numbers North 43 ° 39 ', West 70 ° 13 ' ran through her mind, numbers she couldn't allow herself to forget.

Unattended for a moment, McCall thought about escape. She could certainly outrun the German. Then Richter arrived out of breath, his anger forced under control and as though reading her thoughts sneered, "Run, *Fraulein*, but there is no place to run to, *nein?*"

McCall's shoulders dropped as she realized the truth of his words and allowed herself to be pushed through the archway onto a grassy field. He dragged her to a 30-foot high granite tower that contained a set of stone steps leading to some kind of second level. She could see open ports where guns once overlooked the harbor.

Five minutes later McCall was locked in a ten by ten foot cell. There were no windows. Water leaking through the rotting, limestone ceiling mortar, had formed chalk white stalactites. The walls were solid brick, the floor an uneven stone.

Dampness from unfiltered air crept into her wet clothes making her even colder. Richter had placed a white plastic bucket in the center of the room. She assumed it was a stool and shuddered as she realized it might have to double as a toilet. A rusted iron army cot stretched across one wall and a candle stuck in a crack in the wall provided her only light.

McCall had never been in a situation that tested the envelope of her courage. She found it hard not to cry. "God," she gasped, "I'm in a tomb!"

39

MILLER WATCHING

As Matt drove through the increasing swells McCall's safety pestered at his mind and riddled him with guilt about how he'd gotten her involved. His doubts about his ability to save her left him weak and discouraged. He could only hope that when the Germans called he could think of some way to either discover where they had taken her or get some extension of time for the gold. He knew neither of those was about to happen.

A sudden panic seized him. What if his cell phone's battery quit? How would they contact him...or would they even bother? What if he was in a place where there was no cell phone service...what then? Would they simply kill McCall and find some other diver to salvage the gold? He yanked the phone from his jacket pocket. Satisfied the battery was fully charged, he replaced it. Matt knew the bulls-eye hole in his arm, while not a serious injury, could put him out of commission unless it got some immediate attention.

For the first time in his life Matt was not sure what to do. Should he get help? If so, where? Could he conjure up help before Richter called? And more importantly what would he say when Richter called...the gold was gone!

The best place in the bay to ensure he would receive the call would be the eighty-foot observation tower on Jewell

Island. He headed the boat through increasing swells to the cove behind the island and anchored. Ten minutes later Matt was at the top of the tower. He was wet, exhausted and his arm throbbed with pain.

Twenty minutes after Matt and McCall had left from Sunset Cove to dive on Jack's sub, Detective Miller had arrived and parked his unmarked car under a screen of trees where one of the Yarmouth patrol cars had reported seeing a Boston Whaler moored in the cove. However, when Miller arrived it was gone. Now after three hours of watching he was tired, frustrated and irritable.

He reached inside the vehicle and clicked the mic adjusted to the state police frequency, speaking quickly to the person responding.

Then with a voice that sounded like a knife on a stone sharpener grated, "I don't care *what* you have to do or *who* you badger, alert the Coast Guard and put out an all points bulletin. I want this guy!" He slammed the mic back on its hook.

40

WOULD THE LIE FOOL THE GERMAN?

As Matt hunkered inside the wet, leaking observation tower, he thought about his father and what he would advise him to do if he were here to guide him. Then he remembered there were no paths back to boyhood except those littered with memories, and in his case some of those memories were not so good.

He wondered if he would be branded a sentimentalist if he confessed he remembered his mother singing to herself in the kitchen or the nights she sat on the edge of his bed and listened to his hopes and fears.

Matt shook away the thought and in spite of the cold that crept inside his yellow oilskin jacket, dropped into a fitful dream of a different kind where pirates manned the U-33, the Jolly Roger flew at the top of the periscope.

Instead of the black flag with skull and cross bones, a soggy white sweater fluttered in the breeze and the captain's skull, rammed on the end of the periscope, leered into the wind...his growling stomach pried him awake at four o'clock.

McCall and the missing gold poured into his consciousness as he came fully awake. Matt knew he needed help and in a hurry. Miller by now would have figured Matt was somewhere with his boat and Matt was certain he would have alerted the Coast Guard.

He'd heard nothing from Richter. What did that mean?

The Portland police would be on the alert for any call Matt might make to them and Miller would taint any information Matt might send them.

That left his boss at DMR, but by the time he could confirm Matt's story it would be too late. He gave the problem some more thought then punched in numbers on his cell calling Alex.

Alex answered instantly. "Where the devil are you, Matt? I knew you would dive yesterday but thought I'd see you last night and when you didn't show I called ...well...everywhere! I even tried McCall at her place on Cousins but the gal running the bed and breakfast said she went off with you and never returned."

"She got that right and unless we do something bright and quick she won't ever be coming back." Matt explained what happened early that morning at the sub, the deadline he was under and the fact the gold was gone. "I've got to find her, Alex."

"Matt, what you are suggesting is like saying a cure for insomnia is to get more sleep. We don't know where she's been taken and you don't have the gold. If you had the gold and delivered it, they would kill both you and McCall in a heartbeat!"

"Look, Alex, call your dad he could..."

"No can do, Matt," he said, interrupting. "My mom and dad aren't back from Florida."

That reply left Matt hanging. "What do you hear about this storm?"

"Last night the Channel 6 newscaster, Joe Cupo, predicted hurricane *Albert* would hit Portland some time late this afternoon. I checked the weather again this morning. Kevin Mannix confirmed Cupo's earlier report. He says the storm stalled but winds over a hundred miles per hour will hit Old Orchard sometime around seven tonight. That's just short of a *category two* hurricane, Matt!"

The voice rolling out of the cell phone suddenly sounded scratchy and the speaker crackled as a bolt of lightning announced the return of the storm.

Matt could barely hear when Alex asked, "When will Richter call?"

"Sometime before five o'clock."

"Don't answer the call, Matt, as long as they can't reach you they'll never know the gold is missing. I don't think they'll risk hurting McCall until they know for sure."

Matt shielded the phone under his jacket away from the rain. "I wish I felt inspired by that suggestion, Alex, but I'm not excited. There has to be another way."

"If you think of one, ring me up. I'll be at the yard all day helping Charlie secure his boats. With the weather going sour we're all off duty. Keep the faith." He hung up.

Matt snapped the cover on the phone and tucked it away, zipping his pocket closed. As thin as it was, that cell phone provided the only link to McCall and he'd been worried the storm might somehow screw up the connection.

The question was not whether Richter would call. Matt was certain he would, but what Matt would say when he did. He would have to lie about having located the gold and lie convincingly, not something he did particularly well. Would the lie fool the German? Matt wasn't sure and McCall's life depended on that lie.

By four thirty Matt was getting nervous. Hunger gnawed at his insides. He felt like time had become abbreviated, crushed together like an accordion. He'd moved to Maine, met McCall, held a fortune in his hand and was about to get arrested. The bad guys had his girl and he didn't have the gold to rescue her.

The Coast Guard was probably hunting him right now and the people who could help him didn't believe he was telling the truth. He shook his head, thinking his life was situated on a bad curve.

Matt discarded Alex's idea about not answering the phone. He couldn't be sure what would happen to McCall if he failed to respond. He couldn't take that chance.

Rain continued to whip through the narrow observation slits and waltz through the openings as the wind bounced and changed direction. Matt checked the batteries again, realizing he would soon have to return to the boat to recharge and he dreaded the thought the call might come and he'd miss it.

He began to shake as the chilly, damp wind streamed in through the ports. He hugged himself, drawing his arms tightly against his body conserving the heat.

Suddenly without warning, the cell phone rang, shocking him with its alarm clock jangle. He snatched the phone out from under his coat.

41

THEY'VE KILLED HER!

Matt's "Hello" came out scratchy and incomplete from his nervous throat. He cleared his voice, "Matt Banner."

Someone was breathing into the phone but not speaking. Matt felt hollow and for a moment fear laid siege to his soul. *They've killed her!* Then Richter's gravelly voice asked, "You have the gold?"

"Yeah, I have the gold. Some coins, too."

"*Goot*," he replied. Matt could hear the anxiety and relief in Richter's tone. So, thought Matt, you have nerves...good...that helps.

Matt suddenly found himself listening to instructions on where to bring the gold. Part way through he realized he was being directed to the rock pier on Mackworth Island in Portland Harbor, one of his hot spots for stripers.

"I know where that's located," he replied. *Did they have her on the island?*

"*Goot*," came again. "It is now almost five o'clock. You have until five thirty. I will meet you there. Do not be late!"

"Impossible, Richter. In case you haven't looked out a window lately there's a category two hurricane about to wallop Casco Bay. There won't be a boat on the water. The Coast Guard won't even be out. I could sink with your precious gold on board. Another sunken boat, only this time you won't have a clue about where it's located!" He shouted into the phone.

There was a pause, then a reply, "Ah, yes. I see your point. But the storm will provide you with good cover, don't you think?"

"Richter, both our chances of getting there are somewhere between zero and none! Then when I don't show up, you'll kill McCall. I can't take that chance. You've got to allow me more time to feel my way through this hurricane."

There was a pause and Matt could hear a muffled conversation. Suddenly a voice he didn't recognize spoke into his ear.

"Herr Banner, this is Heinrich von Brockner." The voice rang like steel when he ordered, "You have until seven o'clock!"

Matt's heart felt squeezed as he demanded, "Put McCall on, Brockner, I want to know she's okay."

The sound of a phone being passed to someone echoed in his ear.

In the background Matt heard Richter ordering McCall. "Tell him you are all right."

"Hi, Matt. It's McCall. I'm okay. They've got me..."

Matt then heard a frightened scream. His heart beat faster and in spite of the cold, sweat broke out on his face and the phone he'd worked so hard to keep dry felt slippery in his hand.

"Richter, if you've hurt her I'll..."

"You'll do as I say, *Herr* Banner," Richter interrupted, back on the line. "No heroics. Is that understood?"

Matt let the line stay open while he tried to get his breathing under control. Then in a strained voice replied, "Seven o'clock. Make sure *you're* there."

"*Auf Wiedersehen*!" and the phone went dead.

Matt knew the decision had been Brockner's but even so he was furious that Richter insisted he drive his boat through the storm. Matt hadn't been kidding when he said both their chances were less than slim. But he felt a little thread of hope stitch though his veins.

Normally there would still be daylight at seven but tonight darkness would fall early. It would be overwhelmingly dark which suited Matt's purpose just fine. Who could tell what might happen?

He remembered his dad telling him that character was the wisdom not to do foolish things. Matt wondered if delivering non-existent gold to ruthless killers through the teeth of a hurricane with winds bending more that 100 mph was foolish and would that mean he was going to fall short on the character stuff.

He tore down the tower stairs two at a time, ran down the quarter mile path to the shore and bolted to the tie-off lines holding his *Dawn Raider*. He flipped open the knots, vaulted over the slippery deck and hauled in the stern anchor. By the time he had the motor running, his hair was plastered to his face.

Matt plugged the cell phone into the spotlight receptacle in case the Germans called again and tucked the precious unit in under the console where it would remain dry. "Dry, unless I tip over," he said out loud, and allowed himself a small smile.

When he left the shelter of the island a wall of water crashed against the starboard rail, thundered onto the deck and tipped the gunwale dangerously close to the following sea. The boat shuddered and gave a heavy heave upward into the wind.

42

THE STONE CELL

At the same time Matt was waiting for the call in the tower Richter was thrusting McCall into the stone cell at the fort. Fury almost choked her. She remained absolutely motionless for a fraction of a second then pounded on the door and hurled curses at his retreating footsteps.

When McCall could no longer hear any sound she leaned dejectedly against the door trying to gather her strength and clear her mind.

The sudden capture at the sub, the dash through the approaching hurricane, Richter's man-handling her into this oppressive room was the final insult. The slam of the cell door registered the horrible realization that she was no longer free.

She cast a discouraged eye around her bricked chamber, feeling terribly disoriented. The candle cast wavering shadows around the room and added to her sense of imbalance. She shivered with the dampness. The air smelled dank and lifeless. McCall ran her fingers through her hair feeling a wet stickiness, a mixture of salt and rain. "God, I'm a mess!" she gasped.

McCall did knee bends, slapped her arms around her body and jogged around the tiny room hoping to drive some warmth through her icy veins. In the end she sank onto the filthy cot, mind and body frozen and benumbed.

She hugged her knees, feeling a wretchedness of mind she'd never known and clenched her jaw to kill the sob that welled in her throat. She fought hard against the tears she refused to let fall. Exhaustion finally overtook her.

McCall lay back on the cot and flipped a fold of the dingy green army blanket over her shaking body while trying to ignore the bugs that might live in the grungy cover. She felt the rough wool scratch against her legs, let herself go limp and felt the tension ease out of her back. She forced her chest to relax.

Unfamiliar sounds seeped through the stone walls, thunder boomed and echoed and wind whistled throughout the outside corridors. Just as she drifted off to sleep McCall heard some inner voice shouting at her to take charge, find a way to escape, or failing that, discover some way to signal for help. She found herself replying, "Voice, great idea, but how?"

Later that afternoon warning bells clamored in her brain, yanking her instantly awake. The candle had burned to a nub, only a hint of light remained in the cell. Her clothes had only partially dried and she shivered with the approach of darkness. A glance at her watch surprised her. It was after five o'clock. Would Matt bring the gold?

What would happen to her if he failed to deliver as Richter had demanded? Would they actually kill her? It all seemed so preposterous. A few weeks ago she'd been helping run a Montana cattle ranch. Now she was wondering if in the next few hours she would be shot or drowned or whatever. It probably didn't matter, dead was dead!

McCall's stomach was in a rage of hunger but there was a task that had to be done now. She plucked the remains of the candle from its niche and hugging the wall with one hand carried the flickering light to the end of the cot. She crouched on the floor letting the waning glow from the wick cast enough light so she could see the latitude and longitude she'd scratched on the wall last night,...*N 43 °, 39 '...W 70 ° 13 '.*

From what Matt had said she didn't think the seconds were important. If they were, it was too late. She had forgotten them. McCall burned the numbers into her head over and over until she was sure she could remember them.

Still holding the smelly candle she stood up, strode over to the plywood door, and carefully examined the hinges. They seemed strong and when she banged and kicked the door they remained solid and unyielding. Hunger gnawed at her stomach, her mouth cried out for a drink of water and she was in desperate need of a bathroom. McCall was damned if she was going to use the bucket still sitting in the middle of the room.

When no one answered she banged harder, pounding her fists against the smooth wood. "Hey, Richter, anybody, open up! I'm hungry! I'm thirsty and I need a bathroom!"

McCall wanted out of the cell for more reasons than her hunger and personal hygiene. An idea had taken seed sometime during the night. For it to succeed she would have to be outside of these brick walls.

Richter carried a cell phone. If she could get hold of that phone she could call Charlie, whose number she remembered from calling Matt at the dive office. He would know what to do with the GPS coordinates.

The question was how to get the phone. McCall worried the thick stone walls might keep the phone from working. She would only get one chance. Outside would give her the best shot.

Her thoughts were interrupted as a key grated in the lock, allowing the door to swing open on protesting hinges.

"Ah, *Fraulein!*" Richter's voice rang in the cell room as he opened the door. He sounded like Arnold Schwarzenegger, cloaked over with German consonants. His narrow face appeared almost hatchet-like in the gray morning light surrounding the doorway. A small two-way radio was stuck in his back pocket. The pistol was tucked into his belt.

McCall's searching eyes focused on the cell phone bulging in his shirt pocket. It was no use, he never went anywhere without it. She felt her plan crumble before it even got started. It suddenly dawned on her that stealing the phone wasn't going to happen--at least not in this world.

Richter had few words to say. He bent down and placed a tray of food on the floor. A liter of Pepsi stood next to the tray. He poked his face in her direction and delivered what would for Richter pass for a smile just as he banged the door shut, slid home the lock and raked her with a laughing voice echoing off the stones, "Use the bucket!"

McCall clenched her teeth. She was furious and spat curses at the back side of the door. Her face stormed and she wrapped her arms in front of her and stamped around the bucket. Looking at the food she wondered if it were drugged or poisoned but she was hungry enough to eat rattlesnake and wolfed down the meal.

Then reluctantly, she relieved herself in the bucket, reminding herself the cost of a happy life for Richter just went up a notch. McCall shook out the blanket and folded it at the foot of the bed, pleased that no foreign critters flopped onto the floor.

Her clothes were drying and she was warmer. The candle burned out and she replaced it with another Richter had left her.

McCall threw herself onto the cot and propped her hands behind her head. She remained there letting her resolve to escape take shape. Her thoughts of escape were followed by a driving need for revenge. "If I want revenge, I've got to get out of here."

That's when she first saw the rat. McCall had seen rats in the barns in Montana and she was not particularly afraid of them, but that had been when she had freedom of movement and where the rats had been much smaller.

She thought a football might look small beside this water rat chewing the remains of her breakfast. Its tiny red eyes watched McCall. After every bite it twitched its tail, opened its mouth and allowed a tongue to dart out. The teeth were yellow with age. McCall's bantam-size quarters suddenly felt smaller.

She hugged her feet back away from the foot of the bed, wondering what the rat would do when it finished eating. As though reading her thoughts, the rat darted into the corner and disappeared into a hole where a rotting brick had fallen away.

McCall leaped to her feet, snatched up the paper plate from the tray, and with a burst of speed that surprised her, raced to the wall and stuffed the plate into the hole. She gave it an extra kick with her sneaker to make sure.

The rotting brick gave her a ghost of an idea but when she tried digging with the plastic spoon from breakfast it shattered with the first stroke. McCall trudged back to the cot, sprawling on top of the blanket, satisfied she had defeated the rat, and focused her mind on the problem of how she could signal for help.

Time crept forward. McCall's thoughts were jagged and painful as she thought about what might be happening to Matt. Was the wound in his arm serious? Would it prevent him from diving? Could he recover the gold?

She didn't know much about boats but knew Matt had been concerned about the hurricane. Would he be able to deliver the gold through the storm? What would happen to her if he failed? McCall tried not to worry but her heart seemed to shrink at the enormity of the tasks Matt had to perform.

The Pepsi was almost gone when suddenly, without warning, the door burst open. Richter grabbed her arm and pulled her from the smelly room. He barked a harsh command, " Quickly, *schnell*!"

He marched her along a wide corridor with a rough granite floor, grunting and hauling on her arm until her muscles screamed. When she tripped he yanked even harder. He quickly dragged her into murky rain-laden darkness and down a set of stone steps that spiraled to ground level.

"*Schnell*," he ordered again, pulling her out of the stairwell onto what looked like a parade ground. McCall was drenched before Richter pushed her into a long, rectangular room. Thunder clapped overhead and lightning cast an instant tick of light, a camera flash, into the room.

The room was warmed by some kind of space heater mounted against the back wall near an open fireplace. On each side of the fireplace narrow sally ports had been cut through the granite wall.

Lights from two Coleman camping lanterns filled the room, scaring the shadows from the corners. The ceiling and walls showed broken laths and crumbling plaster. The room that once had been grand now looked like some derelict from an abandoned housing project.

Richter thrust her forward again, causing her to stumble. When McCall righted herself, she was standing directly before an older man seated at a card table. She was meeting the second German. Somehow, here in person, he seemed less formidable than the night she had searched for the GPS at Jack's house. But McCall could tell she would have to be on full alert.

Sounds of the rising storm rushed into the room through the open door and sally ports. All she could think about was Richter's cell phone might work in this room. She was so occupied with her thoughts that she missed part of what the German was saying.

Then hurrying to catch up with his words she replied. "My stay here has gone well thank you, though not the Hilton," she said, making a face. "And the food needed more salt, otherwise..." She let her voice trail off and gave him a smooth smile that showed nothing of her annoyance.

"Ah, our little Montana gem has a sense of humor. Good, don't you think?" nodding to Richter who had moved beside the older German. His voice was absolutely emotionless and an icy fear chilled her to the bone.

McCall sensed this was not a man of delicate scruples and knew that, while he carried a mantle of aristocracy, he was by far the more dangerous of the two Germans.

"Pardon my rudeness," the man said with only a trace of accent. "I am Heinrich von Brockner." The smile he gave her was benevolent but McCall could feel its shallowness. A feeling of evil leaked into the room, gliding toward her, and she noticed how Richter seemed to defer to him.

In comparison to Richter, Brockner seemed refined, almost gentlemanly. In his cultured voice said, "Ah, Miss McCall, I see by my watch it is after five o'clock, time for us to contact your Matthew Banner."

The words were delivered without passion or threat but his eyes conveyed a depravity that had made Brockner the most feared man in German intelligence for the last thirty years. "So, Richter," he said abruptly, "Make the call."

McCall held her breath while Richter punched in Matt's cell phone number and when he was connected she heard him ask Matt if he had found the gold. She could see by the pleased, relieved expression that Matt had confirmed he had the treasure. She let out her breath. There was a short pause while Matt spoke into the phone.

Richter paused and handed the phone to Brockner. "He wants more time."

McCall shivered at the tone in Brockner's voice as he instructed Matt on the seven o'clock deadline.

Suddenly Brockner thrust the phone into her hand, "Tell him you are all right." When she had tried to tell Matt something about where she was being held, Richter had shoved her away, ripping the phone from her hand.

In the end, all her worrying about the phone was wasted. Instead of putting the flip phone back in his pocket where it was always stored Richter placed it on the card table. Then both Brockner and Richter seemed to ignore her as they argued about the extra time and whether the storm would keep Richter from getting to the pick up spot and what they would do if Matt failed to appear.

This was her chance while they were distracted. McCall never hesitated. She swept up the phone and flipped it open. She slowly backed toward the entrance to the room giving the phone a better chance to make contact. There would be only one chance. She took her eyes away from the littered floor and pressed in the numbers for Charlie's as though each one was a life saver.

Thunder boomed, echoing along the walls of the narrow room. As each number was punched, a tiny chirp sounded from the phone. McCall couldn't see how she would ever get the last number entered before one of the Germans heard the electronic beeps.

At last the number began to ring. Horrors trembled through her body, sweat pooled along her back as she watched for the first signs the Germans were alert. She backed closer to the open doorway, to the gray tinged light and torrential rain beating down on the parade ground. Each step put her closer to the open yard and increased her chances of making contact. She could sense the opening now.

McCall felt the lump of plaster under her foot but by then it was too late. As her ankle turned she uttered a small gasp. Richter's piercing eyes were on her like a hawk on a mouse. McCall's eyes opened wide. She struggled toward the doorway and ignoring the pain, fled out into the torrential rain. A bolt of lightning flashed overhead, a flash-boom. The lightning struck the top of the granite fort and sent sparking embers into the frenzied night.

McCall ran with the phone held to her ear, a limping run through high grass. "Come on, Charlie, answer the damn phone!" she pleaded in the dim light. She was desperate. Her ankle was slowing her down. A quick glance showed Richter running smoothly twenty feet behind her and gaining. Even if Charlie answered now she doubted her message could be delivered.

McCall wasn't winded. She was in good shape but her ankle sent splintering arrows of pain upward into her pounding leg. Every time her foot hit the ground her whole body flinched. The sound of the storm threatened to cut off her ability to hear. Charlie suddenly came on the phone.

"Charlie! It's McCall, North 43 ° 39 ', West 70 ° 13 '. McCall could hear Richter breathing close behind her as she repeated the numbers for the third time.

Richter slammed into her, driving his shoulder deep into the small of her back. A knife-driving pain knocked the wind out of her and she struck the muddy, rain-soaked ground.

The pain was excruciating. She screamed and fell on the phone. Muscled arms encircled her waist. Richter's cheek pressed close to hers pressing her face into the mud. She could feel the stubble of his beard. Slime oozed down her face, blood streamed from a cut on her cheek. McCall squirmed under him and jammed her fingers into his eyes. Richter roared with pain, let go of her shirt and covered his eyes with a muddy hand.

McCall shook with impotent rage and leaped to her feet but before she could jump away he tackled her. Richter yanked her onto her back, sat on her stomach, and jammed a powerful, strangling hand around her neck squeezing off her air. McCall's eyes clamped shut and a great pressure formed in her chest as her lungs screamed for air.

"Who'd you call?" He demanded, letting up the pressure so she could respond. She took deep breaths until she was strong enough to lift her head.

Richter plucked the phone from her fingers, looked first at the closed flip cover phone, then into McCall's eyes. She knew he was wondering if she had time to make a call and if so had anyone answered? His fingers returned to her throat and McCall could tell by the expression in his eyes he was about to kill her.

McCall felt her chest pound and her thoughts drift away from her body. Her eyes glazed as the grip on her throat squeezed life out of her body.

Then through the ringing in her ears McCall heard Brockner shout at Richter not to kill her. Richter released his grip at once.

McCall rolled over and struggled free of his grip. Her eyes blazed furiously as she faced him. Her heart was hammering, her breathing ragged and out of control. She rubbed her throat, willing air into her tortured lungs.

Before McCall could move, Richter snatched her off the ground, and with a snarling voice yanked her to her feet, and hurried her back inside the fort. Holding her close, he spoke so softly the words almost died before she heard them. "Smart lady, I'll get even for what you did!"

Richter dragged her back into the derelict room and shoved her in front of Brockner. McCall's ears rang with what only could be a string of violent curses exploding from the older German. McCall saw the red veins over his eyes bulge, his face turn a bright crimson. She could see his whole body shake as he cursed Richter's stupidity for leaving the phone unsecured. Every few words he would point at McCall. His lungs heaved with the effort of his words.

Richter's jaw muscles worked as he fought to keep his temper. But he did. Brockner was not one to fool with. Richter had seen three men condemned to die with only a nod of Brockner's head.

When Brockner was through with Richter, he heaved himself out of the chair. It wasn't until then McCall realized he walked with a limp and held a cane. Brockner took his time placing the walking stick carefully among the rubble before standing directly before McCall. He placed both hands on top of the cane's gold knob.

He was silent as his crafty eyes raked her body. With a lightning move he whipped the cane head across her face. McCall felt herself falling, her brain unhinged, bright lights flashing in her eyes. She didn't remember hitting the floor, only a sense of Brockner leaning over her saying, "Never again, *Fraulein*. I would feed you to Richter right now but I still have use for you."

Then he nodded to Richter who unceremoniously grabbed her by the shirt collar, towed her through the rain and bolts of lightning back up through the tower stairs and shoved her back into her cold cell.

A sob rattled in her throat, her eyes filled with tears of frustration. She pounded the granite wall in anger, she staggered across the room, and sank down on the cot. McCall had never felt so alone, so unprotected, so defeated.

Her eyelids ached from the blow to her head but McCall suddenly was fighting mad. The feeling of hopelessness suddenly drifted away to the place where dread goes to die. Questions flooded through her mind.

Would Charlie understand what she had transmitted to him? Would Matt be able to meet with Richter at Mackworth Island? Would the storm prevent his getting there? Or would Charlie redirect Matt to the fort?

McCall couldn't forget Matt's face, his cracking smile or the humor that danced just beneath the serious expression he sometimes wore. She remembered when he was angry how his eyes squinted, his lips thinned, and his chin stuck out fearlessly. She made a pledge. She would be strong for him if not for herself! There had to be a way out!

43

LATITUDE LONGITUDE

The sound of the ringing phone startled Matt. With a wet hand he hastily plucked the phone from under his jacket. Rain thrashed against his face, and even in the lee of Long Island Matt found it almost impossible to control the boat and hold the phone.

"Matt Banner here," he yelled.

"Matt, where the hell are you?" Charlie's voice asked.

"I'm in the *Dawn Raider* behind Long Island."

"Matt, get to shore. You are sitting right smack in the path of Hurricane *Albert*. It's raking up the shoreline south of Old Orchard Beach and will be into Portland Harbor in a couple of hours."

"Charlie, why did you call me?"

"Had the strangest phone message just now from McCall. All she would do is repeat numbers to me followed by 'send help.' Sounded like she was outside and running. I could hear her breathing and swearing at the same time. Then all of a sudden I heard a scream and the line went dead. What's going on??" Charlie's last words were almost lost in a seventy mph gust of wind that threatened to tear the phone out of Matt's hand.

Matt's heart rhythm changed with Charlie's words. Yet, he enjoyed a dollop of hope. McCall was alive! Trembling hands clutched the wheel as he replied, "Charlie, what were those numbers?"

"I wrote them down...got 'em right here...North 43° 39', West 70° 13'."

"Charlie, those are latitude and longitude numbers without the seconds added to them!" Matt said, shouting over the wind into the phone.

"I'm ahead of you there. You're right. I checked the numbers with my GPS. If those numbers represent her location, she was calling from Fort Gorges in Portland Harbor."

Matt's heart gave a gigantic leap. Part of his duties when he first arrived had been to explore Casco Bay. Department of Marine Resources had been adamant that he become familiar with the waters he would be working. On one of his trips through the bay he'd noticed the granite fortress in Portland Harbor. Intrigued by the unusual architecture, he had joined a Land Mark excursion company for a tour of the fort.

Construction started on the fortification in 1858 and finished sometime after the Civil War. The fort had been armed during that war and the following Spanish American War and while it was never engaged in hostile action, submarine mines had been stored there during World War 1.

Matt remembered the football field sized parade ground and several gun levels where cannons had been mounted. When he'd asked the tour guide why enormous piles of dirt with grass and trees were on top of the battlements he'd been told that was an attempt to bomb proof the fort from newer exploding shells not heard of when the fort was first built.

The city of Portland acquired the obsolete fortification and used it as a tourist attraction. Most of the officers' quarters were in shambles, plaster torn off the ceilings, the walls a collage of spray-painted messages. Matt wondered why the Germans had chosen this particular spot. Matt tried to mold his thoughts, solve the puzzle, but it was like working with dry clay.

A flood of relief, however, washed over him and he felt a great weight lift off his shoulders now that he knew where McCall was being held and that he had at least a clue about what the place looked like.

"Charlie, listen closely!" For the next five minutes Matt related the whole story: his failed arrest by Lieutenant Miller, why he was out in the bay dodging hurricane winds, McCall's abduction, the Germans, Jack's gold pieces, the submarine and the meeting with Richter where he was supposed to deliver gold he didn't have for McCall's release.

"Charlie, call Lieutenant Miller in Portland. See if you can build a fire under him. Tell him whatever you need in order to get him moving. Have him call the Coast Guard. It will take someone with his clout to get them out in this weather."

"What are you going to do, Matt"?

"Charlie, if I knew I'd tell you. It's almost 6:30 now. In this weather I'll never make that meeting at Mackworth Island with Richter at seven, and since I don't have the gold, it's pointless anyway. My GPS was missing right after Richter took her away, so McCall has it and knew enough about how to use it to obtain those numbers. She has to be at the fort! That's where I'm headed now."

"Matt, you'll never make it. The wind here in the harbor is tearing boats loose from their moorings."

"No choice, Charlie. I got McCall into this mess. I can't let her die. Gotta go," he said into the wet mouthpiece. Then with a grim expression, replaced the phone and headed the Whaler out of the lee into the storm.

As Matt pushed the throttle forward he wondered what Richter would do when he failed to show at Mackworth Island. McCall had been resourceful enough to figure a way to signal Charlie and gutsy enough to do it, but had it cost McCall her life? The scream at the end of her call to Charlie. Was that Richter's doing? The thought sent his heart into his mouth.

44

MILLER MAKES HIS MOVE

Lieutenant Craig Miller's eyes opened wide as he listened to Charlie Craft's words pour out of the phone. His eyes narrowed to their usual suspicious profile when Charlie explained McCall's abduction by two Germans and her probable location in Fort Gorges. He thanked Charlie, told him he'd start rescue procedures and carefully replaced the phone on the cradle. He swept one look out through the rain-plastered window and knew the Coast Guard wasn't going out to rescue anyone.

Miller relaxed in the high-backed office chair, slipped on his reading glasses and doodled on a yellow pad as he pondered what he could do to keep himself in the loop of command. He made a quick decision then dialed the number for the Harbormaster.

When he was on the line Miller directed him to prepare his boat for a run to Fort Gorges the instant the storm let up. He then alerted the Portland SWAT team leader, Joe Welch, explaining why he needed him. Welch agreed to assemble his men and hold them available for a raid on Fort Gorges as soon as weather permitted.

Charlie had done all he could to prepare the yard for hurricane *Albert's* arrival. His crew had stacked all wooden blocking out of reach of the expected storm high tide and secured the remaining boats anchored in the harbor. Some were driven deep into the marsh grass a half mile down river where they would be safe from the violent winds.

Charlie was soaked to the skin and physically exhausted. He'd been working without anything to eat since daylight and since noon work had been in a torrential downpour. It was six o'clock when Charlie released his crew and dragged his leaden feet into his office.

He poured a cup of cold coffee and was surprised to find the sky was dark as night. Charlie was tired but he was worried, too. Ever since his phone call with Matt he had half hoped to see Matt's Whaler run up river into the safety of the harbor, but that hadn't happened.

Using the remote on his desk Charlie snapped on the TV and flipped to Channel 6 for news of the storm. Cindy Williams, the evening newscaster, had finished the local news and meteorologist Joe Cupo was on screen pointing to hurricane *Albert*. He advised his audience that the first hurricane of the season was churning its way along Old Orchard Beach on its way into Portland Harbor.

His report was interspersed with video clips of last year's September storms, *Dennis* and *Floyd* that had thundered into the North Carolina coast. Charlie knew Matt Banner was right now in *Albert's* teeth. At least he would be if he were still afloat, but he didn't see how Matt could possibly survive in a 20-foot boat.

45

DAWN RAIDER – A *VERY* SMALL BOAT

There are no complicated nautical tasks to master on a 20-foot fiberglass outboard. No halyards to haul, no sails and spinnakers to control, just the wheel at the center of the boat. Matt was at the wheel now powering the *Dawn Raider* out from the protection of Long Island when a gust of hurricane-driven wind raked the boat and shot him in the eyes with driving rain.

Each time the chasing waves pushed the Whaler sideways, gallons of water cruised over the rail, leaving Matt standing in a foot of water before it funneled out the scuppers. Matt knew the Whaler was supposed to be unsinkable. The question that raced through his mind was...would *he* be unsinkable? With that thought he tightened the life jacket and checked to see that his makeshift life line was secure.

Matt's rain hood popped against his ears, a deafening sound. Wind continued to fling salt spray into his unprotected eyes until they felt raw and blistered. Sea gulls had long since sought shelter, seals had vanished, the only moving object in the wrenching havoc was Matt's tiny boat, a spec in the eye of the storm, flinching with each impact against the hull.

With white-capped waves chewing his stern like a pack of wolves he strained his eyes into the rain and darkness searching for the fort.

There were no longer actual cannons mounted in the fort, only the square firing ports framed in metal where salt spray, he remembered, had eroded the metal frame around each opening, allowing the gun ports to leak tears of rust down the gray stone walls, staining them a golden brown. Without the cannon the fort appeared empty-eyed.

Matt steadied his legs and wiped the salt out of his eyes. If the storm quit, the fort should be in full view. "Piece of cake," he yelled out loud but his face was a road map of doubt.

46

RICHTER

Richter was in a foul mood when he returned from Mackworth Island. He'd hung around the stone pier waiting in the rain with only a poncho for cover, but Banner had failed to show. The wind had driven water down Richter's neck and under his arms. His face was wind burned and his eyes stung with salt spray.

Not only had Banner failed to show but Richter had almost drowned on the two-mile return trip to the fort. The 26-foot Grady White was faster than Matt's *Dawn Raider* but heavier and not nearly as nimble.

Forced to run at an angle to the oncoming waves, his boat suffered gallons of surging water over the windward rail. The boarding waves had smacked Richter to the floor, and unable to regain his feet, he'd caromed aft, crushing his shoulder when he fetched up in the stern.

He had finally reached the fort and tied off the boat to a buoy, then motored the Zodiac dinghy to a shelving beach and secured it to a rock. Richter climbed the slippery ledges toward the fort entrance, wiped water from his eyes and cursed Brockner. He shook a fist at the rain-swollen sky and cursed the storm.

The original plan had been simple. Find the guy with the gold pendant, get him to tell where he found it, recover

the lost German treasure and fly back to Germany far richer
than when they'd left.

Now they had murdered the diver and kidnapped some
girl. Richter wasn't sure exactly where she fit into the
picture, who she was, or where she was from. Brockner had
told him the girl was the key to the gold and he had brought
her to him as instructed.

Richter was not in good spirits when he entered the
officer's quarters to find the lanterns casting a cozy glow
over the room and the good colonel hunkered up next to a
warm heater. His mood turned from sour to ugly.

Richter reported that Banner had failed to appear but the
report apparently had no effect on Brockner. His chiseled
face stared at the brick fireplace. Brockner shifted in his
chair, turned bland, emotionless eyes back to Richter and
nodded his head as though reaching a decision.

While Brockner absorbed the news, Richter waited. He
remembered Brockner's promise to kill the girl.

"What do we do with the girl?" Richter's question was
tinged with anticipation. His face was marked with healing
scratches where she had raked his face. He longed to
destroy the girl.

"She might still be of use. It's possible Banner could
not reach you because of the storm. You had difficulty in
just that two-mile stretch. He had much farther to go. We
will call him again at midnight. If he doesn't answer, then
I'll give the girl to you and we'll find some other way to
recapture the gold."

Brockner coughed and covered his mouth with a silk
handkerchief. He felt tired and age seemed to have climbed
on his back when he wasn't looking. It would be over soon.
Brockner continued to stare into the fireplace, a brooding
expression on his face.

Richter noticed that while Brockner seemed in control, a slight hesitancy had crept into his voice. For the first time Richter lost confidence in the colonel. The strain of searching all these years was taking its toll. Coming this close, and the prospect of losing the gold that had dominated his life, might just be more than Brockner could tolerate. Was the colonel beginning to unravel? He wondered.

In one way Richter hoped Banner would not show up. He savored the chance with the girl. He would use the night to figure some inventive way to dispose of her, some method that would leave no marks, no clues, and preferably be slow and painful. His thin lips narrowed and his eyes sank farther into his head as he relished the idea. He looked at his watch. Ten o'clock. Not long to wait!

47

WHERE WAS MATT?

McCall picked herself up from the floor where Richter had thrown her to find a new candle casting fluttery shadows around the cell. Her watch showed it was ten o'clock and she assumed by the lack of activity that Matt hadn't shown up. A stab of fear shot through her. Had something happened to Matt? If so, would the Germans carry out the threat to kill her? Would it be tonight? Could it be right now? She knew Richter would be in a rush to put her away. Thinking with a mind that was feverishly hot she knew Brockner was her only hope.

She turned her thoughts to Charlie. Had he understood her message? Matt had told her he could find anything in the world if someone gave him the latitude and longitude. Had Charlie called Matt with the numbers? Could he really find her?

McCall had always relied on herself. There had to be a way out of the cell and it was up to her to figure it out. It was time to do that now.

The wall behind the cot was made of solid, tightly-fit granite slabs that would be impossible to penetrate. The brick wall where the rat escaped? The rat would not dig himself into a dead end. What was behind there?

McCall quickly studied the walls. Red powder from eroding bricks lined the floor beside the rat hole. She needed a tool.

There was nothing in the room except the candle and the cot. She quickly threw off the blanket and mattress, leaving the skeletal frame of the cot exposed. The legs of the cheap Wal-Mart special Richter had dragged into the cell were attached to the frame by flat, half-inch pieces of metal. McCall stood the frame on end and placed her foot against the brace and jumped on it as hard as she could. Twenty minutes later, sweat pouring down her face, heart thudding against her rib cage, McCall had a foot-long, wide digger.

48

NOT TO BE A HERO

Suddenly Matt throttled the Whaler back, letting it tread and wallow in between the waves. There was something out there in the night. Matt could sense it. The dull glow over Portland was blotted out by a black square. A few seconds later Matt realized the outline of Fort Gorges was blocking the light. The fort couldn't be more than fifty yards away. It was ten o'clock. Would he be in time?

The tide gripped the Whaler and tugged him toward the gray outline of the fort squatting on a dark ledge. Matt drifted the Whaler onto the lee of a shingle beach and tossed the anchor over the side although the going tide would probably ground the boat. Once satisfied the Whaler was safe he lunged up a set of granite steps toward the entrance to the fort.

Richter had told him not to be a hero but Matt was in no condition to play hero even if he'd wanted to. His hands were stiff and torn and every muscle ached. Hero or no hero, however, he was McCall's only hope.

He couldn't leave her to the Germans who would kill her when they had no use for her. McCall was smart. She would have figured that out. How was she dealing with the thought?

Matt crouched next to the stone archway leading to the interior of the fort. He removed his life jacket, took a deep breath and darted through the dark portal.

Inside the fort he leaned against the wet granite wall. What would Richter do when he didn't arrive at Mackworth Island? If he were in the German's place, he would expect an attempt to rescue the girl and have some plan to prevent it.

Matt was wet and miserable but he was also angry! Those two Germans had screwed his life around enough. It was time to go on the offensive. He suddenly found his mouth no longer parched with fear. A calmness spread over him, and in spite of the wind, a heat wave coursed through his body.

He couldn't just go inside and give a whistle. Or in a loud voice say, "Hey, guys, games over, got to take McCall to a movie, time to go!" No, that wouldn't work. As he thought about the problem, a fraction of an idea sifted into his mind. Not a full blown plan. But it was simple.

He'd do a room by room search until he found her. What would he do when he found her? He didn't have the foggiest. He'd have to play it by ear.

From his position just inside the entranceway Matt looked across the parade ground. He focused his eyes on a granite tower that contained the stone steps he'd used earlier in the summer to get to the second level. To reach it he'd have to run sixty yards across the open field. Even with the shadows and poor light he'd be in plain sight once he left the cover of the walls. He'd have to figure another way.

Every time lightning flashed the dirt and gravel piled on the top battlements looked like distant mountains silhouetted against the sky. When he'd asked the tour guide how to reach the top, she'd replied, "That top level is unsafe. We're not allowed up there."

Matt worried about Richter. He would have some alarm system rigged to warn against intruders and wondered if he might already have tripped it. He shuddered with the thought and peered intently into shadows that a moment ago had given him protection and now seemed to have eyes watching him.

He had no idea where McCall was being held or any real proof she was there at all. His relationship with McCall seemed so messed up sometimes he wondered if his feelings would ever get untangled.

Where was it all going? Seemed like one moment they were like glue and the next like two opposing magnets. Harnessing his feelings and quieting his emotions was like trying to nail jello to a tree.

He didn't like that stone tower. The sally ports cut through the walls would permit anyone inside to see his approach. Once he was in the tower, Richter and Brockner would have no trouble boxing him in. He wouldn't be able to escape in either direction. He needed another way to the second level.

Matt didn't know why he was convinced she'd be up there, but he figured Richter would have squirreled McCall away in some hard to get at spot. There were innumerable stone rooms spread throughout the fort. Each had smelled the same, dank and wet, and was usually hidden away around dark corners.

On the tour he had tried to peek into some of them but without a flashlight the rooms were nothing but black holes, ugly, scary-looking places that he'd thought might contain the souls of the dead. He hoped McCall wasn't in one of those crypts.

An idea struck him. He slipped back through the doorway and moving quietly in the darkness. He crept to the beach where he'd seen the rubber Zodiac. From it he

quickly extracted a small Danforth anchor with attached
nylon line. He opened a white box strapped under the seat.
Matt removed a flashlight, stuffed it into his pocket and
returned to his spot at the base of the wall by the parade
ground.

He paused, checking the field once more before trotting
to the first balcony. To reduce the sound of the anchor
crashing into the stone wall he padded the flukes of the
anchor with his jacket, and coiled the line. Hefting the
anchor, testing its weight, he heaved the homemade grapple
onto the second story balcony. Just before the grapple
landed, the rain jacket broke loose. The flukes slammed
into the stone rail with a loud clank.

Matt held his breath and listened but there was only the
sound of the wind and storm. When there was no response
to the noise, he immediately grabbed the end of the dangling
rope and started upward, hand over hand.

The thin nylon immediately cut his hands and pain
instantly shot into his left shoulder. He fell, skidding along
the rough granite wall, skinning his knuckles before
crashing onto the ground where he lay momentarily stunned.

Recovering his breath, Matt assaulted the wall again.
This time he used his legs to clamp the rope in between each
upward pull with his right arm. Two more grunts and he
could haul himself over the balcony rail. Each pull drained
away his strength; sweat ran down his back mingling with
the rain. Rain made the rope slippery. His hands began to
slide.

49

IN THE CROSS HAIRS

Back in the officer's quarters Heinrich von Brockner's face turned livid, a glowering mask of rage. He paced the room and limped to one of the sally ports by the fireplace where he stared out into the storm. Brockner had tried repeatedly to contact Matt Banner. Each time he failed his anger grew until the veins along his neck bulged, and the hand holding the cell phone shook.

Cleaning his pistol, Richter sat behind the desk. He'd seen these despotic outbursts by Brockner before. He'd learned to keep his mouth shut and wait. Brockner suddenly whipped around, jabbed his gold-headed cane at Richter and with a voice like a hissing snake ordered, "Kill her now!"

McCall was on her knees in a pile of red dust, working at a feverous pace. For the last two hours she had dug and prodded at the wall using the piece of steel from the cot. It was now rounded from gouging against the old brick and rotting mortar.

Her face was streaked with red where she'd wiped away the sweat. Her fingernails were split and worn to the skin; her arms ached from digging at the wall.

Four loosened bricks lay in the rubble at the base of the wall. McCall had dug furiously, each moment expecting Richter to appear, drag her away and shoot her. In spite of her effort, the result of her work was discouraging. At this rate she'd be all night. McCall knew she didn't have that kind of time. Certainly daylight would be the limit. They would come for her then.

McCall returned to the wall prying at the stubborn bricks with the piece of metal, when she heard a noise outside from the corridor. She felt her heart stop as the sound of shoes grating on stone echoed under the plywood door. McCall stopped work. A warning sounded in her brain, a shadow of alarm sprang across her face. Richter!

McCall looked at the size of the hole and instantly realized she could not squeeze through. "Oh God, not now." She bit back tears of frustration, a few more minutes and she would have been free.

Shoes grated again and hands fumbled with the lock on the door. Then Richter's voice penetrated the wood. "Mine at last, *Fraulein*." She heard the sound of the key as it entered the lock.

Back in the officer's quarters Brockner's face suddenly came on the alert. The three-inch square box on the card table next to him began to squawk, a red light blinked in rapid succession. Brockner's watery eyes looked through the darkness beyond the door. He picked up his pistol. Someone had tripped the alarm.

He swept up the hand-held radio and spoke rapidly in German, ordering Richter to stop what he was doing and locate the intruder.

McCall heard the static rasp of Richter's radio followed by Brockner's command. The rattle at the lock stopped immediately. The sound of the shoes on stone retreated from the door.

McCall hurled herself into the corner, flipped over on her back and rammed her feet against the edges of the twelve-inch hole in the wall. Her sneakers made dull thuds as they pounded against the brick. Suddenly she could feel a cool draft funnel into the room. She kicked harder. One brick worked loose. Then another. Without the close support one brick provided to another, a three-foot section collapsed.

Richter ran across the parade ground. Just as he was about to enter the officer's quarters, he spotted a movement along the wall under one of the balconies. Then Brockner appeared and thrust a .270 Winchester scoped rifle and a box of shells into his hands.

Richter loaded the rifle and hurried along the edge of the parade ground until he could see Matt struggling on a rope half way to the balcony rail. Richter quickly threaded his arm through the rifle's sling and took careful aim. Fifty yards. He couldn't miss. The light-gathering qualities of the scope brought Matt into sharp focus. The cross hairs settled just below the left shoulder blade.

McCall flinched at the sound of the shot as it boomed and echoed through the fort, bouncing from wall to wall, skipping through the balconies. She *God blessed* whoever was causing the diversion and gave one more kick at the edge of the hole. Before the dust settled, McCall darted through the wall into a dark passageway.

50

RICHTER SHOOTS

A violent flash of lightning illuminated the interior of the fort. The immediate clap of thunder distracted Richter's aim. The crack of the rifle reached Matt at the same time a pock mark blew from the granite. He flinched away from the splinters of rock exploding from the balcony rail, slivers of chipped stone sliced across his forehead and his chin.

Matt lost his grip on the rope and dropped two feet along the wall. The bounce when he fetched up snapped him around so he was facing Richter, who with the rifle at his shoulder, was lining up for his second shot.

Matt twisted his exposed body around until he faced the wall and dug his feet into the cracks between the granite blocks. His arms strained on the rope.

The skin on his back crawled, as he awaited the bullet. His arms were in agony; shoulders burned as he scrambled up the line, fighting to gain purchase on the rail just beyond the reach of his grasping fingers. He wasn't going to make it.

He brought his feet up horizontal to his waist and ran sideways, zigzagging along the wall. At the same time he hauled himself, hand over hand, up the rope. The crack of the rifle and exploding pock marks followed him until he vaulted safely over the balcony, leaving Richter swearing at the storm.

Richter cursed the flash of lightning that had startled him, destroying his aim. He'd frantically worked the bolt, feeding in another round, firing his second shot just as Matt skittered to one side. The noise sent hundreds of roosting pigeons pouring over the railing, fluttering over the parade ground, interrupting his aim. No matter how Richter tried, the scope filled with nothing but flying birds.

Before Richter could fire again, Banner scrambled over the balcony rail and disappeared. His last futile shot cut the rope. Richter's face was livid with fury as he bolted to the stone block tower sixty yards to his right. There he ran up the stone steps to the second floor.

Matt found himself trapped on the second level. Twenty feet separated him from the parade ground. He couldn't escape that way because Richter had shot away the rope. He didn't want to chance a jump. Even if he landed successfully Brockner could be there to meet him. It was a no brainer. He'd have to find someplace to hide.

Matt had never been shot at before. That someone was actually willing to take his life scared the hell out of him. Beads of perspiration popped out on his forehead. Matt noticed his hands felt cold and when he started to run he had difficulty controlling his legs.

Matt knew his one chance to avoid Richter would be to find a way up to the earthworks strung along the top level of the fort. He stood a chance of losing him in the tall grass and bushy trees growing on the rim. Later there might be a chance of stealing the Zodiac which was light enough to drag into the water. But he couldn't go there until he found McCall.

Matt raced along the second level corridor, feet grinding on the uneven surface where the granite floor had been hammered into rough pits so the gunners serving a cannon wouldn't slip. He tore by gun ports divided by brick archways. After the fifth cannon slot the corridor bent left. Matt was halfway down the 100-foot leg when he heard running footsteps directly ahead.

Was it the other German? He must have heard the shots and seen Richter run to the tower stairs. Once Brockner was on the second level they'd have him boxed. The footsteps behind from the tower were running smoothly, each footfall echoing through the brick corridor. Richter was already upstairs! He was catching up.

There was no place to hide. The corridor was wide open except for the base of the archways. The runner in front was closer. Matt crouched behind the nearest pillar and waited. He could hear whoever it was, breathing hard, the dull thud of sneakers rapidly closing the distance as they pounded on the granite floor.

Matt sprang out from his hiding place, tackling the dark figure, knocking the runner to the ground. A loud grunt echoed through the balcony as the body collided with the stone floor. Before Matt could untangle himself, the runner rolled out from under him, leaped to its feet, and rushed at him unafraid.

As Matt ducked the blow he realized who it was. He grabbed McCall around the waist, hugging her close. In a quick whisper, "Hey slugger, it's me, Matt... quit it! You're hurting me."

Half laughing, half crying McCall flung her arms around Matt's neck and held on.

"Oh, God, Matt, I thought no one would ever come! They were planning to kill me!" She shuddered and squeezed closer.

"No time," he said thrusting her away, "Richter's right behind me and he has a rifle."

"This way," McCall said, leading him back the way she had come. "Stairs," she pointed.

"Where?"

"Up."

"You been there before?" Matt asked between breaths.

"Never! Just saw them a second ago. But they go up."

Matt hesitated.

"You want to try going down? Brockner has a gun, too," she said swiftly. Matt shook his head. Richter was almost on them. One more turn and he'd see them.

"Up... you lead," he said. Checking the corridor, Richter was fifty feet behind, trying to run and sight the rifle at the same time. He fired!

Lead rebounded off the wall next to the stairwell; the explosion from the barrel an ear-crunching sound. The bullet caromed off the wall and buzzed down the corridor. They ran for their lives.

Turning blindly, McCall stumbled into the stairwell. Matt shoved her up the stairs in front of him and scrambled behind. McCall could feel her feet pound on the steps, tear up the stairs, each stride burning her legs with fatigue.

Richter gained the foot of the stairs in time to fire again. Dust and flying pieces of brick ricocheted wall to wall. The smell of burning powder choked the narrow passage. In the dark stairwell the scope was worse than useless. The bullet found only brick and mortar. An icy fear gripped Matt. He could almost feel bullets tear into his back.

Surging away from the probing rifle, he arched forward, urging McCall to climb faster. Suddenly they broke free of the stairs and sped over a gravel pile and burst into the mini forest that crowned the top of the fort. Low-hanging bushes swallowed them up just as Richter exploded from the stairs only seconds behind.

Richter fired at the sound of breaking twigs, swinging the rifle left and right in an arc. Bullets whipped through bushes, clipped off limbs and showered leaves on them as they ran. Matt pulled McCall along so fast and with such force he thought her arm had to be wrenched out of its socket.

He didn't dare stop but kept up a wearing pace. They leaped downed trees, vaulted eroded gullies, and tore through briar patches. Sweat washed down his face, dripped into his eyes and stung them half closed before he stopped to rest.

They collapsed in a protected hollow along an abandoned trail midway between the forty foot drop to the parade ground on their right and the outside edge sixty feet above the rocks.

Matt sucked in air so fast his chest hurt. When he had his breathing under control he asked, "You all right?"

McCall felt the roaring rush of blood in her ears. It was impossible to quiet her erratic pulse. She took a moment to steady her heartbeat. When she replied, her voice sounded far away. "I'm okay. Let's keep going."

Matt could hear McCall's labored breath but she had held up pace for pace. His feelings for this Montana girl went up another notch. He held back on her arm, "No, let's stay here for a minute. He can't shoot at us because he can't see in the dark. He's been firing at the noise we were making. To find a target he has to stop and listen. That's slowed him up. If we stay still he won't be able to locate us."

"You mean until morning. This wooded part is only about thirty feet wide. There's no place to completely hide. All he has to do is station Brockner where he has a good shooting lane and start walking around the top. He'll drive us out like rabbits." As she replied she gave him a brave

smile. McCall didn't feel brave. What she wanted most
was for this whole ordeal to be over. Her face was
scratched and burned where sweat had leaked into the cuts;
her ankle ached.

"Matt, I'm both miserable and mad. I don't like
running, being chased and shot at. I feel like a fox in front
of the hounds. Somewhere here we are going to have to
fight!"

"Got any ideas?"

McCall paused for a second, thinking. "No, Matt, no
plan." Her voice sounded discouraged. Then she thought
about how Richter had treated her in the cell, the bucket,
and the rat. "Only I'd like to get my hands on Richter when
he didn't have a gun." McCall needed to balance the ledger.

The storm began to let up, lightning flashes were less
frequent. The rolling thunder sounded farther away to the
east and the rain had stopped. Matt knew bright, clear
weather would fall in behind the hurricane. He wondered if
either of them would be around to see it.

Two hours later, Matt whispered, "Could you find the
Zodiac? It's on the beach. My Whaler will be aground."

"I could find it."

"Think you could get the outboard started?"

A long period of silence followed his question before
she replied, long enough for Matt to see the first rays of
dawn break against the eastern sky. They were going to
have to move soon. He wished he knew where that would
be.

"I doubt it. Remember, I'm from Montana. Lots of
grass but not many lakes," she finally said, giving him a
weak smile.

Richter's footsteps suddenly sounded fifty yards to their
right. Matt could see him in the gray light, moving slowly,

eyes checking. He wasn't in a hurry. The rifle was held at the ready. Matt could see the pistol in his belt.

McCall's eye's suddenly found Richter and she sucked in a breath putting her hand over her mouth.

Matt whispered, "We've got to move!" His voice was urgent. "That path he's on will lead him right here."

"Which way?" he asked.

"I don't know," she cried in desperation.

Matt could see the lights from Portland fading in the rising dawn. "This way," he said quietly. Grasping her hand he pulled her along a narrow trail. Some of the trees were head high, covering their run along the rim of the fort. Matt let go of McCall's hand, freeing his to grab onto bushes. The trail seemed to disappear, then re-form into nothing more than a dip in the limbs that tore at their clothes.

Suddenly McCall screamed as her feet flipped out from under her and she slid down a gully that would shoot her over the wall of the fort to the rocks below. Matt whirled, shot out an arm, latched onto her shirt.

Rocks and gravel tumbled over the wall, a Niagara of falling earth, sixty feet to the rocks below. McCall's legs frantically back peddled. She hugged his arm as he snatched her away from the edge. "My God, Matt, if you...

"Matt...I..." She didn't know how to apologize for the scream that would bring Richter. He would be on the alert now. Ready. He'd have zeroed in on their location. They had to run.

"Careful." They were still close enough to the edge so loose stones dropped over the side of the fort. Matt noted it was a long time before they hit the ledge below.

A shot split the air. McCall screamed! A branch snapped off directly in front of her face, the bullet buzzing out into the harbor.

"Quick, in here." Then before she could protest Matt shoved her behind a bush intertwined with nasty brambles. Richter was searching but it was unlikely he'd poke around in the thorns. He held her face between his hands and searched her eyes. "Stay put here for awhile. When you think it's safe make a run for the boat.

"It will have a key just like a car. Untie the rope, push the boat into the water and turn the key. It will work. I promise."

Matt understood the fear that immobilized his muscles and tore at his mind like a pack of wild dogs. He knew he must leave now before his courage failed him.

He gave her a quick kiss and spun back on the path where he knew Richter would have no trouble finding him. Matt crouched with one knee on the ground. Adrenaline raced through his body and charged him full of energy. He broke to his feet and burst out of the bushes.

A hail of fire searched through the trees, clipping branches. Matt raced along the rim of the fort ignoring the crack of the bullets that buzzed like bees, leading Richter away from McCall.

Unmindful of the briars tearing at his face, stabbing his skin, he stormed through the heavy undergrowth spreading along the dirt parapet. Vines grabbed his ankles and flung him into the underbrush. In some places the growth was tangled and dense but in other places a running man could be seen from the waist up.

Slowly Richter herded Matt toward the edge of the fort, narrowing his prospects, hazing him out into the open. Matt stopped running, bent over at the waist and gasped for breath. He gulped air, stood on legs that felt like jelly, while anger gave him the strength to continue.

Then as easy as pie Richter stepped around a copse of trees and pointed the rifle directly at Matt's heart. "Well, *mien Herr*, we meet again!" The words were soft spoken like two friends meeting, but the eyes were not friendly. The rising sun bullied its way through to breaking dawn and cast hollow shadows onto his skeletal face. Richter tightened his finger on the trigger. "Please, step backward."

Matt sensed he was only a few feet from the wall and the sixty foot drop. He could see in Richter's eyes he intended to back him over the edge.

When the ground slanted Richter demanded, "More please." The rifle prodded. When Matt's foot stepped into air his body twisted and bounced on the ground; he slid on his back, then rolled over facing the fort, his hands desperately grabbed at bushes as they tore past. There was no question he was going over the edge. His mind whirled, there was no time to think. His belt scraped over the outside rim of granite and for an instant slowed his fall.

With his good arm he snatched at a small tree thriving in a crack. Leaves peeled off, limbs became a slippery rope slowly lowering him over the edge. His flailing feet rammed onto a separation in the blocks and stopped his fall. A groan escaped his lips.

The sound of McCall's cry floated over the wall. Stretched full length, helpless, finger tips tiring, the sound of her cry tore at his heart. Richter hesitated. From where he stood he could not see Matt clinging to the wall and was uncertain if he had fallen to the ledge below. He was also afraid to crawl down over the loose gravel to find out.

When McCall cried out again Richter decided it didn't matter. If they had the girl they would be able to get Banner. Just in case, he hollered over the edge, "I'll be back for you, *Herr* Banner." Then with a grunt he spun away, running back the way he'd come.

Two minutes later he found Brockner had dragged McCall out of her hiding place, and had one meaty hand wrapped in her hair.

Matt didn't have time to see if Richter was trying to trick him. His fingers were slipping. The strain threatened to dislocate his shoulders and the muscles on the wounded arm burned like fire. His feet hunted for the tiny cracks in the stone below. Matt strained upward pulling with all his remaining strength. His whole body trembled as he got a fist over the wall. Then an arm and elbow.

He rested, stuck on the wall like a fly. Then by force of will alone, his mind and face contorted with the effort, he toiled higher until he could get one leg on top. Without waiting he rolled over away from the edge, jerked to his feet and climbed up the slight incline to the safety of the trees.

With the back of an arm he wiped the sweat away from his eyes. His body shook violently as adrenaline tore through his veins. His arm was bleeding again. Where was McCall?

Then he heard a struggle ahead, heard McCall scream, followed by a voice ordering her to be still. Matt understood then. Brockner had found her! The two of them were hustling McCall to the open field below.

McCall was cussing, swearing at Richter. They were two stories below on the parade ground.

"Banner, I know you can hear me," Richter called, raising his voice to the trees. "We have the girl. Come down or I will think of something special to do to her. Believe me, my ideas are a bit crude. Would you like to see me cut off an ear?"

Matt's heart stopped. His mind seemed to be separate from his body. All the effort to get here wasted. He had failed McCall. What could he do?

"Leave her alone, Richter, I'm coming down."

"No, Matthew! You'll be shot!"

"I don't think so. They still need me for the gold. Richter almost made a mistake, Brockner. He almost killed me. Without me you'll never find it!" He could see Brockner jabbing his finger into Richter's chest followed by a short argument. Brockner seemed to win because he looked up and said, "Unfortunately you are correct. Richter is sometimes very short sighted. But he is correct when he says we have the girl."

Matt found the stairs and climbed down to the parade ground. Richter pointed his pistol at them, motioning toward the open door of the officer's quarters. Matt went in first, followed by McCall. He found himself inside Brockner's headquarters.

Matt quickly surveyed the room searching for a way out. He took in the card table, gas lanterns, cots then wondered what was behind a blue tarp that had been nailed over what looked like a doorway.

Bright sun poured through the slits of the sally ports on each side of the fireplace. Brockner took a seat alongside the card table. Richter stood the rifle in a corner, then turned off the lanterns and space heater and stood alongside Brockner. His face held a smirk.

Matt's eyes traveled again to the blue tarp to their left. He arched his eye brows at McCall. She shrugged her shoulders. "I don't know," she mouthed. He glanced at his watch and was surprised to see it was only six thirty. Matt felt like he'd been here since the day the earth cooled. Yet they were still alive!

51

VER IS DER GOLD?

There was no obvious place in the room to sit down and both Richter and Brockner seemed content to let them stand in front of his desk.

Brockner's suspicious eyes narrowed. His lips formed a thin line before he spoke. "You missed the meeting with Richter. The weather, *Herr* Banner? Maybe the wind, the choppy sea?" he raised his eyes in question. Then his voice became icy cold. He rose from the chair, his jowels shaking. Spittle flew from his mouth. His cane banged on the desk. *"Ver is der gold?"*

Matt cast a swift look at McCall. He felt his heart begin to pound. Sweat broke out on his palms. The next few words might be his last.

With a glance at Richter he said, "As soon as your German friend here left with McCall I dove on the U-33." Matt could see Brockner's eyes widen in anticipation. The hand holding the cane began to tremble. "The box was empty, Brockner. No gold. Dead empty. Not even a crab."

Matt waited. Seconds slipped by. McCall drew in a deep breath. The sound echoed in the silent room. The voice that replied was as quiet as a whisper in church and as dangerous as a cobra. Brockner's head swayed from side to side. His breathing seemed to stop.

"Do you expect me to believe that? The gold is there! You lie! If it is not on the submarine you have hidden it somewhere!" He hurled his cane against the far wall. A string of curses flew from his twisted mouth.

Matt could see a tiny avenue, a small street marked hope. "Believe me, Brockner, the gold is not on the sub but I think Jack removed the last of it just before you lugged him off and shot him." Matt watched Brockner carefully. He knew the German's need for the gold was such a driving force he would cling to any response that left lingering hope.

"We were best friends, Brockner. I can find the gold." As he said the words he saw Brockner's body relax. His eyes were still suspicious but his face held relief. For the moment there was no sound in the room as the older German weighed Matt's words.

The remaining warmth from the lanterns and gas heaters felt good. Matt pulled his drying shirt away from his chest, feeling it peel away from his skin. McCall moved over and stood close to him. She could tell by his expression Matt was up to something, but remained puzzled. What was going on?

Brockner struck an inquisitor's pose behind the desk, feet together, elbows on the table top, unfathomable eyes giving Matt an impenetrable stare. Richter took a position next to him, posture military erect.

Richter appeared to be waiting for some sort of order from Brockner. However, there seemed to be a drop of uncertainty between the two of them about what they wanted to happen. Brockner must know that with both of them missing for over twenty-four hours there would be some kind of search going on.

Brockner's gold expedition had for the moment faltered and he was a man who did not broker failure easily. He had limited time to retrieve the gold.

Before Brockner could say anything, Matt threw a question at him, "How did you know the necklace Jack Kilby found was part of a large treasure?"

Brockner inhaled a deep breath deciding if he wanted to answer the question. After an initial pause said, "All my life, *Herr* Banner, I have been in German intelligence. My business was to keep my eyes open for movements against the Reich, and review both foreign and domestic documents.

"I was born during World War II in Frankfort. My father was later reported missing in action and my mother was killed during an air raid over Berlin."

Brockner seated himself behind the desk. "Following the war I joined the German Army. I moved swiftly through the ranks joining the intelligence corps in 1970.

"One day some classified material fell into my lap. It was the full report of Admiral Canaris's plan to fund an expensive sabotage movement in the United States. He had ordered a one-man sub, the U-33, to penetrate the American coastal defenses.

"The submarine carried a small fortune in looted jewels and gold that could be easily turned into cash. Two German agents were to meet the submarine at Parker Point at the mouth of the Royal River and carry away the contents of that chest."

McCall's eyes flashed in sudden understanding.

"Yes, I see you are ahead of me, young lady. The sub never arrived. Or better, it never made shore. Something happened to it. Once I knew about the jewels I searched U. S. naval records for reports of any naval action engaging a German submarine in Casco Bay."

"And you found it," McCall interjected.

"Yes, I did," Brockner replied, slipping her a wintery smile. "A report that a gun battery from Jewell Island had fired on a submarine on August 27, 1944. The coordinates of the sub's last known location were recorded but unfortunately the sinking was unconfirmed and the sub was never found. Those coordinates, however, placed the U-33 near Jewell Island. There was only the slimmest of chances the sub fired on was not the U-33."

McCall gasped, "That's where Jack found my grandmother's pendant. It was part of Nazi gold looted in Europe!"

"Yes, quite so."

"How did you know the necklace was part of that box?" McCall asked.

"Ah, yes. How did I know? Attached to Canaris's secret mission papers was an itemized list of each and every item on board the U-33. With typical German efficiency a complete description of each piece had been carefully cataloged."

As the German answered McCall's question, Matt calculated the chances of breaking out of the room and once again noticed the blue tarp ten feet away. Brockner was seated, which put him at a certain disadvantage. A pistol, however, rested close to his right hand. Richter's automatic was stuck in his belt and he looked to be on full alert.

Brockner continued, "For years I watched lost fortunes from the war surface. None of the items matched the list. None, until your Jack dragged up the necklace. I cross-referenced his find with the list and...as you say...Bingo, a one hundred percent match.

"There was no mistake," Brockner continued, "A piece of Canaris's booty had surfaced and I was the only one who knew." Brockner's eyes became large.

"Can you imagine the feeling after all those years?" He rose to his feet, body quivering, his voice getting louder as he spoke. "A fortune in my hands!" The sound of his voice echoed in the room, and bounced off the graffiti-painted walls.

"All I had to do was locate Jack Kilby and force him to tell me where he found the necklace. I would have all the rest of the jewels and gold coins." Suddenly Brockner exploded. He shook a clenched fist at Matt. Rage turned his face crimson.

"Then Richter killed him and you showed up, spoiling it all with your meddling, chasing after the GPS that held all the secrets, and diving on the sub before we were ready."

A slow smile spread over Matt's face. He gave McCall a wink while shifting his eyes to the blue tarp. Ignoring Brockner's fuming anger, and with a calm face he asked, "Colonel, did you ever wonder what happened to your father? What he was doing when he was killed. What were the circumstances?"

Brockner's eyes became as unreadable as stone. He was slow to respond before replying, "As I grew up, I prayed my father would come and rescue me from my uncle, who was a brutal man. I hated him and hated my father for dying in the war and not taking care of me.

"Yes, *Herr* Banner, I've thought of why he never came home. But there were many who didn't, especially those on the Eastern front. I was told his last posting was as an infantry lieutenant outside Stalingrad." Then Brockner shrugged as though the whole matter was of little consequence.

"Your father was never at Stalingrad, Brockner. He was never in the infantry. He was in German submarines, the *Kreigsmarine.* He was a decorated U-boat commander who had been awarded the Iron Cross."

Brockner looked startled for a moment then shook his head negatively and replied, "Impossible."

"Not so impossible," Matt continued. "Your mother died before the war was over. Paperwork surrounding the actual events concerning your father could easily have been lost. My guess is they were purposely misplaced and the Stalingrad story substituted. The switch worked. You believed it for forty years."

McCall's mind was racing ahead. Could it be possible? No, never... Matt couldn't be thinking...?

Both Richter and Brockner were focused on Matt. Each wondering where this was all going.

Then Matt said quietly again, "Brockner, it was your father who commanded the U-33 sunk by American naval gun fire from the Jewell Island gun battery on August 27, 1944." There was silence in the room, a silence that took on a weight of its own.

Matt could see the smile on Brockner's face slip as he absorbed his words. Matt pointed a finger at Brockner. "I saw your father."

"What do you mean?" he expelled, his face a mask of disbelief.

"In the sub. The U-33. I saw his body, or rather his bones, together with the remains of a German naval uniform and his commander's hat swimming with the fish, Brockner, right there with the gold just like you said, only it was supposed to be Oberlieutenant Hans Deiter commanding or that's what someone wanted us to think."

"I don't believe you!" His denial, a high pitched curse.

Matt knew he needed a distraction and was about to deliver one. He hoped McCall was ready. "I have proof, Brockner, absolute, undeniable proof!"

Brockner threw a questioning look at Richter and eased himself back down in the chair.

Matt pinned his eyes on Richter. "I'm going to reach into my pocket.   Don't get nervous."   Slowly Matt withdrew a soggy, black wallet still soaked from fifty years under water. The leather had been chewed and the stitching pulled away in places, but it still held a driver's license, a military I.D and a photo showing Hans Deiter in full uniform.

"Inside the folds of the leather, Brockner, you will find a document, purposefully hidden, that the commander of the sub should never have been carrying. You'll see that the top part of the document says that in the event of capture the captain was to use the name Hans Deiter. However, in the section accepting command of the U-33 the captain signed his full name, *Hans Peter Brockner*. Your father."

Matt took one step forward, placing the wallet and the identifying document side by side on the table and dropped the Iron Cross next to the wallet.

Surprise slowly siphoned the blood from Brockner's face.   Both Richter and Brockner were focused on the wallet. Brockner reached a shaking hand toward the paper that held his father's name.

Matt stabbed a look at McCall, nodding at the blue door, at the same time swung his foot under the desk, smashing the legs and spinning Brockner's pistol across the floor where it bounced into the fireplace. Richter, momentarily stunned, failed to move. Matt grabbed McCall's arm and thrust her in front of him, shoving her into the tarp.

McCall swept through the door, struggled loose from the plastic folds and raced across the room, dodging chunks of plaster and loose boards. She could see through several doors that had once been interconnecting passageways. Matt yelled at her to keep running.

He stopped and took up a position beside the torn tarp. When Richter stumbled through, he kicked him in the stomach, driving his foot deep behind his belt. When he doubled over, Matt followed the kick with a tremendous rabbit punch at the base of the neck. Richter collapsed. Before Brockner could untangle himself from the desk Matt had followed McCall out through the doors.

With both Germans armed, there was no way Matt could untie the rubber boat, start the motor and escape without getting shot. Then again, he didn't want a repeat of last night's adventure on the roof of the fort.

They ran out of the last room onto the parade ground. Steam rose up from the drying grass and the mounting sun cast a shadow over half the yard. There seemed nowhere to go. Then he directed McCall to the tower and raced over the spongy ground, following McCall who ran smoothly in front of him.

McCall was having similar thoughts about the roof and remembered there were no hiding places on any of the gun levels. Their only chance lay somewhere below. If there were any below.

Matt's knees were thrusting up and down, his feet pounding over the open field as he tried to catch McCall. She was easily out distancing him. Risking a glance behind, Matt saw Richter in a police stance, the pistol bucking in his hand making tiny popping sounds, but they were sixty yards away and running, and the bullets flew by harmlessly. Richter was stumbling after them.

Panting and out of breath they skidded to a halt behind the protection of the stone tower. They looked at each other. "Which way?" they said together.

"Matt...! Richter's coming! We have to make a decision!"

"Come, down here, follow me," Matt said, bolting down a set of steps. The beam of his flashlight stabbed a yellow path through the stygian darkness. Matt swore. The light exposed an enormous cavern half the size of a football field. The roof appeared fifty feet above their heads. Except for piles of jack strawed lumber there was no place to hide.

"It's the powder magazine. If he traps us here we're history."

McCall could already see the problem. Reaching for his hand she skipped back up the stairs, turning left into a short tunnel. She could hear Richter breathing just beyond the tower. They had only seconds. Fear gave flight to her legs.

She suddenly darted left into a black square marking the entrance to another room. There was no chance to check it out. They would make it here or they wouldn't. Matt's light showed a gray cement shelter about ten by fifteen with another doorway to the right. They squirted through and flopped down with their backs against the wall and snapped off the light. A chilled black silence surrounded them.

Matt knew it had to end here. He was at the end of his strength. There were no other places to go and no other way out of this room except through the door they had just entered. Richter was armed and outside hunting them. Now was time to draw a line on the playground sand and dare the bully to step across.

McCall's lungs heaved and a rasping shudder fluttered through her body. Her forehead was wet and her hands felt cold. When she had control of her breath she asked, "What do we do? How do we take him?" He thought it was like McCall to think of offense rather than defense. He hoped he would live long enough to see how the score came out.

"He has to come in here or starve us out. Neither of those guys has time on their side. They need me to locate where Jack hid the gold post haste or they are going to get arrested." Matt followed that with a chuckle.

"What's so funny?"

"The gold."

"For God sake, Matt, what about the gold?"

"I have no idea where Jack would have put it and except for Deiter's bones there's nothing in that sub."

"Nothing?"

"Zip, zero. I haven't a clue where it's at. I told the truth when I said Jack probably removed it."

"Maybe that's good."

"Maybe, McCall, but we both have pieces of our hide invested in this adventure. I'd like to at least get some payback." He paused, "You asked, what's the plan?"

"Yeah."

"I think we'll have to play it by ear. See what he does and take advantage of any mistakes he makes. You got any better ideas?"

McCall thought for a moment. "No...none."

Matt reached for her hand and held it. There was nothing more to say. There was nothing to do but wait.

A few minutes later he leaned over and whispered, "I think I heard him go down to the powder magazine. Give him a minute and he'll be back. The doorway we used will be the first place he'll look." As he spoke Matt absently rubbed his shoulder, willing the pain to go away.

McCall wished there were some light so she could see Matt. She tried to see her hand when she waved it in front of her face. Nothing showed.

Matt's ears picked up. He gave McCall's hand a squeeze and a hushed whisper to be quiet. The sound he'd heard was not of the fort, or pigeons or an errant breeze whistling in the passageway. The slight scraping sound was a man walking carefully, trying not to disturb the debris that lay on the corridor floor.

McCall tried to breathe softly. The sound was very close. Her breath seemed to solidify in her throat.

Matt felt the hair on his neck bristle and a spasm of fear grip in his gut. Then he pushed away the fear and got ready. The next move would be Richter's. Matt leaned over, placing his mouth next to McCall's ear. "No matter what he does, don't make a sound. Don't move a muscle." She squeezed his hand to let him know she understood.

Outside Richter had convinced himself they were not in the powder magazine. That narrowed the choice to the door in front of him.

A flashlight would have helped but he didn't have one. Richter's German pride was damaged. The girl had ripped his face and made a fool out of him. Richter had a pounding headache where Matt had hit him. He promised himself he would shoot and worry about whether Brockner approved later.

Without warning, Richter stepped through the doorway into the first room and quickly flattened himself against the wall. He held his pistol two handed in front of his body ready to fire. Nothing moved.

He listened for sounds of breathing, then reached into his pocket and withdrew a match. He struck it on the wall and immediately threw the splinter of burning wood to the middle of the room. Richter saw the room was empty and the outline of another door five feet to his right.

"I know you are in there, Banner. Come out now and I won't shoot you!" The only reply was the echo of his words rebounding from the cement walls. When his eyes had adjusted to the blackness of the room he could see a faint outline of the other door. He stepped cautiously forward to the edge of the opening, stretched his gun hand into the room and fired three quick rounds.

Fire leaped from the muzzle, a blinding blue red flash splitting the darkness. Lead spun off the far wall, chipping cement and driving splinters of lead throughout the room.

The sound deafened his ears. Smoke spewed into his face making him cough.

Nothing happened. No cries of pain. Absolutely nothing happened...nothing at all.

Richter knew he had a problem. He might be playing soldier outside an empty room! While he wasted his time here, Banner and the girl might be getting away. Then again, maybe his shots had actually killed them both. With a sigh of resignation he knew he would have to enter the room and see for himself.

The shots had plugged McCall's ears, leaving them with a dull ringing noise. Without the ability to see, coupled now with being unable to hear, was frightening. She had felt Matt wince and wondered if he had been hit. She reached for him but didn't speak.

Richter bunched his muscles and launched himself through the opening. What happened next was in flashes, split seconds, bits and pieces. Matt leaped to his feet and struck down with the flashlight with a fury he'd never known. He repeated the blows until he was sure Richter was down and out.

52

MONTANA GIRLS CAN SHOOT

Matt knelt beside Richter's outstretched body, feeling for a pulse along his neck. Assured Richter's heart was still beating, Matt quickly lunged forward and felt his way along the wall to the doorway and the pale light glancing in from the main corridor. When McCall didn't follow he called, "What are you doing? We've got to get out of here. Brockner will have heard the shots and come investigating."

When McCall didn't answer immediately, he spun around and started back into the room cursing at himself for not making sure Richter was not going to get up again.

Her reply suddenly leaked out through the boxy, stone cavern. "In a minute."

"Hurry up!"

"Stay cool, Mr. Banner, I'm sifting around in the dark here. I want his pistol."

"Forget the gun, Richter's not going anywhere."

"It's not Richter I'm worried about. Check outside for Brockner."

McCall felt her skin crawl as her searching fingers bumped into Richter's warm body. It required a deliberate effort for her to continue the search. His breathing sounded labored and ragged. Since she had no idea how hard he had been hit, the possibility of his waking up truly frightened her.

She thought if he never woke up that would be okay too. But McCall was adamant. If either of the two Germans threatened her again, she would be ready.

Then with a cry of joy she called to Matt, "I've got it!"

"Good, now let's get out of here!"

She joined him in the cool shadows at the base of the tower. Both their minds focused on the rubber Zodiac, their ticket away from the fort. Matt's eyes traveled from the pistol McCall held in her hand, to the determined face and tangled blond hair. McCall had a set to her lips and her jaw was clamped shut. It was her "Don't screw with me" face. She held the gun professionally.

"You know how to use that?"

"You don't grow up in Montana and not know how to shoot."

"Then let's see if we can make it out of here."

They bolted across the open fifty yards toward the archway leading from the fort. Every stride exposed them to the possibility of withering fire from Brockner. They were halfway to the Zodiac and freedom, running wildly, hearts pumping, legs eating up the remaining distance, when Brockner casually stepped out, blocking the exit.

Matt would have been hard pressed to say which occurred first. The wop-wop-wop sound of the incoming helicopters or Brockner's sudden appearance. The wop-wop-wop was getting louder each second. Brockner stood with feet wide apart, two hands holding his automatic.

The face over the gun was wide-eyed and no longer confident. Matt instantly froze. He stared at the tiny shells erupting from the top of the automatic like he'd lost the power of thought. Sunlight winked on the flying casings. Harmless-sounding tinkles scratched the air when they clinked and rolled on the stone floor.

McCall tried to shrug away the prickly feelings of revenge. Was it right to hate? She'd been taught to do unto others. Well, she was about to do just that. Her desire to even the score left no lingering doubts.

McCall dropped to one knee and swung her pistol level with Brockner's chest and without hesitation began a slow methodical fire. The pistol bucked and popped in a regular rhythm, mixing easily with the wop-wop from overhead. Brockner's fire plucked away chunks of grass in front of them, blasting turf into the air before whining away over the parade ground.

The wop-wop was now directly overhead. He could hear a loudspeaker directing the shooter by the exit door to cease fire. He was under arrest. Brockner took one look at the arriving choppers and fired a last round. Suddenly his right leg collapsed under him. Matt saw a look of triumph cross McCall's face. Brockner hauled himself painfully to his feet and threw away his empty gun and limped out the doorway.

The choppers landed. SWAT teams ducking under the rotating blades spewed out onto the ground, automatic rifles swinging, pointing, securing the parade ground.

Feeling dull and sluggish Matt ran after Brockner. Brockner staggered through the entrance ahead of him, holding his leg where McCall's bullet had hit.

Matt slipped over seaweed-covered ledges, hurrying to catch Brockner before he reached the Zodiac. As he caught up, he saw Brockner hide something under one of the seats. Matt suddenly grabbed Brockner around the throat and wrestled him to the beach.

Brockner was old and frightened, Matt was young and angry. There was no real core left in Brockner. Whatever fight was left in him suddenly fled. Matt rousted him to his feet and shoved him back toward the fort.

Before leaving the boat, Matt reached under the seat and hauled out a dark green fanny pack. He ripped open the zipper and reached inside. There were the jewels missing from Jack's house. He pawed around for a second before he found McCall's grandmother's pendant. He stuffed it into his pocket, closed the bag and pushed Brockner to the fort, delivering both Brockner and the bag to the waiting helicopters and the SWAT team captain.

By then McCall was surrounded by helmeted men with *State Police* stenciled on the backs of their dark blue bulletproof vests. She signaled two SWAT members to follow her. Dashing over the parade ground, she led them past the tower to Richter. A few minutes later the two SWAT members hauled him out of the dark cement room and dragged him to the waiting chopper. McCall followed close behind, poking Richter in the back while she offered him words of wisdom about how to handle *Hell* when he got there.

Matt ducked under the whirling chopper blades and allowed a SWAT guy to help him into a seat behind the pilot. McCall followed, taking a seat beside him. Loss of blood and lack of food had taken their toll. Without the adrenaline to drive him, Matt was folding rapidly. A medic was busy sticking needles in him, pouring fluids into his arm.

McCall's hand found his and she blinked back tears while wishing she had the words to tell him how she felt, how she admired his bravery and unselfishness. She searched for a way to put into words how she honored him. However, all she could do for the moment was gaze at his mud-streaked face and pray he'd be all right.

Matt spent Monday night in the hospital. Nine a.m. the next day a doctor removed the bandages and examined the wound. "Healing nicely, Matthew," he said professionally. He put on a new bandage, patted Matt's arm, gave him some antibiotics and said, "You're good to go."

McCall hurried into the hospital room and was surprised to see Matt fully dressed and ready to leave, which in some ways made her task more difficult.

"You look a bit battle tested, Matt. She gave him a quick kiss and asked, "You OK?"

"The Banners are indestructible," followed by a weak smile, but a shadow in McCall's face told him what he'd feared.

"Matt, I've got to get home. I've been gone too long as it is. My brother called last night. The foreman got hurt yesterday and ... well, my brother needs me." In spite of how she had rehearsed the words they sounded like she was running away.

Even with his rumpled hair and dark rings under his eyes she thought he was the most wonderful creature she'd ever seen. McCall could see his strong jaw clench at the news she was leaving. She felt his brown eyes searching her face and began to blush.

"We never did stop to talk about where we were going in this relationship, did we?" he asked.

"No, Matt, there never seemed to be time. Ever since I met you it's been a race from one moment of danger to another. Frankly, I'm glad that part is over." Her voice gave a hesitant laugh.

"What about the other part?" Matt asked.

"You and I?"

"I had that in mind."

She met his gaze. Her breath quickened. Then she placed her hand on his arm. "Is there something important going on between us, Matt?"

Matt looked at her freshly scrubbed face, the gold freckles and the swoop of her honey blond hair where it touched her shoulders. He felt a growing ache for his Montana girl. He felt jolted where she touched him, a spark of lightning surging between them. Matt had been slow to admit his feelings and suddenly they rushed to the surface. He could feel his face turn red. "McCall, I..."

"Matthew Banner, you're blushing!"

"Yeah," he grinned, "I am." He paused. "McCall, I'm afraid if you go back to Montana I'll never see you again. You know, the old summer romance trick."

"You think this is a summer romance?" There was a catch in her voice, "Well, it's not. I've never felt this way before," and slipping her arms around him kissed him good-bye.

He suddenly released her and fished her grandmother's gold pendant out of his pocket. He held it by the gold chain and placed it over McCall's head. "It belongs on you, McCall. I got it from a friend of mine," he paused and smiled, "Captain Kidd!" They laughed. "I'll make arrangements with Lieutenant Miller. There won't be any hassle."

McCall seemed at a loss for words. She kissed him again, slid out of his arms and reached into her purse. She withdrew a plain envelope and handed it to Matt with instructions, "You're not to open this until I'm on the plane!" Then with a wave at the door walked briskly down the corridor. Matt felt she had just stolen his shadow.

With an aching heart he hoped she was not out of his life. After all, what did he know about who she might be attached to in Montana? Would the connection she had there suddenly regain its luster and the days in Maine become dim?   Matt's wound was healing, but his heart needed bandages.

That should have wrapped it up. Matt found out later it had been Watts who finally moved the SWAT team to action. Putting together what Watts had known about Jack's murder and seeing the same white boat carrying a girl had been enough for him to fire up his rusty VHF radio. He had connected to emergency channel 16 and insisted the Coast Guard call the state police. The call bounced up against Lieutenant Miller's request for a SWAT team and the police had been launched into the air.

After McCall left the hospital Matt called the yard to ask Charlie if he could come pick him up. By the time they returned to Yarmouth, Matt had given Charlie a blow-by-blow of the whole fort episode. Richter, trying to cop some kind of deal with Lieutenant Miller, had confessed to killing Jack, but under orders from Brockner.

That would be enough to put them both away. Lieutenant Miller had dropped all charges against Matt and sent a fax to Florida recommending the police accept Matt's version of his sister's death.

Everything seemed back to normal except for McCall, who seemed to have ghosted out of his life. He worried about that. Why had she given him that letter? Was there something in there she hadn't been able to say to his face?

Then there was the other issue. After all the struggle and danger no one had located Jack's treasure. Had Black Beard loaded it on board his high-sterned galleon and sailed away to the place where pirates bury their treasures?

Matt chuckled at the thought. But while he was in the hospital he'd given the disappearance of the gold some serious thought. His mind had traveled up several blind alleys before the answer hit him between the eyes. In fact he was surprised he hadn't thought of it before.

The issue of McCall, well, that was a different story. He reached into his pocket and withdrew her letter, the one he had promised not to read until she had returned to Montana. Well, she was gone. He slid the thin piece of paper between nervous fingers and held it up to the light, but no matter how hard he tried, Matt could not bring himself to open it.

53

THE KEY

Matt folded the letter on its original creases and stuffed it back in his pocket. He had one more important task to complete before he could concentrate on McCall, and if the words he feared were written on that small block of paper, it would destroy his day.

Matt knew he would never be satisfied until the gold was recovered. Somehow he felt this would put Jack to rest. He had work to do. The letter would have to wait.

Matt had his own ideas about the missing gold but resisted sharing them with any of the divers except Alex. They'd spent an hour on the phone before Matt left the hospital, banging heads without arriving at a solution to where Jack might have hidden the treasure from the U-33.

While he didn't actually know where Jack had hidden it, he had a pretty good idea of who might know. He knew also that if he was correct and located the treasure he was going to need some kind of legal help to ensure his salvage rights to both the gold and the submarine. He shrugged away those worries thinking Professor Russell would have some ideas about that.

The capture of Brockner and Richter had made headlines in the Portland Press Herald. The evening newscaster, Cindy Williams, developed an expansive report that spilled over for two nights on Channel 6 News. Matt had been featured as the key figure in a rescue at Fort Gorges and during a live interview with Williams had covered his own political trail when he said Lieutenant Miller had played a major role in the rescue.

Williams opened with, *"Lieutenant Craig Miller of the Portland Police Department believes that after further investigation he will locate the missing gold coins and jewels that had been taken from the U-33, a German submarine, recently discovered mired in the mud of Casco Bay. The gold was part of Nazi jewels looted from European estates during World War Two. However, the current whereabouts of the fortune is unknown."*

She finished with the comment, *"Speculation is that the gold was to fund an extensive sabotage operation in the manufacturing plants in the northeast. The submarine was purportedly sunk by gun fire from Jewell Island on August 27, 1944 but naval records concerning the sinking are unavailable."*

Tuesday afternoon proved to be warm and muggy. High cirrus clouds hung lazily in the sky and Matt could feel a slight breeze on his face as he lounged in the shade of a forty foot catamaran stored in Charlie's yard. He squinted down river past The Cannery Restaurant and watched the dive boats coast up river, one behind the other. He waited patiently for the dive crews to moor their boats and hike up to the dive shack.

Each diver had a tank slung over his shoulder, fins and mask threaded on their black snorkels. The guys had unzipped their rubber jackets and trailed behind Kiki who trudged happily up the gravel road in her yellow and orange wet suit. With a slight flush on her face and the soft afternoon sun bouncing from her blond head, Matt thought she looked radiant.

Matt hadn't seen his team since last Friday and they swarmed over him, gathered him up and swept him into the shack.   When the gear was stowed, Matt found himself beleaguered with questions about the fight at the fort and they all wanted to see the bullet hole in his shoulder.

He gave them the short rendition, but even then it was close to six o'clock before everyone drove off. Lance was the last to leave. He shut the shack door, locked it behind him and was seated in his car reaching for the ignition key when Matt approached.

Matt leaned inward on the window ledge, moving inside Lance's personal space. "Lance, we need to talk," he said in a controlled voice.

"What about?"

"I think you know." Matt kept a positive timber to his voice because what he was about to say was pure speculation. The slightest hint he was bluffing and Lance would be history.

"I don't know what you mean."

"Jack's gold, Lance.   The stuff he took from the submarine." Matt watched Lance carefully.

"I still don't follow." However, his eyes shifted straight ahead.

"Well, Lance, let's look at it this way. Jack had no way to get the metal lid off the box in the sub and yet I found the box open, so something happened. Jack was an inquisitive guy. He'd have pressed after somebody to open it for him. He couldn't just go to Tommy's Dive Center in Portland, waltz in and say, 'Hey, guys, I've found a sub sunk during the war with a mystery box on board. I need someone to cut off the top', now could he, Lance?

"So he looked closer to home. Looked to his dive team and someone he could trust. Maybe you, Lance! The guy who can *weld* under water. The guy who can probably use a cutting torch as well!"

Lance's face turned pale. "Maybe I did cut off the top," Lance said, eyes shifting. "But I don't know anything about any gold."

"Okay, have it your way, but when I tell Lieutenant Miller you lied to him when you said you had no idea about the gold, he's going to be an unhappy dude." Matt tapped the window, "See you around." He turned and walked away.

"Matt! Wait!" Lance sat stiff-armed holding the wheel with both hands. He let out a long breath. "You're right. I cut off the lid. And you can bet I wanted to see what was inside that box but Jack wanted no part of that. He chased me to the surface. That's all I know."

"Close, Lance, but not *all*." Matt had to go carefully because he was guessing. His eyes bored a hole into Lance's face. "I think Jack knew he was being followed and asked you to hide the gold."

Lance squirmed in his seat. "Awe, come on Matt. I've admitted cutting off the lid. What more do you want?"

"Where'd you hide it?" Matt could almost hear his watch tick while he waited.

"Yeah," Lance finally said in a resigned voice. "He handed me a large metal suitcase. The silver kind. Thing weighed a ton. He had me take the case to the Portland Jet Port and put it in one of the storage lockers in the passenger area."

"The key, Lance. Where is the key?"

"Beats me, Matt. I gave it to Jack."

Matt knew Lance too well, "The copy you had made. Where is that?"

Lance looked trapped. "If I tell you and Miller finds out I'm cooked."

"You produce the key, Lance, and I'll get you off the hook with Miller." Then letting that sink in he added, "You have no claim on that gold, Lance. But I do. My whole body earned every penny."

Lance suddenly gave up. He reached up under the dash and tore loose a piece of duct tape securing the key. The tiny piece of brass looked too small to be the solution to a gruesome murder and McCall's abduction.

54

THE GOLD

That night Matt took a chance he could catch Professor Russell at home and phoned him. When Russell answered, Matt asked him how to preserve his interests in the gold that had been stored on board the sub.

"What you are looking for is called salvage rights," he replied. "I can help you there, Matt. I have a graduate student specializing in that area. Give me your fax number. I'll have him prepare paperwork and send it to you first thing in the morning." Matt thanked the professor and hung up.

At ten o'clock the next day Matt tore the papers out of the fax machine at the shack and read them carefully. Then, satisfied his interests were protected, he called Lieutenant Miller at his Portland office.

As soon as Miller picked up Matt started right off, "Lieutenant, I can solve the mystery of the missing gold. With that in hand you'll have the physical evidence as motive in Jack's death. I want you to come with me when I pick it up."

Miller hurled a string of questions through the phone. Ignoring him for the moment Matt continued. "There are some stipulations. I know there are European agencies working on return of stolen paintings, jewels and other art work to their rightful owners or descendants.

"The jewels, when you get them, go to those agencies except for that first pendant Jack found. That belonged to McCall's grandmother and I've already given it to McCall. Full salvage rights to the gold coins, however, are mine since they could never be traced."

Matt needed to obtain clear title to the coins. While part of him rationalized they belonged to him for the effort in recovering them, another part said, "The missing coins should go to Jack's family, except for one coin for Alex. The navy can have the sub. Get someone to call and I'll give them the coordinates."

Matt listened as Miller's voice poured through the phone, then answered, "Good question. 'Where's the gold?' Meet me at the Portland Jet Port in an hour and we'll solve that problem."

Lieutenant Miller arrived along with an attorney, an efficient-looking man in his early forties with thinning hair and round, silver glasses. After reading Matt's terms spelled out in the salvage papers he agreed to the conditions and signed them. Then Matt produced the key.

Miller located the correct locker and applied the little piece of brass to the lock. When it clicked, the door swung open. The silver metal suitcase was inside. Matt thought the case a far cry from the chests of pirate gold the day Jack discovered the necklace and pendant. There were no buccaneers defending it with cutlass and pistol, no Captain Kidd, no Jolly Roger, but valuable all the same.

56

MCCALL'S LETTER

Later that afternoon Matt returned to his apartment and in honor of McCall fired up his CD player and put on Shania Twain's *Feel Like a Woman.* Her voice vibrated out of the speakers and filled the room. Matt dropped onto the bed and pulled McCall's letter from his pocket. As he slipped the blade of his jackknife along the seam, he felt his heart speed up. The end of his world could be inside!

McCall had entered his life at breakneck speed, and with a few well-chosen words in her letter she might spurt out of it at the same velocity. His need to explore his feelings for her had always been postponed by some impending danger they faced. The close moments had been interrupted by the need to stay alive. Had they had time to manufacture enough glue, and if so would it be enough to stick them together?

He tapped the envelope. If he left it unread, maybe he could write the end to their relationship any way he chose. To open it paved the way to an end of a script he might not like.

He felt a rash of panic when he realized there really had been no option. Her parting instructions had been for him to open the letter once she was airborne. He was well overdue. He suddenly realized there might be another explanation, a good one, and he'd messed up by procrastinating!

Matt ripped the letter out of the wrinkled envelope and whipped his eyes across the message McCall had written in a neat flowing hand. There were surprisingly few words.

Look in the glove compartment of your truck.

Warp speed propelled Matt out the door. At the truck he punched an impatient thumb on the glove box lock, allowing the door to flop open, exposing an airline ticket with a yellow sticky note attached.

The ticket was for Matthew Banner, good one way from Portland, Maine, to Billings, Montana. The note said, *I love you. Call me*!

Matt raced back inside and reached for the phone.